CARNIVOUROUS TIBETAN MONKS ... Trade quotas ... A pair of kung-fu bodyguards named Floss and Betty ...

Ray Sharp has his hands full, just as Hong Kong is being handed back to the Chinese. A fizzled fireworks display marks the end of an era, though it seems that the more things change, the more they stay the same. Worker exploitation—both factory and flesh—remains a booming business.

And Ray is once again caught up in a whirlpool of sex, intrigue, and trying like hell to do the right thing. With the help of his Chinese-Mexican colleague and pal, the diminutive Ms. Wen, Ray hopes to get to the bottom of some shady trading, though like most tasks Ray undertakes, there's a danger he (and his friends) may get swept away ...

Also by Eric Stone:
The Ray Sharp series:
Flight of the Hornbill
Grave Imports
The Living Room of the Dead

Wrong Side of the Wall

SHANGHAIED

THE FOURTH RAY SHARP NOVEL

BY ERIC STONE

BLEAK HOUSE BOOKS

Published by
BLEAK HOUSE BOOKS
a division of Big Earth Publishing
923 Williamson St.
Madison, WI 53703
www.bleakhousebooks.com

Printed in the United States of America
12 11 10 09   1 2 3 4 5 6 7 8 9 10

978-1-60648-030-4 (hardcover)
978-1-60648-031-1 (paperback)
978-1-60648-032-8 (evidence collection)

To Eva, again,
for too many reasons to list here.

CHAPTER **ONE**

One of the monks is missing."

Warner holds a finger to his lips to shush me. "Later."

We move down the line of the five remaining monks, shaking their hands, wishing them well, ending with Bokar, the head lama, who we assure we are on the case. They squeeze into a taxi, the driver scowling at them and muttering foully under his breath. He can't be too upset, he'll find some way to overcharge them on the drive to the airport. We wave goodbye as they careen away from the curb in front of the Mandarin Hotel.

"So, Bill, what's with the missing monk?"

"He seems to have found another calling on Portland Street. Honing his tantric practice, I imagine."

Portland Street is famous for its yellow-sign girls; hookers who work in small apartments with yellow neon signs that are often elaborate word play on Chinese names. "Isn't there a long tradition of horny monks?"

"I don't know. I don't want to know. Bokar couldn't convince him to leave."

"How ya gonna keep 'em down on the lamasery, after they've seen Hong Kong?"

He scowls at me. "What's keeping you here, Ray? Now that the commies have taken it back."

"Haven't figured it out yet. I still don't know if guys like us are going to be an anachronism or not."

"In the new Hong Kong?"

"If that's what it is. Meanwhile, I'm still working. What's up with our monks? The missing one got anything to do with the job?"

"I wouldn't think so, but you know how these things go, take your eye off even the little things, and they can bite you in the ass."

I'D MET THE MONKS at dinner, two nights ago. About halfway through our main courses, it occurred to me they were eating meat, and that seemed odd. I asked about it.

The chief lama finished chewing a large bite of the gore-rare and charred black porterhouse, put down his knife and fork, and took a deep draught of his non-alcoholic beer.

He dabbed below his lip with the starched linen napkin. Then he smiled and answered me in perfect, clipped Oxford English.

"According to the *Pali* texts, Mr. Sharp, this steak is blameless."

Lei Yue kicked me, hard, under the table. I would've kicked her back, but it would have been childish. Especially in front of six Tibetan monks who might be clients, and our boss, Bill Warner. I couldn't even look at her. We'd both break out laughing. We have that affect on each other. If this had been a big Thanksgiving dinner, we'd be at the kid's table.

I'd directed my question to the head guy. I'd forgotten his name, but his robe was a rich, extra-sharp-cheddar orange. The others wore robes that matched the small dollop of bright yellow mustard he'd wiped off from under the right corner of his mouth.

"Blameless? I'm sorry if my question seems rude, but you must know our Western stereotypes of Buddhist monks living an ascetic life. I would have thought you'd be a vegetarian."

"No, please, Mr. Sharp, do not concern yourself with the decorum of your inquiry. It is not the first time such a question has been asked. The *Majihima,* the *Anguttara Nikayas* and the *Vinaya* all make reference to the 'blamelessness' of eating meat. The condition is simply that the monk must have no reason for suspicion that the animal was killed specifically for him."

I couldn't help raising my eyebrows.

The big cheese chuckled in that annoying way that monks often have, the one that has "I'm the more enlightened one here" hiding somewhere not too deep behind it. Or maybe that's the way I heard it.

"Even his Holiness, the Dalai Lama, has said, "I am a Tibetan monk, not a vegetarian." He cut another big bite of his steak and hoisted it halfway to his mouth.

"We are in a restaurant, Mr. Sharp. This cow would have been slaughtered for consumption regardless of our patronage."

It's the time honored, 'if I wasn't doing it, someone else would be,' excuse. I've employed it myself from time to time. It took an effort, but I kept my mouth shut. So was it the cow that was blameless? Or him? Where did the restaurant fit in? The butcher? The cook? The waiter? I didn't think the boss would be happy if I antagonized the guy, so I didn't ask. I smiled, cut myself a chunk of my own beef and appreciated my position at the top of the food chain.

It must have cost Warner a bundle. Steak houses in Hong Kong aren't cheap, and we were in the swankest of them all. Aren't Tibetan lamas supposed to be poor, impoverished by the Chinese occupation, something like that? I wondered how they'd pay for whatever it was they wanted us to do. What did they want with a corporate investigation firm, anyhow?

Maybe it was an excuse to show up for the parties. The night before the dinner, at midnight, July 1, 1997, the British Crown Colony of Hong Kong had been handed back to China. More than a few of the local Brits spent the past month drunk, grumpy, packing up. Some fellow Americans, too. I'll be losing plenty of friends who are heading home over the next few weeks. A lot of the local Chinese are worried about whether or not they should have a Canadian, Australian, hell, even a Costa Rican passport—just in case. A contingent, a regiment—how many is that anyhow—of People's Liberation Army soldiers occupied the barracks where the British colonial troops, who were mostly Nepalese, had been the day before.

But none of us were talking about that. We were busy eating. The cleaned steak plates were taken away and the monks all ordered dark chocolate brownies topped with coconut ice cream to pack in on top of their beef. They weren't watching their cholesterol.

I sipped a top-shelf Portuguese *aguardiente*. The main monk asked what it was. I told him it's a type of extra strong brandy. He asked if he could sniff it. I passed it over. He inhaled deeply from my glass and a transcendent, slightly sorrowful look washed over his face. "At times I feel it is a shame that the texts have found no way for us to consider the finer alcoholic beverages blameless."

He enjoyed another whiff before passing it back. I took something larger than a sip, then held the glass up in his direction. "Too many of us try to blame alcohol for those demons it summons from within ourselves. The booze itself is, I think, not to blame."

What was that, that I said? Some forlorn, off-the-cuff remark from the crossroads between pop psychology and Buddhism? Or was it the booze babbling? Luckily a loud, deep, window-rattling boom shut me up before I could say anything else.

It was followed closely by a bright flash of red light and the oohs and aahs of diners. The show got underway and, with a table by the huge picture windows overlooking the harbor, we had front row seats.

The night before, the departing Brits spent some eight or nine million U.S. dollars on a farewell fireworks display. It lit up the low hanging clouds and reflected off the rain as the Queen's yacht *Britannia* chugged out of the harbor, taking the last British governor and the whiny Prince Charles with it.

Once the colonists were gone, three fireworks barges were towed into the middle of the harbor and anchored in place. One in front of the stock exchange. One roughly in front of Government House. And the third not too far offshore of the girlie bars in Wanchai.

The Chinese, not to be outdone by the Brits, spent thirty million U.S. dollars on their skyrockets. It was guaranteed to be the biggest, brightest, loudest fireworks display in recorded history. Not counting atmospheric nuclear explosions. I'm sure that if they thought they could set off a nuke in the middle of Victoria Harbor with relative safety, or at least without catching hell from the rest of the world, they would. It couldn't be much louder than the explosion that interrupted us.

The whole thing was set to last an hour, with more than half the bang saved for the grand finale, the last five minutes. I was surprised that the windows facing the harbor hadn't been taped to prevent shattering, as they are for an approaching typhoon.

I needed another drink, blameless or not. As everyone else pressed forward to the windows, I edged back to the bar. Lei Yue was already there, a margarita in hand, standing on a barstool to see over the heads of the crowd.

I ordered my drink, then turned to her. "Monks wouldn't let you get in front?"

"Got no respect for short people, I guess. Maybe they don't like *chicas*."

"Maybe you'll get lucky and be reborn as a man. Then you'll have a shot at enlightenment."

"Isn't that the way it always is for us women. The glass ceiling even gets between me and nirvana."

"Or fireworks."

"I can see fine from here, *amigo*."

"Me too." We clinked glasses, *sympatico*, and watched for a little while, flinching when the big ones went off.

When a particularly giant-sized burst rattled the windows, I tossed down the rest of my drink, turned and ordered another. Lei Yue did the same, then plopped down to sit on the stool.

"You're not going to be able to see from there."

"*Chingate, cabron*, I don't want to get sliced up by flying glass."

"I wish you'd stop calling me 'asshole.' And was 'fuck you' really necessary? You've got a really foul mouth. Do you realize that?"

She threw a drunken arm over my shoulder. "You know me, just being affectionate, Ray."

"You've got a rough way of showing it."

"What do you expect? I'm a Chinese Mexican dwarf living in a town that's been taken over by the very same *pendejos* that chased my family out of their ancestral home. There's only so smooth I can be."

I eased one of my arms around her shoulders. We make an unlikely pair of best pals, but there you have it. She actually took a bullet for me, a couple of years ago. I'd do the same for her if I had to. She says she'd do it again if necessary, but she wouldn't step in the way of a knife. She hates knives. She sure does swear a lot though. In three, maybe four languages. Lei Yue's impressive in a lot of ways.

She sat there, me standing next to her, sipping our cocktails, watching the bombs bursting in air. There was someone's idea of grand musical accompaniment on the radio. It'd been building and swelling since it started. It sounded like a battle to the death between a Western symphony and a traditional Chinese one. The Chinese orchestra was winning, as one would expect on the occasion.

The monks were silhouetted against the bright colors blaring through the windows. Red, then yellow, then white, then mostly more red and not much blue or green flared against their bald scalps.

The end was approaching. The Western music overcome, the pentatonic clamor triumphed. It swelled mightily for a brief moment, then subsided as the twinkling of the penultimate burst of colored gunpowder flitted down into the waters of the harbor.

It was a very pregnant pause. A deep thrumming of drums, rumbled low but built almost imperceptibly. I looked at my watch. Six minutes to nine. In a minute we would be subjected to eighteen million dollars worth of fireworks going off in five momentous, ear stabbing, eyeball scorching minutes. I was ready for it to hurt.

Lei Yue clambered back up to stand on the barstool to get a view. I rose onto my tiptoes. It seemed like the whole room held its breath.

A rising thunder of enormous brass gongs ripped from the radio speakers. It rolled into a nearly unbearable stomach churning bass that sounded, and felt, like an earthquake I'd survived in Jakarta.

Just as I was looking for somewhere to dive for cover, it broke into a terrible, shattering clatter and clanging of cymbals and whiny caterwauling of one, two and three stringed instruments. It felt like it was splitting my bones. I closed my eyes against the turmoil of it.

But I forced them open again. If it was the end, I wanted to face it. I wanted to see it, at least for the moment or two before it blinded me.

The music roared and crashed and banged and took form into *March of the Volunteers*, China's national anthem.

But the harbor stayed dark. There were no more explosions. No more colors. Nothing.

Everyone in the room waited until the music stopped. The ringing and buzzing in our ears died down. Then we all looked at each other, not sure what happened.

After a couple of quiet moments, Lei Yue tapped me on the shoulder. She leaned into my ear to whisper. "*Que paso*, Ray?"

I answered back in my normal voice. The whole room looked at me from the first word. "Damned if I know, Lei Yue. Nothing happened, apparently."

CHAPTER **TWO**

The head lama had an otherworldly look on his face as he munched a strip of bacon. A bite of Denver omelette, skewered on his fork, was poised at the ready. Warner put down his coffee cup and leaned slightly forward.

"Lama Bokar, I hate to risk indigestion, but perhaps it is time for you to enlighten my colleagues and me as to why you wish to hire our services."

Lei Yue nudged me in the ribs. "Indigestion, enlighten…" Does Bill Warner, ex-CIA guy, actually have a sense of humor?

Bokar finished his bacon and set down his fork. "Yes, that is, after all, why we are here. The enjoyment of a good breakfast is at most secondary to our purposes."

He's no more than fifty, not old enough to have learned his English in the 1800s, no matter how it sounds.

"I'm glad you're enjoying it. But what is it that brings you to a corporate investigation firm?"

"Indeed, Mr. Warner. We adhere to ancient traditions, but we must suffer our present incarnation in the modern world. As is the case with many, perhaps most, religious institutions, we have a portfolio of investments. We have been made aware of developments that concern us regarding the health of our financial matters."

"Do you have a financial advisor, a brokerage? Perhaps these are questions for them."

"That, Mr. Warner, is the source of our concern. Our advisor has recently—'jumped ship' is, I believe, the proper colloquialism—to a bank of which we have heard troubling rumors."

"What bank?"

"Bank Central East Asia."

I've heard of it. It's had a meteoric rise. Which is an odd expression when you think of it. Don't meteors fall? In any event, the bank rose so fast, suspiciously so, that if it does fall, it'll plummet.

"That's Suwandi's bank, isn't it?"

Warner nodded his head in my direction, acknowledging me. "Ray knows the family, at least the old man and one of the sons."

Pak Suwandi is one of the grand old men of the Indonesian-Chinese business community. He'd taken one small *kaki lima*, a three-wheeled peddler's cart, and built it into the second largest conglomerate in Indonesia, Kakima International. When Samuel, his eldest son, came home with a degree in economics from Stanford, the two of them turned it into one of Asia's most modern, best run big companies. Its shares sell in Jakarta, Hong Kong and as American Depository Receipts on the New York Stock Exchange. It's one of the few companies in a developing country that makes money for even its small investors. When I worked as a journalist, I'd interviewed both the old man and Sam several times.

Then Thomas, the second son, came home with an MBA from Arizona State University, and he wanted a company to call his own. Like a lot of companies, Kakima needed a bank to handle its international trading business. And like a lot of companies, most of that trade involved China and the U.S. So *Pak* Suwandi put up the money to start Bank Central East Asia, which most people call "BC." The headquarters were in Hong Kong, with offices in Jakarta, Singapore, Tokyo and Los Angeles. About a year ago, Thomas, president of the bank, moved the headquarters to Shanghai.

There've been rumors ever since.

"Yes, Mr. Warner. I am hoping that your firm will have the wherewithal to investigate this matter for us. Discretely, of course. If our suspicions are unfounded, we do not desire them to become known."

Warner smiled as reassuringly as he could. "Let's finish breakfast, then go to our office."

There was no need for the other monks to come back to the office. Bokar had to sign the papers and give us what we needed to get started. The others wanted to go sightseeing.

But first they wanted to know what happened to last night's grand finale. Everybody looked at Warner. He was the best connected guy at the table, the only one likely to know anything.

"So, Bill, you hear anything? Why'd the fireworks fizzle?"

He started chuckling. It took an obvious effort to stop. He took a sip of water and fought back more laughs. "Yeah, I've got my sources."

"So, *que?*" Lei Yue looked like she was going to come out of her seat.

"Well, apparently they put all the munitions for the big bang on one barge, the one in the middle. It was computer controlled, but they needed a couple of men on board to keep an eye on things. One of them was smoking."

"Oh, no." Lei Yue and I could guess what was coming.

"Oh, yes. The cigarette got away, something started sparking and they pulled the plug."

"The plug?"

"Yes, the plug, Ray. In case of an emergency. They pulled a lever, the barge sank, fast; eighteen million bucks worth of fireworks went down with it."

"But the fireworks were all going to go off anyhow."

"Yeah, but in a controlled fashion. They'd spent months figuring out how not to blow out all the windows around the harbor. The guy must've panicked."

"What happened to him?"

"For his sake, I hope he's a good swimmer. Maybe he's halfway to Taiwan by now."

"The Taiwanese will probably give him a medal. Like one of those Chinese air force pilots who defect in their jet. What're the Chinese saying about it?"

"They're keeping it quiet. Very quiet. I doubt you'll see anything about it in the papers. It was, according to everyone, a glorious celebration."

"Loud, at any rate."

"Not so loud as it was supposed to be."

"Maybe there's hope for this handover business working out yet."

CHAPTER **THREE**

So, really, Bill, what, exactly, are we supposed to do for these guys? And what's with the missing monk?" Warner's standing behind his desk, looking around to decide where to put the newly signed contracts. His office is bigger and a whole lot less cluttered than mine.

"Forget about the monk. The job's due diligence, as usual. Find out what all the rumors are. Find out how true they are, or not. Find out what it means for the client and come up with a plan for what they can do about it. Simple."

"Yeah, right. These jobs always start out sounding simple, but they never turn out that way."

"That's why I hired you, Ray. You're a guy who appreciates the complexity of things. What's your thinking?"

"I'll make some calls, stir up some contacts. When I've got something to go on I'll call Sam Suwandi, see if I can get anything out of him, but I doubt I will. He doesn't like his brother, but he's loyal.

After that, I might have to go up to Shanghai, poke around there some. I'll need to take Lei Yue with me. My Mandarin's useless."

"You need anyone to go over the financials?"

"It couldn't hurt. The Bank's only listed on the Shanghai and Jakarta exchanges, so there's not going to be as much there as I'd hope for. But they're registered here and the U.S., if you've got anyone with an in at those banking authorities, they might be able to give us a little something more to look at. You need me to do this fast and cheap, or something?"

"Why?"

"The clients. Hard to imagine they're flush."

"You'd be surprised. I'll let you know if we need to cut back. But it's not going to be a problem."

"So, what rumors have you heard?"

"The usual for a family run bank. Sweetheart loans to friends and associated companies, some political shenanigans, a little creative accounting when it comes to fulfilling Bank for International Settlement requirements, nothing all that extraordinary."

"I thought it wasn't all that easy to get around the BIS."

"If you're doing business with people who aren't too picky about that sort of thing, it isn't that hard."

"*Caveat emptor.*"

"That's all the lama is trying to do."

"What's that?"

"He's the buyer, he's hired us to take care of the beware."

"HOW MUCH MONEY are we talking about, Ray?"

Lei Yue's in my office, perched on a tall stack of annual reports that I'd filed on the guest chair. She's looking down at me.

"That doesn't look too stable. I can take those off the chair for you."

She looks around the small, windowless room. "I don't think there's room for them anywhere else, *amigo*. You want me to sign a waiver in case I fall?"

"Warner might. I'm cool."

"Okay, so how much?"

"A few million, at least. U.S. dollars."

"Where'd a bunch of Tibetan monks come up with that?"

"Damned if I know. Sold some relics? Yoga classes?"

"I don't think Tibetans do yoga."

"I don't know, meditation workshops then. You know what I mean. Wherever they get their money, they don't want it mismanaged."

"Can't say as I blame them. So, what do we do, *hombre*?"

"We start off finding out what we can about Bank Central East Asia. I'll call around to the English speakers, maybe a couple of Indonesians. You get on the phone with whoever you can think of who speaks Chinese."

"I don't know many financial types."

"Yeah, but you know some of the Chinese press guys and some business people in China who might've dealt with them. See if anyone's heard any juicy rumors."

"What sort of rumors?"

"I don't care, anything. We can sort out what's worth looking into or not after we make a list."

THE PARTIES HAVE BEEN going on for days. The only people I can think of to call locally are still going to be hungover. I'm okay, I haven't been in the partying mood. Last night I begged off hitting the town with the monks. Other than one particular thousand-year-old, drunken Jesuit in Macau, who I've shared many a "Scottish tea" with, religious figures make me nervous.

Offices in China are closed. It's still a holiday. I call Juli in Jakarta. She's working and she doesn't drink, much. She knows the Suwandis better than I do, through family and work connections. She's one of the better business journalists I know, and a good friend.

Juli's assistant, Iris, answers the phone and recognizes my voice about halfway through my "hello."

"Boss man." I used to be her boss when I lived in Indonesia. "How's it going? Haven't heard from you for a while. Too busy *cau loi?*"

"No girl chasing lately. Where're you picking up Cantonese slang, anyhow?"

"I spent the last week showing some Hong Kong correspondents around town. I feel sorry for you living there. That is too hard a language to learn. You should move back here. *Bahasa*'s easier."

"So I can chase you?"

"I'm not your type."

"Maybe I've changed."

"Maybe, but then you're not my type."

"I'm not Juli's type either, but I need to talk with her. She in?"

"What, that's it? You're not going to ask me how I'm doing?"

"Okay, how're you doing?"

"Good. I like this job. I've started writing some pieces for local papers."

"That's great. What sort of stuff?"

"Features, some reviews. I did a piece on Emmy."

Emmy was a mutual friend, sort of an ex-girlfriend of mine. Last I heard she'd gone to Holland to marry a geologist.

"How is she?"

"Not so good. Her Dutch guy dumped her. Brought her to Amsterdam with a one way ticket. There was an ugly scene when he introduced her to his parents. That was the end."

"That's terrible. How'd she get home?"

She hasn't. She's stuck, trying to get money for a ticket."

"Have you got an address? A phone? I can send her the money."

"Nice of you to offer, Boss Man, but she says she's done taking money from men."

"How's she making money to buy her own ticket?" I'm pretty sure I know. She'd been a part-time hooker in Indonesia. That's how we met. She was also a chambermaid in the hotel I'd been staying in.

"She can't get a real job, so, you know."

"Talk about taking money from men."

"You know Emmy. She's proud. It's more like she won't take *charity* from men."

"Hell, she can pay me back if she wants."

"I'll tell her, but I can't get in touch with her. She calls me once a month."

"Next time she does, ask her to call me, okay?"

"Will do. What do you want Juli for?"

"I need to pick her brain."

"Ouch. I've always hated that Americanism."

"Regardless, that's what I've got to do."

"Okay. Hang on, sir. I will see if Ms. Samsudi is available."

Before I can say anything else I'm switched to hold and assaulted with the lugubrious strains of *keroncong*, the type of music that President Suharto likes to have crooned to him at public events. It seems like an eternity before Juli comes on the line.

"Hey, Ray. What's up?"

"Juli. There's gotta be better hold music than that available."

"Oh yeah, I keep forgetting to change it. This was a *Golkar* party office before we got it." *Golkar* is Suharto's political party. It figures.

"Sorry to rush you, Ray, but I've got to leave for an interview in a few minutes. Iris says you want to mine my head, or something like that."

"Pick your brain, she hates the expression. What do you hear about Tom Suwandi and BC? Not boilerplate—rumors, scandal, any juicy stuff?"

"Some. Our usual deal?"

Our deal is that anything between us is off the record until I tell her it isn't. But then, if there's a story in it, she gets it first.

"*Gung hai lah.*"

"What's that?"

"Cantonese for 'of course.'"

"The old man and Sam are tearing their hair out. They called Tom onto the carpet and it turned into a shouting match. Tom walked out on them. I heard he threw a crystal ashtray through a window, went straight back to Shanghai and won't answer their calls."

"Okay, so far so good. What's it about?"

"The bank, of course. He's loaned it out, all of it. To friends, for pretty much anything they want. From what I hear, the bank has bounced a few big commercial customers' checks because they didn't have sufficient funds."

"Who didn't? The customer? What's so strange about that?"

"No, the bank didn't. They've loaned out almost everything they've taken in. Until they start getting paid back on some of their loans, the depositors are out of luck."

"What about the investment banking? Stock market's up. They must be sitting on piles of shares."

"They are, but a lot of that's no good."

"How so?"

"Chinese companies, not much liquidity. They've accepted a lot of options that haven't vested yet for collateral. But they haven't vested yet."

"So they've been playing with funny money."

"And even that's about to run out."

"Where are the bank regulators in all this?"

"That might have something to do with why they moved the headquarters to Shanghai."

"What's going to happen?"

"From what I hear, it was a three-way argument. Tom wants the old man's company, Kakima, to bail him out. The old man is willing, but only if he takes over the bank. Tom doesn't like that. Sam doesn't want the old man to do it at all; he thinks it might bring down the whole empire."

"Would it?"

"Nothing would surprise me at this point, but your guess is as good as mine."

"Who are these pals of Tom's that he's been throwing money at?"

"That's a worry, too. No one knows for sure. There's been talk about a lot of Chinese Army companies into dodgy businesses. They're always looking for money and they can claim to deliver good connections."

"Can they?"

"Some can, some can't. Depends on where in China and what you want. But some of them have a nasty habit of treating loans as simply fees that the banks are paying for their connections."

"Know anyone in China I should talk to?"

She rattles off a few names, then hustles me off the phone.

CHAPTER **FOUR**

No one's home in China. They must be too busy celebrating the return of Hong Kong, or figuring out how they're going to make money off it. I don't care if the old farts in Beijing claim to be communists. China's the most nakedly capitalist place on the planet.

Lei Yue hasn't got much more than I have. A journalist pal of hers has heard that BC's heavy into garment and toy manufacturing with some of its Chinese friends. He assumes that means sweat shops. But in those businesses, there's nothing new about that.

Still, it's a start. I know a guy who makes toys. He's got a factory in the New Territories and he's always at work. I call him. He says we can drop by anytime. We take the subway to the train, then the train to Shatin.

The first time I was in Hong Kong, in 1978, I took the train to the Chinese border. It bombed right through Shatin. There wasn't any reason to stop. The small village had a population of fewer than

300 rice farmers. Its only claim to fame was that there was a time when the rice raised there went exclusively to the emperor.

Now there's no emperor and the only rice in Shatin is brought there in twenty-five kilo sacks. It's home to a million and a half people living in high-rises, Hong Kong's largest horse racing track, and a whole lot of "factories" where no one actually makes anything.

Cal's factory is on the fourth floor of a twenty-story industrial building. He greets us at the door, having buzzed us in from the front entrance.

"Ray, dropping by to see the Hong Kong economic miracle in action?" He dwarfs my hand in one of his enormous mitts and pumps it up and down a couple of times.

I look out across the quiet, huge expanse of concrete floor. There're a few women at tables at the foot of towering piles of cardboard boxes in a far corner. I can't tell what they're doing from this distance.

"Looks like the miracle's on break at the moment, Cal."

He chuckles, then casts out a hand at Lei Yue, wrapping it all around one of hers. "And what are you doing in the company of this old reprobate, young lady?"

She smiles up at him, way up. Calvin used to play basketball for Kentucky. He was one of those centers who was never quite fast or agile enough to make it into the pros, but tall enough for the college job.

"Cal, this is Wen Lei Yue. She's a colleague." He unwraps his hand from around hers and lets it drop loosely at his side.

"Collegial, how? Remind me, Ray. It's been a while." He's trying to find out if I'm still a journalist. It'll be a different conversation if I am.

"We're working for DiDi, Bill Warner's outfit. Due diligence, that sort of thing. Any secrets you've got, Cal, they're safe with us." I'd never burned him for any of his confidences when I was a reporter, so I'm guessing he'll believe me.

He walks us to his office at the far end of the big, mostly empty room. We pass the three women sitting at the tables. They're sticking labels on plastic wrapped Rambo dolls they're taking out of unlabelled boxes.

Cal's office isn't very big, but his desk is oversized. There's a cheap sofa, a coffee table piled high with catalogs and a few photos of our host posing with basketball greats. We sit on the couch, he leans far back in his chair and props his feet on the desk, carefully pointing them at me out of courtesy to Lei Yue.

"Sorry I can't offer you anything. If you want the full, wall-to-wall, corporate hospitality treatment you'll have to come see me in my main office in Central."

Lei Yue picks up one of the most recent catalogs and leafs through it. She looks at me, wanting to ask a question, not sure if it's polite.

I smile back. "Go ahead and ask."

She holds the catalog up for Cal to see. "Does your company make all this?"

He beams at her, takes his feet down off the desk and leans a little forward. "Most of it, little lady."

I grimace and try to make sure Cal sees it. Lei Yue hates being called that. It's never a good idea to make her mad.

Her voice is calm, scarily so. "Where? Not here, certainly."

"No, of course not. Most of our factories are in China."

"So what, exactly, do you do here? Your catalog says that your toys are made in Hong Kong. Do you have another factory here?"

Cal looks at me for help. I shrug my shoulders. He can't quite believe Lei Yue doesn't know the answers already. I know that she does. She has a nasty habit I admire. She delights in coaxing uncomfortable truths out of people. It makes her a great partner.

He leans a little further forward. "Well, I guess it's no secret. At least it shouldn't be, by now. Hong Kong's expensive, Miss Wen.

Rent's expensive, labor's expensive, regulatory compliance, too. People want toys, clothes, wrist watches, electric devices, all the stuff that used to be made here, and they want it cheap.

"Now China, it could make all the cheap stuff the world might ever want. But the U.S. and Europe won't let it. They've got quotas. You can only export so many G.I. Joes and Barbies and t-shirts and pairs of socks and CD players that are made in China.

"So we set up this factory here and it doesn't really make anything. We buy quota and slap on the Made in Hong Kong label and Americans and Germans and French people get their stuff a lot cheaper than they would otherwise. Everyone's happy."

"Is that legal?" She knows that already, too.

"It is, and it isn't, Miss Wen. Since no one makes much of anything here anymore, Hong Kong's got more quota than it can use. Same with Macau, Singapore, Japan, South Korea. There's brokers who sell that extra quota, so the same amount of exports that are legal to send to the U.S. and Europe, are getting sent there just the same.

"But if you're doing that, you're supposed to make a certain percentage of whatever it is you're making, in the place that the label says it's made. For example, if you're gonna put a Made in Hong Kong label on a sweater, you gotta attach the sleeves to the sweater in Hong Kong.

"But that's stupid, and expensive. So I've got this fake factory here and another one in Macau. Soon as they build some more real factories in Indonesia, I'll probably open another fake one in Singapore, too. But they're a little tougher on that sort of thing down there. Now that China's taken over here, well…"

Lei Yue's about to ask something else, but I stick up a hand to interrupt. "Sorry, guys, enough economics class for the day. We've got other fish to fry."

Cal leans back again in his chair, puts his hands behind his head. "Fried food's bad for you, Ray. You're looking a little like you might want to lay off it."

Lei Yue snickers and pats me on the knee. She's been teasing me lately about how I've gained some weight. I'm not exactly buff, but I'm not bad for a guy in his mid forties. I decide to ignore the whole thing.

"You do any business with BC, Cal?"

"The bank? Yeah, a little. They handle some of our trade finance and put us together with a few suppliers in China. Why?"

"You have any trouble with them?"

"What sort?"

"Whatever. Doesn't have to be major, anything that might seem fishy to you."

"This got anything to do with my company, Ray?"

"Nope. It's a due diligence job on BC for another client."

"Anything I ought to know?"

"Not so far. If I find out anything you do, I'll give you a shout."

"I've heard a few things."

"Like what?"

"This is all totally off the record, right? I don't care if you aren't a journalist anymore, not even a peep to your old pals, no matter how many vodkas you toss back at the Foreign Correspondents Club."

I make the zipper across the mouth motion and try to stick a reassuring look on my face.

"I've heard some stuff I don't like about some of the factories they've hooked me up with. Bad conditions, unsafe, maybe some indentured workers, kids."

"You check any of it out?"

"It's China, Ray. What am I gonna do? Those people need the jobs, no matter what. If it wasn't me, it'd be someone else."

I've heard more than I can stomach of that excuse lately. But I manage to keep my mouth shut.

"Where'd you hear it, Cal?"

"I'd rather not say. I promised."

"Okay. Who at BC set you up with the factories?"

"Came straight from the top. A guy I know in Shanghai intro-duced me to Tom Suwandi. He made the calls."

"You think he knows anything?"

"I don't know. Maybe. All he told me was that they were depend-able and would give me a good price."

"Who introduced you to Suwandi?"

"Garcia, Eduardo Garcia. He's with the Mexican trade mission there."

Lei Yue perks up at the mention of her home country. "Mexico? What've you got to do with Mexico?"

"We've got a factory there. One of those *maquila* something or another deals, near Mexicali."

"*Maquiladora.* It's a cheap, free trade manufacturing zone along the U.S. border. It might not be such a big deal anymore, now that NAFTA's in place. Is it a real factory?"

"Yeah, we assemble some of our higher-end toys there."

CHAPTER **FIVE**

"I told you this was going to get complicated, Bill. Tibet, Hong Kong, Shanghai, Mexico, the U.S., Indonesia; I haven't even spent a whole day on it. By the time it's all over I'll have to write a travelogue." I'm back in his office, filling him in.

"Happy?"

"No, I'm getting tired just thinking about it."

"So, what next?"

"Find some more people to talk to around here. Once they stop celebrating in China I can make some calls up there. Lei Yue and I'll probably have to go up to Shanghai pretty soon."

"Think you can get into any of the factories?"

"If I can't, Lei Yue might be able to. She can pretend to be a buyer from Mexico, something like that. If they've got anything to hide, she's less likely to make them nervous than I am."

"How's that? She makes me nervous."

"No she doesn't. She scares you. That's different. Mexico's not as picky about the little things, you know that, like child labor and safety. And they don't have a Foreign Corrupt Practices Act like the U.S. Why do you think Chinese companies are opening up factories along the U.S. border? A Chinese company's going to think a Mexican will raise less of a ruckus over the niceties than an American will."

"So if she finds anything, they'll be victims of their own stereotyping."

"Something like that. They oughta know us Yanks are as capable of sleaze as anybody."

"You're telling me. You know I used to work for The Company."

It's the first time he's ever owned up to having been with the C.I.A. "I thought you weren't supposed to admit that."

"Nothing you didn't already know. Plus, maybe I was one of those guys who spend long, dull days pouring over international newspapers and putting clips in files. That's what most of them do."

"And I was hoping you were about to issue me a secret decoder ring. Damn."

"Nope, you're the brawn. If anyone gets the ring it's going to be Lei Yue. She might scare me, but she's the brain."

I try flexing my arm. It isn't all that impressive. Maybe I should start going to the gym.

"HAND ME THAT WATER BOTTLE, will you?" John Montgomery's hardly breaking a sweat on the treadmill. He's doing eight minute miles, but his voice is rock steady.

I hand it to him. "Do I look like the waterboy?"

He eyes the motionless belt I'm standing on. "I wouldn't ask if you had that thing moving. If you're not here to work out, what do you want?"

"I've got some questions."

"Concerning Wellfleet?" Montgomery's the managing director of the shipping division of one of the biggest Hong Kong conglomerates. I'd met him in the course of an investigation into the trade in stolen Cambodian antiquities. He'd become DiDi's client, and was happy with the results. Wellfleet, his company, does a lot of business in China.

"Not that I'm aware of. It's due diligence on BC."

That gets his attention. He stumbles, but recovers quickly, shoots me a look then hits the stop button on the machine. When it slows enough, he glides to the end and steps off, motions for me to follow him.

He walks over to a leg press, sits down, adjusts the weight to a hundred and twenty five kilos and kicks out a quick set of ten before stopping and looking up at me.

"BC? It's Pandora's Box, Ray."

"I'm beginning to get that impression. What do you know?"

"I do know some things. And my gut is telling me there's more to it."

Montgomery's got great instincts.

"What can you tell me?"

"I have an eight o'clock dinner with my big boss, Chau. I may be getting the sack. I could use some fortification. I'll meet you at the Dogs in twenty minutes." He turns away from me, moves the weight up to a hundred fifty kilos and slowly begins to work the machine.

I walk down the stairs, out the door and into the parboiler of the late afternoon streets of Central. Mad Dogs pub is a block away. By the time I surf the waves of sidewalk crowds to get there, I'm drenched. It's as much condensation, having come from the dry, cool air of the gym, as it is sweat.

They pull the Guinness very slow from the tap at Mad Dogs, so I order a Carlsberg to hold me over until it's ready. It works wonders. What is it about that first swallow of cold beer when you're hot? If every sip could taste that way, I'd drink a whole lot more of the stuff.

I've finished the cold, light Danish brew and had the first, nutrient-rich draught of the dark, malty Irish beer when Montgomery sits down across the table from me.

"You buying?"

"DiDi is. If you've got something for me, I can expense it."

A waitress, a cute, baby-faced Chinese girl with a nearly impenetrable Scottish accent and no more than about four and a half inches of skirt moves up very close on his side. He's a handsome guy, his face practically glowing with recent exercise and a hot shower. "Wot i' it yo want, love?"

Both our eyes take their time travelling from the bottom of that skirt up to her face. By the time they get there, she knows what both of us want. But that's the idea, isn't it? Montgomery orders his own Guinness, and an eighteen-year-old Macallan to sip while waiting for it. The single malt whisky's about the same age as the waitress. She walks away making it clear she's aware we're watching.

"At least the whisky's old enough for you, John."

"She's legal."

"Yes, but no doubt inadvisable."

We'd met at an exclusive auction that also offered bidders companionship. I hadn't stuck around for the after party, something Montgomery has taunted me about ever since. It doesn't bother me. I'm no stranger to the pleasures of the flesh, but I prefer to engage in them privately.

"So, John, turning to more mundane matters, what can you tell me about BC?"

"You didn't hear any of this from me."

"Of course not."

"They're insolvent. From what I hear they have no performing loans, none. And they took a lot of paper, more like options on paper, to back up those loans, and the paper's worthless."

"But these are Chinese guys, Indonesian-Chinese in any case. Aren't they all about property? Don't they hold any mortgages?"

"Sure they do, but it's almost all construction loans. You know all those half-finished buildings in Macau, Zhuhai, Dongguan?"

"Those are theirs?"

"Theirs and the Chinese army's. There's no foreclosing on that bunch. Even if BC could, what would they do with a bunch of half-built office and residential towers there's no market for?"

"Okay, but if this is all true, why aren't their doors closed?"

"They've still got some money coming in. The old man is fearful of what will happen to Kakima if BC comes tumbling down, so he's been helping prop it up. I'm fairly certain that Tom talked his father into putting up Kakima assets to back up the bank."

"How long can they get away with that?"

"A little while at least. It is one of the largest family fortunes in Asia. But there is also more money coming in, and that's the bad part."

"They running a laundry?"

"That's the least of it. A lot of those construction loans were meant to wash money in the first place. But things might really blow up, even in China, if the whole deal falls apart. It's sort of sweet. If everyone involved doesn't prop up everyone else, they'll all get hurt."

"Could you speak English please? I'm beginning to get a headache trying to follow you."

The waitress sidles up to Montgomery with his Guinness. She sets it down near his hand and he takes ahold of hers, looking up into her eyes. "Where are you from, hon?"

He knows damn well where she's from. I'm an American and even I knew the moment she opened her mouth she was from Glasgow. Montgomery's a Brit. She leans an over-sized enhanced breast against one of his shoulders and purrs an answer into his ear.

He whispers something that makes her laugh. It's a heavy smoker's laugh, harsh and dry. It's not in the least bit sexy but he leans into her and follows up with something that makes her laugh even harder.

I reach across the table and tap Montgomery's hand. He looks over at me, a little annoyed at the intrusion.

"Could you ask your friend if maybe she can bring me another beer, a Carlsberg this time?"

He does, and asks her for another scotch as well, and watches her walk away.

"Cheer up, Ray. Perhaps she has a friend, or an older sister." I shake my head.

"You were saying, John? In some language I can understand this time."

"Every party involved is a crook of some kind, and they need each other. An international bank tied to a large, publically-traded conglomerate gives the Chinese crooks, a lot of them connected to the army, a respectable front for handling their financial affairs. The bank makes for an excellent middleman to put some distance between foreign, particularly American, companies and some of their dodgy suppliers, the Chinese crooks. And, because of that, the bank's in a perfect position for laundering money for either side. Since both sides need the bank, they're not going to let it go under, even if on paper it's already bankrupt. They'll pump money into it, as long as they can, in the form of commissions and fees and small slices of their pies."

"Is this illegal?"

"It depends on whose laws and what pies the bank's taking slices from. Some of it is, some of it isn't. A lot of the peripheral activities are illegal, even in China."

"Like what?"

"Violation of environmental and trade laws and treaties, unsafe factories, using indentured or forced labor, hiring children, probably some human trafficking to the U.S., maybe Europe. I wouldn't be surprised if some of the money that needs laundering comes from drugs, guns and whores. It's what I meant about Pandora's Box."

"What's this all mean for a regular customer? Say, someone who's got a few million bucks in a portfolio parked with BC's investment bank."

"Is that your client?" I nod my head. "It means that they've helped finance some rather unsavory behavior and they'll be lucky to see any of their money again. Sorry, Ray. Let Bill Warner break the news to them."

"Anything they can do?"

"Tell them to put in sell orders on everything, quick. Or try to transfer the account to another bank. Anything. But I suspect it is too late."

"How do you know all this? Can you prove any of it?"

"I do a lot of business in China, Ray. At high levels. You think we big business fellows don't talk? I hear things. I'm not an attorney, or a journalist. Or even a gumshoe, like you. I don't have any need to prove any of it. Luckily my company has no significant dealings with BC."

"Gumshoe?"

"What? Do you imagine they didn't show those old movies in London when I was growing up? Do you suppose I've never read Raymond Chandler? He was an Englishman, you know."

"And a drunk."

Montgomery raises his glass and then tips it down his throat. The waitress has been keeping an eye on us. She scurries over.

CHAPTER **SIX**

How dependable do you think Montgomery is?"

I'm trying to fight off the stench of burning coffee. Warner gets into the office early most mornings, puts on a pot, then lets it boil into sludge before drinking any of it.

"Plenty, Bill. Wellfleet does a lot of business all over the region."

"You think Chau gave him the sack?"

"He was having dinner with him last night. If he did, we'll find out soon enough. A lot of the old companies are doing what they can to Chineseify. There's talk that Beijing's going to steer all its development to Shanghai, and away from here. A big shipping and trading company's probably got better *guanxi* if it isn't run by an Englishman."

"Relationships?"

"Yeah, in every sense of the word."

"So, is Montgomery any use to you up in Shanghai?"

"Sure, he gave me some names. He's been doing business in these parts long enough that even if he did get the boot, his connections will still be good. At least for a little while, until everyone knows whatever it is he's going to get up to next."

"What does a guy like that get up to next?"

"Lands on his feet. That's all I know."

"Okay, what do you get up to next?"

"People ought to be crawling back into their offices in China by now. I'll make some calls. I've got to come up with some believable reason to set up a meeting with Tom Suwandi."

"Any ideas?"

"Shouldn't be too hard, sounds like they're desperate for money. Maybe Lei Yue will be looking for partners to set up a factory along the border in Mexico. I'll make the introductions, for a cut of course, business as usual."

"Sure, but isn't BC going to want to check out her credentials?"

"Her family runs a few restaurants in Tijuana and Mexicali, and I think they've also got a frozen eggroll business. Shouldn't be too hard to set something up."

"Keep me up to date. Let me know what you need."

"Will do. One thing. I know it's probably nothing, but could you find out for me what, if anything, the missing monk did for the lamasery?"

"He prayed, chanted, I don't know, what do monks do?"

"Come on, Bill. These guys've got an investment portfolio worth millions. There's got to be someone on the inside who had something to do with it, even if it was only stuffing cash into envelopes and delivering it to their money manager. I want to know what that monk's job was. If it was sweeping up and making beds, I'll leave him alone with his libido in Mongkok. It's a loose end until I know he didn't have anything to do with the money, that's all."

"I'll call Bokar."

"SOUP OF CHINA? What kind of name is that for a company?"

"*Caldo de Chine S.A. de C.V., cabron.* More like a stew. My parents started out with a pushcart they bought off a taco vendor. They kept the name."

"Do they have any fancy letterhead you can use?"

"I'm way ahead of you, Ray. I keep a supply at all times, just in case. I am, after all, on the board of directors."

"Okay, what're we going to tell Tom Suwandi your family wants with him? What do they need from China?"

"There must be something, my father's the egg roll king of northern Baja."

"Does that make you the dumpling princess?"

"Smile when you say that, *cabron.*" I am.

"Maybe they want to expand. Your family wants to start opening a bunch of Chinese fast food shops around Mexico, sort of like Panda Express, that sort of thing, only in Spanish. They'll need kitchen equipment, chopsticks, lots of stuff."

"*Pronto Chine,*" not at all a bad idea, *mi amigo.* I might suggest it to the family for real."

"You do that. In the meantime, dummy up a nice letter of introduction to whom it may concern from your *padre, el* chairman of the board. I'll make some calls."

THE MORE ANGLES WE CAN WORK, the better. I get Cal to call Garcia at the trade mission in Shanghai and let him know we're going to be in touch. I put in a call of my own to Sam Suwandi in Jakarta. Three layers of assistant later, I've got him on the phone.

"Ray. I haven't heard from you for a while. Now that you're no longer a journalist, you don't need me for anything."

"I didn't want to bother you, Sam. I keep hearing you're a busy man."

"I suppose. But if you run your company right, you're not as busy as everyone thinks you are."

"You running it right these days?"

"Right enough."

"How's your father?"

"Good, you know the old man, he's got more energy than I do."

"How about your brother?"

"Is that what this is about?"

"What do you mean?"

"Let's see now, Ray. I haven't heard from you since you left *Asian Industry*. I hear you're working in corporate investigations, due diligence. You're based in Hong Kong and the whole world's beating a path to China to do business. My brother, who I don't think you know if I recall correctly, runs a bank in China. I can put these things together."

"Maybe you ought to be the investigator. You're right, it's due diligence. How much do you want to know?"

"Nothing. It's better that way. What do you want from me?"

"An introduction. No details, something simple, along the lines of 'this guy I know wants to meet with you about something, can I have him call you?'"

"He'll ask me what I know about you."

"Fine. Tell him what you want. What've I got to hide? I just want him to take my call, hopefully take a meeting."

"I don't want to know, Ray. I was going to call Tom this evening, anyhow. I'll drop your name, then you're on your own."

"Thanks. Drinks are on me next time I'm in town. Give my regards to your father, will you?"

"Will do. But, Ray... Tom's my brother and that means a lot. But you and I go back a long way. And I consider you a friend. So be careful."

"Huh?"

"That's all I'm going to say."

WHEN I GET OFF THE PHONE, Warner's at the door of my office, holding a couple of sheets of paper. He looks anxious.

"What's up, Bill?"

"You were right, there might be something more to the missing monk." He hands me the papers. One page looks like a personnel file of some sort, the other is a contrasty faxed photo. "He's the lamasery's bookkeeper."

"Think he's still in Mongkok?"

"That's the last place anyone saw him."

"Fine, but where? It's an easy place to disappear."

"Even in Mongkok there can't be a lot of Tibetan monks wandering around. Especially tall ones. Apparently he could play center on the Tibetan national basketball team, if they had one."

"So, Lei Yue and I are headed across town before we head to Shanghai."

"Why do you need Lei Yue? I figure you for being pretty familiar with the sleazy side of Mongkok."

"I don't know whether to be complimented or offended, Bill. My vices are, I don't know, at least a little more refined. However, my Cantonese is terrible, Mandarin non-existent. I'll need Lei Yue if I'm going to talk to much of anyone."

"Okay, aren't you gone yet?"

"YOU'RE NOT GOING TO TRY and hold my hand, are you?" Lei Yue isn't crazy about going to Mongkok.

"Maybe we ought to tie ourselves together with rope, like mountaineers."

"We're not facing an avalanche, it's only people on the street."

"In Mongkok it's pretty much the same thing. If we had to walk up or down any hills I would insist on roping us up."

I like Mongkok, when I'm in the right mood. It's the world's most densely populated neighborhood and its sidewalks are canned sardine close with pedestrians for about twenty two hours of every day. Once I was there between 3:30 and 5:30 in the morning and it was relatively quiet. At 5:31 I blinked. When my eyes opened again I couldn't see more than ten feet down the block through the crowds.

We get on the subway at the Sheung Wan station and easily find seats. The train fills a little more at Central, then the wave breaks in through the doors at Admiralty. We cross under the harbor and when the doors slide open at Tsim Sha Tsui you can almost hear what little air remains rush out as more people hammer into what little space is left, taking its place.

Lei Yue starts to get up. I pull her back down on the seat. "Where do you think you're going?"

"Mongkok's only three more stops. We've got to start trying to get to the door."

"Where do you think all these people are going? We can stroll on out after they've stampeded."

"I missed my stop that way once."

"Worse comes to worse, we'll get off at Prince Edward and walk back."

I know that will earn me a scowl. And it does.

"Chisin gwailoh."

I suppose I am a crazy white guy. I've been in tropical rainforests that were cooler and drier than Hong Kong in July. I smile at her. At least the air conditioning in the subway is ferocious enough to fight off the cumulative body heat.

"Ray, where do we look for a monk in Mongkok?"

"Warner seems to think he was visiting yellow-sign girls."

"Oh great, so we go from crummy apartment to crummy apartment asking if any of the *putas* have seen a horny monk?"

"Something like that, unless you've got a better idea. Hope you've had your shots."

"I don't think they make shots for the kind of stuff you catch in those places."

"Just don't sit down or have sex with anybody. You'll be fine."

"You ever been with a yellow-sign girl?"

"I'm going to have to do something about my reputation. No, I haven't."

"You've got nothing against hookers. So, why not?"

"True, but I prefer the sort where you can harbor delusions that it's something more than dropping by the convenience store to get your rocks off."

"Delusions are right."

"Let it drop, will ya? Some of my best friends are…"

"Girlfriends, too. Forget it. We're here."

The throng surges toward the exits even before the train stops. The last out are likely to get stomped to death by the crowd charging in if they lose their footing when the doors slide open. Miraculously, no one does and Lei Yue and I manage to get out behind them.

It takes strategy to take your time doing anything in Hong Kong. I wouldn't be surprised to discover that the government pumps methamphetamine into the water supply. Dawdle at the front or middle of the herd and you're likely to be trampled underfoot. Lei Yue and I straggle at the back, sticking close to the edges so as to provide plenty of room for the hurrying crowds to hurry past. By the time we get to the long escalator up to ground level, we've got it to ourselves. It's a rare joy to have anything to yourself in Hong Kong.

For the moment, at least, the decibel level is even reduced to less than cacophonic. Lei Yue doesn't have to shout to be heard.

"Where do we start?"

"Portland Street's as good a place as any. It's got the biggest concentration of yellow signs."

"Why yellow signs, anyhow? Isn't it supposed to be a red-light district?"

"I don't know, I guess they're cheaper or something."

"It's only ten-thirty in the morning. Are these places going to be open?"

"Remember what I said about convenience stores? They never close."

"What's the protocol? Do we talk to their pimps, mamasans, who?"

"Technically it's legal so long as it's one woman working for herself from her own apartment. There are a few illegal brothels where we'll need to talk with a mamasan, but mostly it's going to be knocking on doors talking to whoever answers. The triads keep close tabs on it all behind the scenes, though. Word'll get to some bad guys quick enough."

"Great, what then?"

"We get some visitors."

THE YELLOW SIGNS TEND TO BE PUNS, two to four characters that could be someone's Chinese name, but can mean something else if spoken with other tones. "Tight Soft Kitten" is popular, as is "Hungry Wet Mouth," "Hot Banana Peel" and "Dragon With Two Backs."

A thin man with a wispy beard, shirtless to show off a chest sporting a tiger tattoo, bared teeth dripping blood, opens the door to Precious Carnivorous Flower's apartment. He's holding a large, rusty cleaver, with a gleaming, freshly sharpened edge pointed in our direction. He looks nervous. Me too.

It's only the fifth door we've knocked on, all in the same building. Word does get around fast.

"Di mah, gwailoh?" It's a friendly enough way to ask "what's up?" But he says it as sharp and nasty as the blade he's holding. I can see Precious Carnivorous Flower behind him, sitting on her small, hard bed, pretending to leaf through a fashion magazine while keeping an eye on the door.

I hold my hands up and smile. "Sorry, *moh mah fahn*. I'm looking for someone."

The guy looks confused. Lei Yue elbows me in the hip. "You told him something that sounds like you don't have any rice. What'd you want to say, *cabron?*"

"I don't want any trouble. I'm looking for somebody. You know what to say."

"Then let me say it."

I don't understand much beyond *chun gwailoh*, which means she's called me a stupid white guy. In any case, it relaxes the cleaver man, who slowly lowers his weapon to his side, then finally waves us into the room.

It's a small room, lit by a dim overhead bulb with a pull string. The back wall has a tiny window that's entirely filled with an air conditioner that is managing to keep the place cooled down to hot, but less than volcanic. A single bed runs the length of the room. There's about four feet of space between the bed and the door. The walls and ceiling are covered with posters of pop stars and fashion models. It reeks of citrusy perfume with another, acrid ammonia note that I don't want to think about.

Precious Flower has scooted up into the corner at the head of the bed. She doesn't look happy that we're crowding into her space. She's wearing a loose, blue silk robe that she's holding tightly closed. I can see bruises on her legs, but nothing so severe that they couldn't be the result of occasional clumsiness in close quarters. She might be twenty. Or she might be forty. She's caked with so much makeup that I can't tell. She looks neither precious nor floral.

Cleaver Guy takes a seat on a red plastic stool in front of a low vanity covered with bottles and tubes and brushes. He looks at us and rhythmically bounces the flat side of the chopper on his thigh.

The only other place to sit is on the bed. Rather than loom over everybody, I take a seat. Flower tightens her arms around her legs and scrunches even further from me. Lei Yue frowns and stays standing in the middle of the room, as far from everything as she can.

Flower rasps out something under her breath to the guy. He doesn't say anything, but looks hard at Lei Yue, then me.

"She wants us to pay her, Ray. She doesn't care what we do, but she gets paid for her time."

"How much?"

Lei Yue doesn't have to translate. "Five hundred, *gwailoh*," she spits at me.

Maybe I've never been with a yellow-sign girl, but I have heard something about what they charge. Sixty-five bucks U.S. is way too much for a few minutes of conversation. I pull out my wallet, take out two hundreds and a fifty and lay them at her feet. It's fifty more than she'd usually get for about fifteen minutes of sex.

She kicks at the money and begins to protest, loudly. Cleaver Guy laughs, then barks at her. "*Ng hau tsho!*"

She shuts up and settles back into her corner, an abused look on her face. I almost feel sorry for her.

Lei Yue and the guy jabber back and forth at each other for about a minute. She holds her hand out. I figure she wants the faxed picture of the missing monk. I pass it over and she hands it to him.

Cleaver Guy looks it over, then shakes his head "no." He says something to Flower and passes it to her. She barely looks at it before pushing it back at me, saying "no" too fast. She knows something.

I get out my wallet, fish out another hundred and wave it at her. She reaches for it, then pulls her hand back and holds up two fingers. I ease out another, but hold on to both of the bills tight when she grabs them. I nod in the direction of Lei Yue.

She speaks rapidly, in a staccato burst of words and exaggerated tones. When Lei Yue smiles and nods at me, I let go of my end of the cash.

"She says she was having tea this morning with some other women. One of them was talking about a monk from China, with a strange accent, who she'd been with earlier."

"What's her name? Where can we find her?" Lei Yue turns back to Flower and asks.

She shakes her head and rolls her eyes when telling me the answer. "Big Breasted Korean Housewife."

"Great. There's a bunch of those around here. Find out which one."

She wants more money. Lei Yue talks her out of it. She tells us.

Before we leave I want to make sure we're not going to have more triad trouble. Lei Yue talks with Cleaver Guy. He wants to know what's in it for him.

What never ceases to amaze me about gangsters is that they'll take whatever they can get. A big score is great, but when one isn't available, anything else will do. A cop friend of mine in Boston told me about a mafia bigshot who, when he wasn't making million dollar dope deals, would take out parking meters with a baseball bat to collect the quarters.

Cleaver Guy wants a thousand bucks. He settles for three hundred and is on his mobile phone when we walk out the door.

Flower shouts something after us. I look to Lei Yue, who's laughing, for the translation.

"She said to come back sometime without your bodyguard. She'll fuck you to death."

"Bodyguard?"

"Me, I suppose. I'm always getting your ass out of trouble."

"You are, at that."

CHAPTER **SEVEN**

The Big Breasted Korean Housewife we're looking for is on Shanghai Street near the corner of Mongkok Road. We surf the crowds on the shady side of the street, pausing every so often to paddle out of the flow and move aside to catch our breath in the narrow entryways of shops.

There's a block of stores selling expensive paper maché luxury goods for the dead to take with them into the afterlife. A fistful of million dollar "Hell Banknotes" might cost a hundred Hong Kong bucks. A mansion, complete with servants and a two-car garage housing a couple of Rolls Royces can cost twenty thousand. And it all gets burnt up in an oven at the funeral home or temple, the smoke transporting it beyond the grave.

The next block is full of cookware and cutlery shops. Then a block of gold dealers, then tea and spices, then birds. No matter how many times I walk down Shanghai Street, I still feel like a tourist.

I can't read Chinese, not much at any rate. I can recognize enough characters to know what bus number I'm getting on, to keep from going into the women's restroom and then no more than another dozen or so I've picked up somewhere. It takes about 3,500 characters to read a newspaper.

Lei Yue isn't a whole lot better, but she recognizes the character for "big" and another for "housewife." We head up the narrow stairs.

The building reeks of spilled rice wine, stale cigarette smoke, incense and greasy takeaway meals. There are eight small apartments on each floor, sixteen floors in all. A riot of TV and radio noise spills out from most of the doors, about half of which are plastered with yellow paper facsimilies of the signs outside. The other doors are decorated with good luck symbols and pictures of the Goddess of the Sea, Tin Hau.

The elevator's not working and the building isn't air conditioned. I'm drenched with sweat by the sixth floor and there's five more to go. Lei Yue's in better shape than me, but her short legs make her work a lot harder.

When we get to the eleventh floor we pause on the landing. I wipe my face the best I can on the sleeves of my shirt. Lei Yue takes deep breaths and fans herself with her hands.

"I hope Big Breasted Korean Housewife doesn't mind sweaty customers."

"I'm sure she gets her fair share. When we get to her door, you stand to the side. She might not let us in if she sees both of us. She'll probably take me for another disheveled john."

"I know you guys have got a thing for big breasts, but why a Korean housewife?"

"Couldn't tell you. I expect she'll be in some frumpy housecoat, her hair in curlers, ironing when we walk in. Not my idea of sexy. You can ask her."

She's got a high-security set of doors, metal bars on the outside, another metal clad door behind them with a large peephole. There's some kind of loud, heavy metal Chinese rock coming from inside. There's a stick of burning incense stuck in a plastic cup full of sand between the two doors.

I motion Lei Yue back around the corner, reach through the bars, knock, then stand back far enough for whoever's inside to get a good look at me. I hear shuffling noises, the rock music is turned down, the space behind the peephole darkens. I hear deadbolts being thrown.

The door opens on someone who isn't at all what I was expecting. She's tall. She does look Korean, but mixed with something else. She does have very large breasts. She's young, made up to look older. She doesn't look much like a housewife. With her short, bright pink curly afro and the loosely laced black leather bustier, she looks like she ought to be fronting a punk band. She's got a towel wrapped around her waist, torn fishnet stockings reaching down from where it ends above her knees. I can't help myself, there's something strangely sexy about her.

"Uh, hi. I'm Ray."

"And sweaty, too. Why don't you come in, Ray, we're letting all the cool air out."

Her English is accented with a faint tinge of the deep south, the American south.

"You speak English."

"Yep, Korean, Mandarin, Cantonese and some Japanese, too. None of that's helping us keep cool. You coming in?"

"Uh, yeah, sure." She begins to undo the outer gate.

"Hey, Ray, aren't you forgetting something?" Lei Yue moves up to my side. She and the Housewife look each other up and down, then turn to look at me.

"Sorry, pal. I don't do women and I don't do doubles. I think the girl down in 5-G might be what you're looking for." She begins to move back to close the door again.

I put out a hand. "No, sorry, you got us wrong. We're looking for someone. I want to ask you some questions."

She pauses and looks me over again. "What kind of questions?"

"If you let us in, I'll explain."

"Nope, sorry. You can explain it standing right there. Then I might let you in."

"We work for a corporate investigations firm." I get out a business card and hand it to her. "We're looking for a monk, a Tibetan. One of the girls you had tea with this morning said you might have seen him last night."

"Hell, I thought that guy might be trouble. Okay, come on in, but I charge for my time, fifteen minutes at a time." She opens the gate and we walk into a room about the same size as the last one we'd been in, only decorated more tastefully and with three shelves crammed with books on one wall.

I dig my wallet out of a sweaty pocket, pull out a five hundred and hand it to her. "How much time does this get me?"

"About twelve minutes, but I'll give you a discount, call it fifteen."

"I thought the going rate was two hundred, two fifty."

She pats her hair and jiggles her breasts. "I'm an exotic. Can't you tell?"

"You don't look much like a housewife."

"Maybe you don't know the right housewives. I've got a different wig I can put on if you insist."

Lei Yue is standing in the doorway, watching us, not sure what to do with herself. The woman smiles at her, sits down on one end of her bed and pats the mattress next to her. "Have a seat, hon. I don't bite, the bedspread's clean. Your pal here can sit on that." She points at a tiny pink plastic stool next to a water bucket and a plug-in tea kettle.

I move the stool to where I can sit with my back against a wall and my legs stretched out in front of me. I don't have particularly long legs, but there isn't a lot of room for them. Lei Yue does sit down next to the woman, introduces herself and sticks out a hand to shake. The woman takes it and holds onto it.

"Can I get you something to drink?"

"No, that's okay." Lei Yue looks surprisingly comfortable, but then twists up her mouth in a way that means she's trying to figure out if she should say something. She decides she should.

"Do you mind if I ask you a question?"

"No, not at all. He's paying for my time." She nods in my direction. "You can have it for free."

"Why 'Big Breasted Korean Housewife'? What's sexy about that?"

The woman laughs and clasps Lei Yue's hand tighter, bringing it down onto the towel around her thigh. "Why, don't you think I'm sexy?"

Lei Yue blushes, but then also laughs. "Well, yes, I do. But why 'housewife'?"

The woman looks serious, giving it real thought. "Some men feel more comfortable with the illusion of something simple, something homey. And a housewife, well she's that, but she might also have experience in other things."

"Why Korean?"

"Well, hon, I am Korean. Half, anyway. My daddy was a soldier from Mississippi. Besides, I think a Chinese housewife might seem a little too close to home for some of these guys."

I can tell Lei Yue's about to ask something else, but my legs are falling asleep and the clock's ticking on my five hundred.

"Hey, why don't you two girls gab later. Can I ask my questions now?"

They both look at me like I've interrupted something important, then begin to laugh. The Housewife is the first to get control of herself.

"Okay, yeah, ask away."

I take the perspiration-limp picture out of my shirt pocket and hand it to her. "Is that the guy you saw?"

"Yeah, he's the one."

"When was that?"

"Must've been around one, one-thirty this morning."

"How long did he stay?"

"About a half hour. He wanted longer, but I kicked him out."

"Why? You said he might be trouble, what sort of trouble?"

"He was all clingy, like he thought we were going to fall in love or something. That and he wore me out, wanted a whole bunch of strange positions and kept moving in and out of them too fast. I'm not exactly small, but he tossed me around more than I like."

"You don't look like you toss too easy."

"I don't. But he was huge, and strong. Something about him gave me the creeps. I didn't want to challenge him or anything."

"How'd you manage to get him out?"

"I told him my pimp was coming soon to collect the money and I was tired and could see him again tomorrow."

"You got a pimp?"

"Not that it's any of your business, but no. I pay some protection money, but I work independent."

"Did the monk make a date with you for today?"

"No. He said he had some stuff to take care of, but he'd try to come back in the evening."

"Any idea what kind of stuff?"

"He did ask if there was a good place to get computer equipment. I told him about Golden Arcade. He wrote it down."

"Could you do me a favor and call me if he shows back up?"

She starts to rub a thumb and a finger together, but then stops and looks at Lei Yue. "Would it be a favor for you, too, hon?"

"Yes, it would. We work together. We're friends. Ray's a good guy, you just need to get to know him better."

"I'll get to know him better if he's got another five hundred bucks. That's the only way I'm interested. But since he's a friend of yours, sure, I'll call if the monk comes back. Can I call you?"

Lei Yue gets a business card out of her pocket, asks for a pen, then writes her mobile number on the back. The Housewife looks at it carefully, then in a low, shy voice asks if she can give Lei Yue her number. Lei Yue blushes again, but nods "yes."

She scribbles her number on a piece of paper from a pad by the side of her bed and hands it to Lei Yue. "I'm Winnie, by the way, Winnie Park." She kicks the bottom of one of my feet with hers. "And you, you can call me Big Breasted Korean Housewife anytime you've got some money you want to spend." She grins, but I think she means it.

As I get to my feet I look her up and down. I laugh and shake my head. "I'm tempted Ms. Housewife, I really am. But don't wait up."

CHAPTER **EIGHT**

Golden Arcade is the place to go for anything having to do with computers. You want the latest software? You'll find it there in any way you want, from cheap, buggy and counterfeit to as legal as it gets at a discount. You can buy pretty much any hardware you'd ever want. If I wanted to spend the next year building a mainframe to rival anything they've got at the Pentagon in Washington D.C., that's where I'd go for the parts. It's a rundown, multi-storied labyrinth inhabited by crooks, spies, nerds and even some legitimate business-people, all set to prey on whoever finds their way in.

No one gives you anything for free in Golden Arcade, so Lei Yue and I stop at a Hongkong Bank money-wall on our way back to the subway. It's a long, curvy, two stops from Mongkok to Sham Shui Po and there are no seats available. I steady myself holding on to an over-head metal bar. Lei Yue tries balancing on her own until she gives up and takes light hold of my belt.

We emerge onto the street by the market. It's a remarkable jumble of commerce. Fruit, vegetable, spice, meat, fish and fowl vendors line the streets, intermingling with stalls selling clothes, toys, electronics, household goods, auto parts; the entire miscellany of daily life.

And snakes. The Queen of Snakes has her shop here. It's across the street from The King of Snakes, her competitor. According to the papers, the business is in turmoil. Three weeks ago, the King was bitten by a banded krait. He lingered for two agonizing weeks, then died. It's not clear who's going to take over his business. The Queen was poised to buy it out, but then she told a reporter the King deserved what he got because he was careless. That made the King's eldest son mad, and now he's not about to sell.

Things are escalating. A couple of nights ago two king cobras got loose in the Queen's warehouse. In the winter, when it's cold, that wouldn't have been a problem; they'd have simply curled up somewhere and slept. But it's summer, and it was dangerous, tough work to get them back in their boxes.

I'd interviewed the Queen once. She was sort of sexy and a bit flirtatious. I might have flirted back if she hadn't been holding the fanged end of a sixteen-foot king cobra.

When Lei Yue and I walk past she's in front of her shop, tending to a tall stack of wire cages with a lot of squirming snakes inside. I say "hello," but it's clear from her look that she doesn't recognize me.

There are at least several hundred shops in Golden Arcade and we have no idea where to start. We stop at a shop on the ground floor to make a photocopy of the faxed photo of the monk. It isn't very good, but it will have to do. We agree to start at opposite ends of the shopping center and meet in an hour. Lei Yue takes an escalator up. I enter through a narrow door into a clogged hallway. It's barely wide enough for me and the remote controlled guard dog coming right at me.

It doesn't look much like a dog. It's emitting what is supposed to be a yip, but it sounds more like the poor thing is shorting out. If it poses any threat at all, it's from electrocution if it comes too close. I flatten myself against a stall selling a bewildering variety of computer games in a babel of languages and let it roll by.

The guy in the stall, tall, lanky, wearing a fraying blue knock-off Izod shirt and a pair of old Coke bottle bottom thick glasses, barks at me. If I'm not leafing through what he's got to sell, I'm in the way. I pull out the monk's picture and show it to him, asking if he's seen this guy. He shakes his head "no," says he doesn't speak English and motions me away with a flutter of his hands.

I get pretty much the same reception at every shop and stall along the first three sides of the long, square ground floor hallway. About halfway down the fourth side, at a stall selling short lengths of wire, tiny light-bulbs and blank motherboards, a man dressed in a perfect recreation of a mid-1950s television rocket scientist nods his head "yes" at the picture.

He doesn't speak enough English to tell me what I want to know, but he's patient with my comical attempts at communication. Finally I piece together that the monk had been here recently, maybe less than an hour ago, and that he was looking for a portable computer. The shopkeeper had sent him up to the third floor.

Even the stairs are lined with people selling stuff. They hold out photo albums stuffed with pictures of what they have to offer. Mostly it's counterfeit branded goods: Gucci and Louis Vuitton handbags, Montblanc pens, Hermes scarves, every kind of expensive watch. They brag about the quality of their counterfeits. "Best Rolex, real Seiko inside." Citizen and Seiko watches are among the few things still actually made in Hong Kong. It's not rare that a shipment of their interior works "fall off the truck" and end up in fake Rolexes. It's arguable as to whether the real or the fake watches keep better time.

If you want to buy something, they'll go get it. It's not illegal to show photos of phony products. If you're caught with the real, fake deal, you get fined according to how many pieces you've got. The laws have many fine points. Most crooks could teach a course in them.

The shops are larger on the third floor, more like showrooms. There's a mix of legit dealers of big name brands and technical geeks who cobble together exotic custom computers from scratch.

I'd once bought a hot rod of a desktop from one of the nerd outlets. For six months it was the envy of everyone at *Asian Industry* magazine, where I was deputy editor. Then one morning I turned it on, there was a loud pop, a bolt of what can only be called lightning, a lot of smoke and it nearly burned the office down. By then, the shop I'd bought it from was out of business.

Three stores specialize in laptop computers. They've all seen our missing monk. He'd bought an IBM Thinkpad at the third and hurried away a few minutes ago. He'd asked directions back to the subway.

I dash up to the fourth floor and find Lei Yue coming out of a shop that builds mainframe computers. "Got him. He's headed back to the subway. Maybe we can catch him if we hurry."

There is an elevator, but the building's getting crowded and it will take longer than the stairs. There's only so fast Lei Yue can go on her short legs. I'm tempted to pick her up and carry her, but I don't want to risk the bodily harm she'd inflict on me if I tried.

At the bottom she stops me. "Go ahead, Ray. I'll catch up." I smile at her and tear off in the direction of the subway.

There're at least four entrances at Sham Shui Po. I figure he's headed back toward Mongkok or Central. I'll have to look for him on the platform. I don't think he knows anyone's looking for him, and so far as I know he doesn't have any reason to be worried that anyone is.

He shouldn't be too hard to spot in the crowd: tall, shaved head, wearing saffron robes. Hong Kong isn't Lhasa, he'll stand out.

It's lunch hour and the subway's filling fast. I enter the platform at the tail end of a train that's disgorging one horde of passengers and taking on another. I think I see the monk getting into the train about halfway up. I manage to shove through the crowd and in before the doors shut.

I squeeze my way through the packed train. I can see the monk's shiny head bobbing above the pool of black hair around it.

Hong Kong's subway cars are open at each end. When they're coupled, they become one long tube that bends and twists and turns with the tracks. If they're empty, you can see from one end of the train to the other when it's on a straightaway. But this subway is jam-packed and the monk drifts in and out of sight on the curves.

We pull into the station at Prince Edward. As some of the crowd piles out I can see him a little more clearly for a few moments. He's clutching a black satchel protectively to his body. He looks wary.

I keep moving toward him. He sees me, or someone, or something, and gets a stricken look. I follow his eyes and catch sight of the top of another bald head moving purposefully toward him. He moves toward the door, but the new crowd is pouring in and he can't make it out against the tide. The doors close before he can get out. He looks back in my direction again, then turns and starts forcing his way through the crowd toward the front, the other bald man forcing his way after him.

As the train weaves, I catch flickering glimpses of them. The monk still pressing forward, the other man crashing after him. They come into sight, then go out again, then appear again. The monk keeps looking back, terror building on his face as his pursuer flashes in and out of range.

I work harder at making my way toward him, but Mongkok's the next stop and the crush of people headed there for lunch is nearly impenetrable. Again I see his head appear and disappear down the length of the train. He's progressing no faster than I am. The distance between us isn't closing.

I'm about as far from the doors as I can be when we stop at Mongkok. I bully my way as quick as I can to the exit, hoping I can pick him up on the platform if he gets off the train. By the time I do get out I catch a glimpse of him at the top of the escalator, shoving through the hordes, his head rotated behind him, his face twisted in panic.

The other bald head is moving its way up fast behind him. Now I can see the guy chasing him more clearly. His head's heavily tattooed. The body underneath is round, but in that way that looks powerful, not gone to flab. He's hard to miss in bright red, shiny sweatpants and a sparkly blue, tight-fitting, sleeveless t-shirt. His arms are also covered in tattoos. He's working his mouth rapidly and the people on the escalator move as far to the side as they can to let him pass.

No one's on the stairs. I take them three at a time. Hong Kong people will push and shove and race to get on and off the subway. They'll make a mad dash for the escalator. Then they'll freeze, standing patiently and quietly in place as the moving staircase transports them at its own pace.

I look around when I get up to the street, but I don't see the monk or the round man. There's no way I can cover all the exits from the subway. On a hunch I head toward Shanghai Street. Maybe the monk is thinking he can hide out with Winnie Park. When in doubt, head home to Big Breasted Korean.

The streets are nearly as swollen with lunchtime crowds as the subway. I've come up at the farthest exit from where I'm going. It takes a while to get there.

When I get to the narrow entrance to the Korean housewife's stairs, there's a chattering, nervous looking crowd of young women blocking the way. I ask what's going on. Two of them simply point inside, the rest part so I can pass.

I walk in and he's there, just after I turn the corner at the top of the first flight, sprawled in a position few people can pretzel into when they're alive. The walls are splattered, as if Jackson Pollack had been practicing for a red period. Rich, nearly maroon blood oxidizes in a pool spreading out from the gaping slash in the monk's throat. Paired with the yellow of his robe, it looks almost festive. The satchel is missing.

There are muttering voices. I look up and a gaggle of yellow-sign girls has collected at the top of the next flight, looking down on the scene, their mouths covered with their hands, their eyes wide.

"Did any of you see another man? A fat bald man with a lot of tattoos?"

They stare at me with blank faces. Either none of them speak English, or they figure it's not a good time to admit they do.

"*Binh doh, dai loh?*" I rub my head then put my hand at about where I guess the fat man's height.

Either I got the tones wrong, or none of them has any idea where the big man is. They turn and walk away.

I hear a commotion at the front door. I don't want to be standing over the monk's corpse when whatever it is finds its way up here. I step carefully around him, avoiding the blood, and trudge up the stairs to the eleventh floor.

After I knock it takes her a while to open the door. I have the impression she's been watching me through the peephole.

"You're back soon. I didn't think I was your type."

"There's been a murder in your stairwell."

"You're not the killer, are you?"

"No. It was your Tibetan friend."

She looks startled. "He killed someone?"

"No. Someone killed him."

She deflates back into the room. I follow, closing the door behind us. She sits down hard on the bed and puts her head between her hands. I stay still, standing over her.

"I think he was coming to see you. Someone was chasing him and I don't think he knew where else to go. I saw the guy who was after him. That's probably who killed him."

She looks up, reaches out for my hand, pulls me down next to her. "I didn't like him. He scared me. But..., do you think it had something to do with me?"

"No, I don't think so. He was carrying a black bag, holding it tight like he was worried about it. It's missing. Did he have it when you saw him?"

She looks thoughtful. "No. He had a small backpack, like students carry. It was orange, or red, I think."

"Do you have any idea what was in it?"

"No. He was careful with it though, like it was delicate."

"Anything about its shape? Was it lumpy? Flat?"

"I don't know. Flat, I think, like it had books or something in it."

"Anything else?"

"He grunted a lot. He shouted, in Tibetan, 'ooh, baby,' like that, it wasn't Chinese."

"I don't mean while you were doing it, I mean anything else, where he'd been, where he was going, something personal?"

"I don't think...no, wait. When he asked about where to get computers and I told him about Golden Arcade, he wanted to know if there were any travel agencies there. He was muttering, talking to himself. I think he might have said something about Shanghai, but a lot of it was in Tibetan and I couldn't understand it."

"That might be useful, thanks."

"What's going to happen now? My visa isn't up to date. Are the police going to come?"

"Yeah, they are. But you're on the eleventh floor. If you've been home all day it won't seem strange to them that you didn't hear or see anything. But once they find out the monk was with you last night, they'll take you in for questioning."

She brushes her breasts up against me and dangles her other hand high up along my thigh. "You won't tell them, will you?"

It's tempting, but I'm not going to take advantage of it.

"I'll have to. I've got to tell them I saw the guy who probably killed the monk, then they're going to be full of questions. It'll be impossible to leave you out of it."

She starts stroking the inside of my thigh and I'm struggling not to fall for it. I pick up her hand and move it onto her own lap.

She lets go of my other hand and moves away from me on the bed with a pout and a small huff. "What're you going to do?"

"Talk to the police. They're probably already here, so I'll have to see them on my way out of the building."

"What about me?"

"It's the police, not immigration. Be friendly, straight with them, tell them the truth, be as helpful as you can. They'll probably leave you alone."

"What if they don't?"

"I'll give you my numbers. Call me if you have any problems, I'll do what I can to help. That's the best I can do."

"What about your friend? The little one?"

"What about her?"

"Can I call her? She gave me her number. I trust her. I don't know if I trust you."

Lei Yue's my partner and probably better suited to deal with someone like Winnie than I am. I tell her I don't think that'll be a problem.

CHAPTER **NINE**

The patrolmen on the scene speak terrible English. It'd be simple to finesse them, go back to the office and deal with the whole thing through cops I know. They might get in trouble, though, and it's always a good idea to keep the police on your good side, even the little guys on the street. So I smile, nod and let them know I'll stick around and wait for the detectives to get here.

The air at street level is simmering. I point to a convenience store across the street, mime having a drink, then cross over to get something cold and wet.

I'm standing in front of the shop, sucking back a too-sweet iced-coffee, when Winnie comes out the front door. She's wearing a mousy brown, shoulder-length wig, severe glasses, a big gray blouse, shapeless brown skirt and sensible shoes. She looks like a big breasted Korean housewife. The cops stop her. She points at her yellow-sign and they smile. While she talks with them, she sees me across the street and looks worried.

I figure whatever she's up to is her own business. I toast her with my drink. When the cops are done with her she crosses the street and walks past me into the convenience store. On her way back out she pauses inside the door where the cops can't see her, but close enough that I can hear her.

"Thanks. I'll call your friend." She brushes gently against me as she walks away down the street.

The detectives are taking their time about getting here. The highest ranking cop I know is a Brit named Colin Cotterill. He's retiring in a month to follow his lifelong dream: opening a whore house in the Philippines. I give him a call on my mobile.

"Cotterill." I hear the lilt in his voice in even that short burst.

"You're sounding chipper, Col. It's Ray Sharp."

"Ray, old chum, how ya going?"

"Not as good as you from the sound of things. What's up?"

"Just got back from signing the lease on a beautiful old hotel on the beach in Cebu. Found a top notch *mamasan*, too. Life is good, mate. Life is good."

"Sounds it. In the meantime, you got time to help me out with a little jam?"

"Who'd you top this time, mate?"

"You're sounding more Australian all the time. Maybe it's too much exposure to the sun. I didn't kill anyone."

"That's a relief. What'd you do?"

"Came across the body of a guy I was following."

"You *sure* you didn't kill him?"

"Yep, I'm sure. I'm pretty sure I saw who did, though." I give him the short version.

"Okay, hang tight. I'll have the detectives give you a ride down here to Arsenal Street. I can vouch for you so long as you're straight with us."

"I owe you."

"Come on over to Cebu in a month or two—and bring a lot of cash."

THE DETECTIVES SHOW UP and they look like a Chinese Cheech and Chong with badges and notepads. The street cops point at me and I walk over to talk with Chong. Cheech has already gone inside.

His English is precise, his heavily accented voice measured and slow. "The officers have informed me that you have been waiting. They do not know why."

"I tried explaining, but my Cantonese and their English weren't up to it. I'm pretty sure I saw the killer."

"What makes you think he was the perpetrator?"

"He was following the victim, chasing him."

Chong nods, puts his pen to his notepad and looks at me. I give him the best description I can.

"Do you recall any of his tattoos?"

"He was too far away. I didn't get a good look. There might have been a red triangle on a black background on his forearm."

"That would mean that he is with the Sun Yee On triad. There are many thousands of them. He will be difficult to find."

Sun Yee On's the biggest of the triads. No one knows for sure, but it might have as many as sixty thousand members, worldwide. It's active in China, with the Army in some places. I start connecting dots that I don't like to see connected. Maybe I'm wrong. I hope so.

Chong asks what I'm doing here. I give him Cotterill's number and tell him I'll wait around for my ride to headquarters at Arsenal

Street. He doesn't like it. He clenches his fists and moves up closer. But standing out on the street, he isn't about to try and beat anything out of me.

He points to the ground in front of me. "Don't you move."

I'm well enough trained to do as he says, even when he disappears inside.

ABOUT TWENTY MINUTES LATER Cotterill pulls up in a beat up old Toyota that looks like it used to be a taxi. He honks and gestures me into the passenger seat. I get in and sit down after moving the styrofoam takeaway lunch containers onto the floor. There's a steambath I like going to in Taipei that's about like this. Except it doesn't smell like greasy duck fried rice.

"Hell Col, they trying to chase you out of the force before your last month's up? Why'd they give you this piece of shit to drive?"

He glares at me. "Stay put. I've got to talk to the detectives."

"You mean Cheech and Chong?"

"Huh? Who? Button it. I'll be back."

He takes the key. I can't even get power to roll my window down. I open the door slightly and stew in my juices while I wait.

TEN MINUTES LATER Cotterill returns. He's tinted a nauseous green.

"Bad in there, huh?"

"If your monk was going to get his throat slit, I wish he'd had the decency to do it on a cold day, or at least somewhere air conditioned."

"The air in here isn't any too good, either."

"It's nothing like in there. You want to see for yourself I'll wait."

"No. I'll take your word for it."

He turns the key and the Toyota rattles to life. He veers into traffic accompanied by the screech of brakes, followed by the angry honking of horns.

"Practicing to drive in the Philippines? Does this thing have air con?"

"Maybe you'll have better luck getting it to work than I have."

"Okay, can we roll down the windows, open the vents, something?"

"You really want to let that air in here?" Cotterill motions out the window with his chin.

The air is foul. We're on Nathan Road and I can hardly see the buildings by the harbor. It isn't far. The prevailing winds whip right through the massive, mostly unregulated, industrial and agricultural hellhole that has become the Pearl River Delta to the north. They bring soot and smoke and toxic steam and pesticides and herbicides and even worse things that you can't see, all of which hunker down over Hong Kong. It's the fart of progress. And it's a bad one.

"Do you mind if I put the fan on recirc?"

He shrugs. I fiddle with the controls. Nothing helps.

Cotterill rolls down the windows when we go through the cross harbor tunnel. There's surprisingly little traffic and we can go fast enough to get some exhaust moving through the vehicle. Maybe it's better for us than the other pollutants on the surface. Maybe.

Workers are scraping off all the "Royals" in front of "Hong Kong Police" on the headquarters building on Arsenal Street.

"They plan to replace it with "People's," something like that?"

"None a my concern, mate. I don't give one wit for the wankers in Beijing, or Buckingham Palace, when it comes down to it. Why d'ya think I'm kiting off to the Philippines?"

"You Brits, no loyalty."

"Loyal enough to my mates. Watch yourself in here. What with the new bosses and all, it could make someone's career to bust a Yank for topping a Tibetan."

"You think I did it?"

"Nah. You're not the throat slitting sort."

"What is the throat slitting sort?"

"No one you'd want to meet, mate, take it from me."

WARNER'S IN THE INTERROGATION ROOM, working his way through a pack of Marlboros. There are also a couple of high-ranking cops. Cotterill comes to attention and salutes when he sees them. We're waved into seats around the table and the three of them keep yammering away in Mandarin, punctuated with bursts of laughter.

I've never seen Warner smoke. Maybe he just does it to put cops at ease. I knew he spoke some Mandarin, but I didn't know it was this good either.

Five fidgeting minutes later he turns to me. "I've filled them in on the background, Ray. Pick it up from when you went to Mongkok and tell them everything."

So I do, but I leave Lei Yue out of it. It'll save her a trip to the cop shop and if Winnie knows anything she didn't tell me, Lei Yue might be able to get it out of her if she doesn't think Lei Yue's also been talking with the cops. I tell them what Winnie told me, and try to convince them, and myself, that's all she knows. A half hour later I'm free to go.

LEI YUE'S BACK IN THE OFFICE, writing her report. She knows nearly everything. When I ran ahead she had the same thought I did; our monk was heading back to Winnie's place. She'd been walking down Shanghai Street and run into Winnie. They went into a noodle shop, where the yellow-sign girl filled her in.

"Lunch? Well, what was it, sort of a first date or something?"

"What do you mean?" She knows what I mean, she blushes when she asks.

I raise my eyebrows. "Get anything new out of her?"

"No, only what she'd already told us."

"You like her, don't you?"

"So?"

"Just curious. She's smart, and pretty, in an offbeat kind of way, sexy. I didn't think you played on that team."

"Team? What?" She screws her expression up in thought, then gets it, then blushes again. "You're the sports enthusiast, Ray. When I want you to know anything about my sex life, I'll let you know."

I'm usually a pretty nosy guy. I kind of want to know. And I kind of don't. A couple of times in the past she's told me how much she hates it that she attracts fetishists, guys who are into her for her size, not who she is. She's never said anything about women.

I've always thought Lei Yue was kind of sexy. It's as much to do with her mind as anything to do with her body, which isn't at all bad from the waist up. But that's a line I never wanted to cross. She's a friend, my best friend, and we both like it that way. If she wants to tell me about her sex life, she will.

I've been standing. I sit down on the edge of Lei Yue's desk. It's always clean in one place, like it's intended to be a guest chair.

"This murder's got me nervous. The killer was with Sun Yee On. They've got a lot of connections to the same kind of Chinese Army companies that BC's hooked up with. Our monk was the accountant for a group that's got millions of bucks tied up with these guys. I don't like it."

"LAMA BOKAR IS NOT HAPPY, RAY."

Warner has called Lei Yue and me into his office. He's just got off the phone with the Lama.

"I wouldn't think so. What'd you tell him?"

"His accountant's dead. His money's gone."

Lei Yue doesn't look or sound happy, either. "Is that it, then? Are we done with the job? We can't just let it drop."

"That's what Bokar said, Lei Yue. He's insisting we keep looking into it. He doesn't trust the police."

I don't trust them either, at least not in China, which is where we'll have to go if we keep on this thing.

"We'll have to go to Shanghai, Bill. That makes me nervous. BC, the triads, that's their turf."

"I can tell Bokar 'no,' Ray. Send him a final bill and call it quits. If that's what you want."

Warner's tone of voice makes it clear that isn't what he wants. I don't know what more he thinks we can do, but he's usually got good instincts.

"No, he's the client. But what's he want us to do?"

"Poke around. Find out enough about what's going on and who's involved that we can turn it over to the authorities who can do something about it."

"What authorities? Who's going to do what about it?"

"I think Bokar still believes in the power of the press, Ray. You might be jaded about it, but he seems to think that if we make it public we'll put someone in power in a position where they'll have to do something."

I suppose that does work sometimes. Even in China.

"So let me get this straight, Bill. He doesn't want his money back so much as it's one of those, 'we can't let them get away with this,' sort of things."

"You got it."

CHAPTER **TEN**

That must hurt, Mr. Sharp. It is said that a burn is the most unpleasant injury of all."

It does hurt, but I'm trying not to show it. I don't want to look weak in front of Tom Suwandi.

"And on the face, too."

The sadistic bastard. He's trying to feign sympathy, but not doing too good a job. What's he got against me, anyhow?

Lei Yue nudges me in the ribs and whispers when our host turns away to call over a waitress. "Embarrassing, too." She's trying not to laugh. I scowl at her.

A waitress scurries over with a bucket of ice and a small towel.

I really don't want to sit in a restaurant in Shanghai holding ice to the blistering tip of my nose. What sort of tough guy am I, anyhow?

"I must say, Mr. Sharp, I would have thought you would have had enough experience with our *xiao long bao* to avoid biting fully into one until it had cooled."

They were hotter and fresher than I had expected. The soup inside the dumpling was scalding.

"These are excellent, Mr. Suwandi. I got carried away."

"Please, do not stand on ceremony, apply the ice to the tip of your nose. You are developing a nasty blister, Mr. Sharp."

Maybe this is a good thing, after all. Perhaps it will help put him off guard. Lei Yue likes to say that being a little person works to her advantage because people underestimate her. How much trouble can a guy who burns his nose with a dumpling be?

I wrap some ice in the towel and hold it to my nose.

"Now, Mr. Sharp, once again, what is the business you desire to conduct with my bank?"

It's a little tough to talk with my face freezing up, but I manage. "Not me, Mr. Suwandi. I'm simply making an introduction." I gesture toward Lei Yue.

He picks up my business card from the table and looks it over. "Is it you making this introduction, or your firm?"

I can't see where it matters. "Both, Mr. Suwandi. I know your father and brother from when I worked as a journalist. Ms. Wen is my colleague. Her family has a company in Mexico and would like to find business partners here. Naturally they came to our firm hoping to find contacts."

There's no harm in telling him that. Business in much of the world is incestuous.

"Are you conducting due diligence on my company, Mr. Sharp?"

"There's no need. We are simply asking for introductions to other companies. If Ms. Wen's family wishes us to conduct due diligence on whatever company you introduce them to, then that will come later."

He looks thoughtful, wrinkling his brow, his long, droopy mustache rising first on one side, then the other. He's a big man for an Indonesian. He packed away more than his fair share of barbecue dinners and beer at frat parties in Arizona.

He chews on a cooled dumpling before putting down his chopsticks and turning his attention to Lei Yue.

"Yes, Miss Wen, what then is it that your family's company wants with Bank Central East Asia?"

She runs through the story we'd cooked up earlier. "We'll need a bank here, Mr. Suwandi, to handle trade finance and joint venture accounts."

It's gotta take all he's got for Suwandi not to drool at the prospect. He puts up a good front, but he's desperate for business.

"We can certainly accommodate your banking needs, Miss Wen. And I imagine we can introduce you to some suppliers and potential partners here."

They put their heads together to discuss business and I bend to the task of eating my no longer dangerous dumplings.

WE'D ARRIVED IN SHANGHAI THAT MORNING. The only other time I was here, in 1978, nothing new had been built since the 1930s. Now the city's a forest of construction cranes, a clamor of building noise, a maze of closed streets and sidewalks. Whole neighborhoods are being razed, restored or newly erected. The taxi ride from the airport to the Peace Hotel on the riverfront seems to take forever, moving through a bewildering landscape of new high-rises that we cruise past on elevated roads, at the level of their tenth to fifteenth floors.

I'd stayed in the Peace Hotel before, too. Then, it was the only place non-Chinese foreigners were allowed to stay. It's got a fantastic view across the river from the rooftop bar. In 1978, it was all farmland on the other side. I could just make out mud-covered people driving water buffalo through the fields.

Now, not quite twenty years later, a science fiction skyline is going up across the way. A huge, garishly lit TV tower, set on a gigantic tripod with two massive globes along its length, looks like something out of a Star Wars movie. Ornately shaped and colorfully illuminated skyscrapers rise around its base. A clutter of construction cranes bob and weave like feeding spiders around more construction sites than I can count.

The only thing that hasn't changed is the room in the hotel. They've been renovating the place, slowly, but they haven't got to the wing I'm staying in yet. The room is big, with a huge, too-soft bed. The fuzzy TV screen shows a heavily censored Chinese version of Rupert Murdoch's Star Satellite Network, as well as a bewildering variety of propaganda channels. The plumbing makes noises like an old steam engine with leaky gaskets, but scalding water eventually comes out.

I've got a view down onto Nanjing Bei Lu, the bright-lights big-city main shopping street. Last time I was here it was lined with Chairman Mao billboards and crowded with bicycles and shuffling hordes dressed identically in blue. Now it's packed with cars, motorbikes, jittery colorful pedestrians hopped up on a booming economy and laden with shopping bags. The room's windows are thin paned. I hope the tumult below stops before we get back from dinner with Suwandi and I want to go to sleep.

After dinner, Lei Yue and I turn down a ride back to the hotel. It's a warm night, it's not all that far, we want to walk.

"So, what'd you and Suwandi work out?"

"You were there, weren't you listening?"

"Nope, I tuned out, concentrated on my food and tried to keep my mind off my nose."

"That was great, Ray. I thought I was going to fall off my chair laughing."

I shoot a scowl at her and crinkle my nose, which hurts. Actually, I think it's pretty funny, too.

"What'd you work out with Suwandi?"

"He's got some people for me to meet, a couple of factories he thinks I should see."

"He must be really hard up for business."

Lei Yue stops, puts her hands on her hips and gives me a hard look. "Why?"

"Face it, the eggroll king of Northern Mexico is pretty small potatoes in the international scheme of things."

"True, but I may have exaggerated a little, and tossed in a couple of hints about other sorts of business."

"I hope you didn't get too creative. We need to be able to back up your story if he checks."

"It should be okay. I made it sound more like ambition than reality. That and, well, there might have been a little something about the kind of activities they'll have a hard time checking out, the sort that would give us cash we'd need to launder."

"I thought I saw him drooling."

"Maybe he was drooling over me. His foot kept wandering over to brush my leg."

"What's got into you lately? Big breasted Korean housewives. Oversized Indonesian-Chinese bankers. I can't keep up with who's your type." I smile in a way that's meant to assure her I'm teasing, but I'm also wondering.

"I don't have a type. And I wasn't happy about his foot."

"It's one of the things I like about you."

"You're not my type. I do know that."

"Me too. As I said, it's one of the things I like about you." I'd like to take her hand and walk quietly and comfortably like that for a while. But she'd have to reach up to me and it would be awkward. As is I have to make an effort to slow my usual fast pace so I don't get ahead of her.

We finish the night with drinks in the jazz bar back at the hotel. It's a beautiful, 1920s flapper swank room. The musicians are all in their eighties, at least, one of the sax players looks a whole lot older than that. They play music that's appropriate to the setting. It's more amusing than good, but provides a comfortable backdrop for conversation.

There's a matched set of red *cheongsamed* hookers at the bar, scanning the room for prey over the rims of large glasses filled with fruit cocktail, and presumably some booze. I consider their company for a moment, but only a moment. I'm not feeling all that rich and I'm too tired anyhow.

CHAPTER **ELEVEN**

Suwandi's car picked up Lei Yue at nine the next morning. I stayed behind, walked around town marveling at how it was changing so fast. I found a few old, traditional neighborhoods to walk through, but they're rapidly being hemmed in by high-rises. I had lunch with some journalist friends who didn't have anything new to tell me about Suwandi. There were things I could have told them, but I held back. It still feels uncomfortable at times, but I'm on the opposite side of that wall now.

Lei Yue got back at four and went straight to her room to take a nap. I had a dishwater-weak espresso at the hotel and went back out to walk around in the rush hour traffic.

I had company. I passed him when I walked out the front door of the hotel and he fell into line, keeping pace about a half block back. He looked almost like anybody else. Maybe I wouldn't have noticed him if he hadn't been wearing a fedora. You don't see too many of those in Shanghai these days. I made sure by taking some random turns, then walking in a circle for a block. He was still there.

He didn't look like he wanted anything from me other than to know where I was going. And he was trying so hard to not let me know he was there, and failing so badly at it, that I took pity on him and pretended I didn't notice. I took him for a tour into a neighborhood I was curious about.

We strolled north along the riverfront from the hotel, the loud sputter of motorbikes ratcheting against my ears, exhaust sizzling up into my nose. At Suzhou Creek, where it runs into the river, I turned left and walked up along the bank to the first bridge I came to. I crossed and walked up along Sichuan Beilu into an area where the aroma of baking sesame overcame even the emissions from the passing tailpipes.

It's a Muslim neighborhood behind the huge Broadway Mansions. People from China's western, desert provinces line the streets selling food and products you don't usually see in Chinese markets. One storefront was selling what can only be described as bagels. I bought one and it was one of the best I've ever had, far better than the soft, doughy things that try to pass themselves off as bagels these days, even in New York's Jewish neighborhoods.

Knots of skullcapped men sat in cafes, sipping sweet, strong-smelling coffee and sucking smoke out of the tentacles of large, shiny hookahs. The odor of fruit-laced tobacco entwined with the baking sesame. I strolled along the sidewalk with my eyes half-shuttered, so as to enhance the sense.

I was struck by a wave of crisp perfume and baby powder. I heard a low murmur of "baby." I widened my eyes and looked at the shopfront I was passing. It was a salon. Maybe a man *could* get a haircut there, but at most that was merely a sideline.

There were five women, dressed in what would be demure, professional, powder blue smocks if they hadn't been hiked up to exhibit expanses of thigh. Two wore fishnet stockings. They were all heavily made up, almost as if for a Chinese opera, playing the part of courtesans. But they weren't playing. They made it clear they were available by the hour. Or more likely, ten to fifteen minutes.

I smiled, with a bit of flirt in it, back at them, but kept walking. There were a lot more. Nearly every third business in that neighborhood is some sort of salon or barber shop or front for a brothel. The men sitting in the cafes ignored them, as did the street vendors. A few younger men pulled up in front of the shops on their motorbikes. They and the women eyed each other, sometimes exchanging a few words. Every so often a guy would park his bike and enter a salon, surrounded by women striking attitudes in the hope of being the one he takes to the back.

A couple of cops walked by and everyone quieted down. No one ran or hid. What's the point? The police know they're there. Every so often there's some political pressure to put on a show. They'll ship a few women out for "rehabilitation through labor" in the countryside. But no one really gives a damn. There's too much money to be made. And profit margins are always higher when something's illegal. The catchphrase by which everyone lives in China these days is: "to get rich is glorious."

From the looks of it, the women aren't the ones getting rich, though.

I paused to watch the cops in a mirror in front of a salon. I wanted to see if the guy following me said anything to them. He didn't. He could have been with the government, but I didn't think so. They don't bother following most foreigners anymore. I was pretty sure he reported back to Suwandi. I walked on.

I don't know how the three old men with their pipes tuned out the ear scarring loud heavy metal that poured out of a "barber shop" next door to their café, but they seemed undisturbed. Perhaps they were deaf. Maybe it's what was in their pipe, but it didn't smell like anything other than a rich, dark tobacco.

I sped up, trying to hurry past the cacophony, but a young woman stepped quickly out of the place, snapped out a bright red taloned claw and latched onto my arm. She leaned into my ear.

"Mister, why man follow you?" She spoke with a sibilant accent made even more so by a bright silver stud run through her tongue.

She must have been watching me for a while to have noticed. She looked serious, curious and a little concerned. I smiled and shrugged my shoulders. I wasn't up to anything that would matter to Suwandi or anybody else, anyhow.

She tugged on my arm. It might have been a ploy to get me inside, but that wasn't the worst thing in the world. I followed her down a few steps into the shop. A Chinese band screeched out a cover of a Def Leppard song. I held my hands over my ears and waggled my head back and forth. She walked over to a large boombox that pulsated under a photo of Deng Xiaoping, his face wreathed in cigarette smoke, and shut it off.

Moans and panting sounds and soft whispers spilled out of the rear.

She parked me in an old fashioned barber chair. The place smelled like perfume, baby powder and a faint note of ammonia. She disappeared briefly into the gloom at the back, returning with a hot mug of tea that she placed on a small table next to me.

She dropped onto a rolling stool in front of me, a grin on her face, her legs spread in a way that hiked up her skirt. She wasn't wearing any underwear. Something glinted down there, too.

She touched my leg to get my attention. As if she didn't already have it. Tilted her head toward the front window. "Man."

A shape was silhouetted from the feet to about mid-torso, on the sidewalk in front of the place. I couldn't see the fedora, but it might have been him.

"Who do you think he is? Police?"

"Do not know. Not police, not party."

"How do you know?"

She shrugged her shoulders, leaned both her hands on my legs and ran them slowly up toward my thighs. "You stay here short time. Maybe man go away."

My eyes were adjusting to the dark. She was plenty good looking. Short bobbed hair, light gray eyes, full, dark red lips. She worked her tongue and its metal stud around a lot. It was a tempting promise. If my tail was all that interested, he'd wait.

I was still trying to make up my mind, but her hands didn't give me a whole lot of say in the matter. She undid my belt, unbuttoned the top of the fly and slowly worked the zipper down. She stared at me. Her tongue wet her lips, polished stainless steel flicked against the plump red.

She pulled my pants down to my ankles. I didn't say anything as she slithered up along my legs. The warm, moist, touch of her lips suctioned lightly on my skin, a slight scratch of metal as well. She bent over and trailed the flat of her tongue high on my inner thigh. She traced a line up and over the swollen vein on the underside of my cock and it rose with her, toward her, feeling its way to her lips which nipped and nibbled at the head, then pulled back to outline its contours with the warm sphere of metal.

She paused, mouth poised above me, then slowly lowered her head, engulfing me fully, the soft, fleshy, living warmth of her tongue bathing my shaft as she eased down on it, the point of steel adding punctuation to her movements. All the way down, she laved me with her tongue, only that part of her moving between us, moving on me. She pulled her head back up again, slowly, reversing what she'd done. Then again, and again.

I had no sense of time, no sensation other than where I was engorged in her mouth. At some point she worked a lever, reclining the chair. I was on my back, legs stretched out in front of me, the liquid of her spreading out against me, her mouth and my cock the center of my world.

I got close, throbbing against the inside of her cheeks, lightly tapping the edges of her teeth, my whole body straining toward that one focal point. She ran her hands up and under my shirt and levered herself up against me, her mouth sliding off me, her flooded labia muscling up my thigh. She lifted her body slightly and I was inside her, wrapped in heat and wet.

It's a new, ugly world. One in which sex can kill you. That's become part of my instinct. I reached down and felt where we were joined. The slight rubber ridge of a condom reassured me and I lost myself in her again. She must've put it on with her mouth. I hadn't noticed.

Then it was the slow, sure, steady pistoning of me inside her, the smooth flow of her silk blouse against my stomach and chest where she'd pushed up my shirt, the soft "uh uh uh" percolating out from between her lips.

I got close again and my own, deeper, breathier "uh uh uh" mingled with hers and our rhythm picked up speed and she ground down harder onto me, scraping her clit along the top of my cock, banging it against my pelvis. Everything between us was soaked with sweat and the juices that poured from her. I teetered for a moment on the edge. Then the synapses fired in my brain like so many sparklers and a long, nearly painful gush of relief jetted from me.

It made me clumsy and awkward. I lost my rhythm. But she still worked herself against me, not finished yet, wanting something more out of this than just my money. I got myself under control, matched her movements, reached down between us to add fingers to the friction.

It didn't take long. A *whoof* sound punched out of her gut. Her insides flexed, gripping me tighter in short, quick spasms. She stiffened briefly, then fell limp against me. I hugged her. Kissed her on the shoulder, softly stroked her ass.

She pushed herself up and looked at me. I looked back and she blushed. She was young, maybe in her early twenties. I wanted to say something, something other than "thanks" and "how much." But I didn't know what to say.

She pulled herself off me, put a hand on my chest to tell me to stay put. She padded away and then came back with two warm, moist towels. She used one to pull the condom off, then wiped me down with a second one.

I was beginning to feel silly, reclining in a barber chair, my pants down to my ankles, my shirt shoved up under my chin. I found the lever and yanked the chair back up. She pulled my pants up past my knees and I pulled them the rest of the way, rolled my shirt down and tried to smooth out the wrinkles.

She sat down on the wheeled stool.

"Good, mister?"

"Yeah, very good. What's your name?"

"Mei Lin. What your name?"

"Ray." I stuck out a hand to shake and we both laughed at the absurdity of it.

"Where are you from, Mei Lin?" Something made me think she wasn't from Shanghai.

"From country, small village. Hunan."

"How long have you been in Shanghai?"

"More one year."

"Why'd you come?"

"Get job factory. No good. Boss bad man. Run away. Need money."

I didn't know what to say. I felt a little guilty. I looked away, into the darkness at the back of the shop.

She stroked my arm, gestured to the window. "Man go away."

I walked to the door and peered out. My guy was gone, or hiding.

I went back in and put a hand on her shoulder. "Mei Lin. I should go. How much should I give you?" I knew she didn't fuck me for free. Maybe she enjoyed it. It seemed like she did. But that's not why she was there.

"Up to you, Mister Ray."

That was smart. I'm a foreigner. She knows I'm likely to overpay. And I did. I gave her five hundred *yuan*, about sixty U.S. dollars. It put a big smile on her face.

"You see me again, Mister Ray?"

I kissed her on the cheek. "Sure."

CHAPTER **TWELVE**

Ray, why do guys in wheelchairs always dance so funny?"

"What?"

She indicates the dance floor with her chin. There's a foreigner, an American by the look of him, maybe a veteran, whirling around in his wheelchair, his hands doing that '80s "come hither" thing, and every now and then throwing in one of those '70s, cup-your-ear-as-if-you're-trying-to-hear-better moves. I have to admit it looks pretty silly.

"Lei Yue, that might be one of the most politically incorrect things I've ever heard *anyone* say. And you, of all people."

"Why, because I'm short?" She looks angry. "I'm only allowed to be politically incorrect about my own kind?"

"I think that's the way it's supposed to work."

"So, am I supposed to stop calling you *gwailoh*?"

"Nah, I'll give you special dispensation on that one. But you could cut back on calling me an asshole in Spanish."

"*Pinche cabron gwailoh.*"

"Maybe I am a cheap asshole ghost person, in two languages, yet. But it's not very nice of you to say so. At least you smile when you say it."

"You know who he is, don't you?"

"Who?"

"The dancing-challenged guy in the chair. Is that better?"

"No. Someone I ought to know?"

"He's the creepy guy I told you about earlier, the one who oversees the food factory."

"He doesn't seem so menacing."

"It's the chair. I don't seem menacing either, because I'm little. We special people can get away with a lot, when we want."

WE'D TALKED ABOUT LEI YUE'S DAY OVER DINNER, after I got back from my walk. The last stop on her tour was a meeting with Eduardo Garcia, the Mexican trade office guy. She hadn't liked him, either.

"He looks like a stereotype of a Mexican *bandido,* Ray. He's got the big handlebar mustache, only instead of crossed ammunition belts and a *sombrero* he was wearing an ugly wide pin-striped suit. He's into bad stuff."

"Like what?"

"I told him about my family's business. He asked if we wanted Chinese workers. He said they were even cheaper than Mexican ones."

"You mean here? Or in Mexico?"

"In Mexico. I told him we couldn't afford to bring over workers from China and we'd have trouble with visas, things like that. He said it wasn't a problem. It could all be arranged."

"For a price, no doubt."

"That was the really creepy part. I don't know if it was because it was the middle of the day and he was drinking tequila, or if he was just *stupido* and boasting, but he was totally upfront about it."

"About what?"

"The Chinese pay to have themselves smuggled to Mexico on freighters. They get delivered to our factories or restaurants or whatever. We're supposed to provide housing and food, but pay their salaries to the *coyotes* that brought them over, until their debt is all paid off. They're like slaves until they pay all the money back."

"Nice racket, when you can get slaves to pay their own way."

"He said he works with a couple of shipping companies. I just need to tell him how many people we need and when and where we need them."

"I'm not sure I get it. You don't have to pay anything?"

"That's what he said. He said it was the beauty of it. The workers pay for everything themselves, we just pay a small salary to the *coyotes* and give the workers a little food and somewhere to sleep when they get to Mexico."

"Where do they come from?"

"All over, rural villages mostly. He said they were usually the workers like the ones I saw in the factories today. They come from the country to the city to get factory jobs, the *coyotes* get to them here, tell them how much better they can do overseas. You know the routine, 'sure it's expensive, but once you pay off the debt you can make a lot of money and send it home to your family, a better world,' and so on. People have been falling for that line of *mierda* for years."

"No offense to your home country, Lei Yue, but why would anyone pay to have themselves smuggled into Mexico? The U.S., sure, but…"

"I asked Garcia that. It's because it's next to the U.S. and it's easy to get across that border once you get to Mexico. In some cases the workers we get will only work for us for a few weeks or months before moving north. But then we can always get more."

"Anything else?"

"He did mention that he could arrange for us to import other products as well."

"Other products?"

"He just hinted. He wasn't so clear about those. I'm pretty sure he meant counterfeits, pharmaceuticals. I wouldn't be surprised if he also meant drugs and guns. He was clear about that sort of thing requiring cash in advance."

"What's the connection to Suwandi and BC?"

"Other than their having made the introduction, and Garcia mentioning that BC can handle *any* trade finance I need, I don't have anything solid, yet."

"What about the factories you saw today?"

"I just saw one food factory. It was run by an American guy in a wheelchair. He gave me the creeps. He kept leering at me, and there was something wrong about the way he talked about the women who worked there."

"Like what?"

"The workers were mostly women and he talked about them the way you'd talk about machines, or farm animals or something. They all looked unhappy, really poor. Some of them looked way too young to be working. The conditions were lousy. They lived in cramped little dorms. There were rats. The place stank. If I worked in a place like that, I'd be looking for something better, too."

I pushed my bowl of sesame chicken noodles away. I love Chinese food. But sometimes China doesn't do much for my appetite.

"Enough dinner for me, Lei Yue. What do you want to do now?"

"Suwandi's driver kept telling me I ought to go to some place called the Red Harvest nightclub. He kept insisting I'd like it. It was pretty clear he wanted me to go there, but I don't know why."

So that's where we were, watching the creepy guy in the wheelchair.

"NOW DOES HE SEEM MORE MENACING?"

"Yeah. And he still dances funny, too."

"So much for politically incorrect."

"Doesn't mean everyone in a wheelchair dances funny."

She throws me a grin, shakes her head in disbelief and changes the subject back to an earlier conversation.

"Are you sure you were being followed?"

"Yeah. Mei Lin saw him, too."

Lei Yue rolls her eyes at me. "I'll bet she did. What makes you think it wasn't just a smart sales technique to get you inside?"

"What makes you think the guy in the chair's a bad guy, other than the way he talks about his employees?"

"Gut feeling."

"Well, my gut's got feelings, too, you know."

"So, what are we going to do about it?"

"About what?"

"You being followed, the bad guy in the wheelchair."

"Not much to do at this point. Watch our backs, keep our eyes open, see what develops. You think wheelchair guy's why Suwandi's driver wanted us to come here?"

"I can't imagine why. But we ought to talk to him. Since I met him earlier, it might seem strange if I don't say hello."

"You going to head out to the dance floor, cut in on his partner?"

"He'll stop wheeling around soon enough. We can buy him a drink, pump him for information. Only thing is, I forget his name. You'll have to introduce yourself quick before he expects me to do the honors."

HE'S ROLLED UP TO A LARGE TABLE in a black lit corner on the far side of the club. It's the place to sit if you want to see everyone coming your way. A matched set of identical twin bar hostesses in tight royal blue Chinese dresses hold toothpick skewered pieces of melon from enormous fruit platters up to him. He waves them off to watch us approach. He has a wary look, like he's trying to focus on our next move.

"Ray Sharp." I stick a hand out at him. "I gather you met Ms. Wen earlier."

He tilts his head as if to better inspect me. He doesn't take my hand. He motions to one of the hostesses with the fruit. She holds a piece of honeydew up to his lips and he wraps them around it, then takes more time chewing than is necessary. When he finishes, he reaches for a napkin on the table, pats his mouth with it, then rights his head.

"Homer Bellevue. Pull up a chair." He has a faint Texas accent.

We sit and he pushes one of the platters in our direction. He keeps both hostesses to himself, though. That's all right. I can feed myself and I'm not in the mood.

"My company introduced Ms. Wen to Mr. Suwandi. She mentioned that she visited your factory today, Mr. Bellevue."

"Homer will do nicely. Let's cut the crap, Sharp. We're Yanks, we're supposed to talk straight."

"Straight about what, Bellevue?"

"Think I can't do a little due diligence of my own? I might be stuck in this chair, but I've got people. What're you two really up to?"

"That's a mite suspicious, Bellevue. Sure, my company does due diligence. It also makes introductions. We do what we can to turn a buck."

"I'm in this chair because I wasn't suspicious enough, Sharp. I don't make the same mistake twice."

"How's that?"

"Urgent Fury's how. Remember that?"

"Medical students, wasn't it?"

"That's more than most people remember, Sharp. Fucking rich kids, can't get into med school in the States so they go to some quack factory in the Caribbean. Then the commies take over, so in October 1983 we invade Grenada. I was a Ranger. We drop in. I'm on the beach and some urchin starts bawling, says come and help his mom. I follow him smack into an ambush."

"So, you're a war hero."

"Yeah, right. Reagan sent me a nice letter, probably one of those mechanical signatures, got a few medals. Heroism's for suckers, Sharp. They should've killed me. At least I put away the kid and his mom before the medics took me out of there."

"There's a lesson in that somewhere, I suppose."

"Don't get smart with me, Sharp. Yeah, I should've blown away the snot-nosed little brat when he first come up to me on the beach. Shoulda known better. What's a kid doing out in a free fire zone, anyhow?"

"Okay. What do you figure we're up to if it's not what we say?"

"I don't know, yet. But if you think I don't know the egg roll queen of Mexico here isn't working with you, then you must think I'm some kinda jerk."

Jerk is an overly polite word for what I'm beginning to think he is. What I haven't figured out yet is whether he's actually dangerous, or just full of himself. If it's his ego, maybe I can pry something useful out of him. If it's not, I don't want to rile him up too much.

But, poking him a little can't hurt.

"Was it your people following me this afternoon?"

He smiles, crooked, like one side of his mouth was paralyzed along with his legs. "Nice piece of trim, that one. I could go for that tongue stud thing, myself."

Lei Yue looks at him, a question splashed across her face.

Bellevue chuckles and wags his tongue at her. "That part of me still works fine, little lady. Come on over here, sit on my lap and I'll show ya. Never fucked me a midget before."

"Do lei loh moh chau hai, chingate maricon!"

She rises up on her chair and reaches for the fruit platter. The whole day — the factory, Garcia, Homer's story — must have finally got to her. She doesn't like being called a "midget," but it's nothing she hasn't heard before. I put a hand on hers before she can throw the platter at him.

I want to throw it at him, too. But I resist. "Fuck you and your mother, Homer, in three languages. I'm with Ms. Wen."

"You think I give a shit, some Spic Chink shrimp calls me a faggot?"

He obviously doesn't care about the fucking his mother part. "I think if you don't apologize, quick and sincere, Ms. Wen and her friends are going to make you sorry."

Underestimating Lei Yue is a mistake I've seen other people make before.

Lei Yue is muttering under her breath, drawing and quartering Bellvue with her eyes. She's tensing and I'm wondering if I'll have to pull her off him. I don't have to wonder for long.

The hostesses pull out guns, point them at us and move to stand at our sides. They're big, too, 45s or magnums or some such thing. I don't know all that much about them. But I can see they're being held more than steady enough in the delicate, alabaster skinned, perfectly manicured, bright red nailed hands. I liked the girls better when they were feeding Homer fruit.

Bellevue's smile shifts to the other side of his face and looks more like a sneer. "Do I look worried, Sharp?"

He doesn't. It seems unwise for a foreigner to pull guns on someone in a public place in China, but what do I know? His hostesses, despite how cute and slight they are, clearly know what they're doing.

"Maybe you should be, Homer. This isn't Texas."

"You obviously haven't been here that long, Sharp. This place is more like Dallas than you'd think."

I'm not going to argue. "So, Homer, what've you got in mind? I thought we were merely exchanging some friendly little multi-lingual insults. Unpleasant, sure, but this might be an overreaction."

"I don't like you, Sharp. You've got a smart mouth, but stupid things come out of it."

He's got me there. I think my father's the first person who ever told me that. Except for the not liking me part.

"That hurts me, Homer. It really does. I don't know what you're going to do next. Hell, you probably don't even know. Neither one of us wants to die finding out. Why don't you call off your girlies and we can get back to the verbal abuse."

"Why don't you shut up and let me think for a moment, Sharp. I have a decision to make. The efficient thing would be to have you and the shrimp disappear. Happens all the time here. Hell, with a billion people a few are bound to get lost in the stampede. But most of those are locals. There's always some stink when a foreigner goes missing."

"You've got people, Homer. We've got some of our own. And they know we're here. They'd raise a plenty big odor. That worth it to you?"

"I don't know yet, Sharp. On the other hand, if I have Floss and Betty here take you out back and rough you up, that might not be enough to get you off my back. Shit, son, you might even like it and then I'll still have your pal the shrimp to deal with."

Lei Yue looks at the sylph holding the gun on her and says something in Cantonese. That gets her a blank look. She tries Mandarin and the girl nods and smiles.

"Ray, my girl's Floss, yours is Betty, they're sisters. But Ray, if *you* ever call me a shrimp I'll cut your dick off and feed it to a giant catfish."

"Ya know, Sharp, I kind of like Miss Wen. I don't know what she's doing with a shit for brains like you."

"She's got bad taste in men."

He looks like he's come to a decision. "Okay, so maybe I did over-react a little. I'm excitable sometimes. I'm not one of your heartwarming cripples."

He waves a hand and Floss and Betty sit down. They keep their guns out, though.

Lei Yue is tenser than I've ever seen her. My right foot is shaking like it wants to tear away from my ankle and run out of the place screaming. Bellevue is leaning forward, elbows propped on the arms of his chair, eyes unblinking, mouth set back into tight neutral.

"Now, why don't I simply ask, nice and respectful like, what it is you two are up to? That better?"

I need to salvage what I can from all this.

"It's pretty much what you think, Bellevue. You're right, Ms. Wen does work with me. But her family in Mexico does also have a Chinese food business. They're looking to expand, they know she's in Hong Kong working for a due diligence company. It's only natural they ask her to look into possible partners, manufacturers, shippers, a bank for trade finance, all that. She asked for help. I know the Suwandi family some. And here we are. Sure, we're looking at your operation, same as you'd be looking at ours if the tables were turned."

He sits back in his chair and takes on a contemplative look, his fingers knit in front of his face. I still don't know what it was about Lei Yue's visit to his plant that made him suspicious, but something did.

There are two ways that people deal with their worries. Either they look into them until they're convinced they don't have anything to worry about, or they eliminate them, not wanting to take any chances.

Bellevue's the second kind, but he's smart enough to weigh the consequences. I'm pretty sure he's not the top bad guy. Not in Shanghai. Not a white guy. Whoever he answers to isn't going to be happy if any shit rolls uphill.

"I still don't like it, Sharp. Trouble costs me money and you smell like trouble. Why don't we all step outside."

"You picking a fight, Homer? I'm not going to help. If you're going to shoot us, you'll have to do it here."

"No, Sharp, I just want to have a little fun. You're right—dead, you'd probably raise a ruckus. But I don't mind giving you to Floss and Betty for a little while. They need the practice and I'd enjoy the entertainment."

The hostesses are simply gazing off into the ether. If they understand anything we've been saying, they're hiding it. Other than the guns, they don't look all that dangerous. But you never know. I don't think a sex show is what Bellevue's got in mind.

"Don't think it isn't tempting, Homer. They're attractive girls. Maybe some other time. For now, Ms. Wen and I are going to get up, say our night nights, wend our way through the crowd out of here and back to our hotel."

He barks at the hostesses, who lift their guns back up and point them at us. I'm pretty sure he's bluffing. I smile as I stand up and gesture for Lei Yue to do the same.

"'Sweet dreams' would have been a nicer way to say goodnight, Homer." I maneuver myself behind Lei Yue as we turn and walk away. No one shoots us.

CHAPTER **THIRTEEN**

I don't have time to figure out whose dainty foot it is before it slams me on the side of the head and sends me reeling into the alley. The sole of another foot finds my stomach and my back cracks against a brick wall. A flurry of fists like a rapid fire nail gun pins me in place. It's happening so fast I don't even hurt yet. But I'm gonna.

I'd like to fight back, but where do I throw a punch? The beating is coming out of the air around me. I hear yelling, screaming, Lei Yue. But she's far in the background, her voice nearly drowned out by the drumming on my body, the explosions pounding through my skin and into my bones.

Steel hard toes crack into my crotch. That hurts, right away. I need to double over, fall to the ground, writhe in agony, but the fists and feet won't let me, they hold me up. What's wrong with my body, my brain? Why can't I black out?

Time slows and that's worse. Is this going to go on forever? It can't. Can it?

It stops. My body takes a while to figure out that it can fall down now. Finally, it gets the message. The paving stones come up at me and I'm happy to see them. They look like soft pillows, somewhere to rest. They're wet when I crumple onto them. That's the fleeting impression I have before I get too busy with pain to give a shit about anything else.

Willing myself unconscious doesn't work. If I had the energy, maybe I could smash my head against the ground, knock myself out. But I can't do that either.

I can gasp for breath, though. I think I can moan and writhe, too. But I hurt so much I can't really tell what I'm doing. My ears work. They're pounding like a jackhammer. But whether it's trying to chisel into or out of my skull, I don't know. There's a shrieking in there somewhere, too. It could be the high whine of an electric drill.

I've been beat up a few times. Nothing permanent's ever come of it. But it's not anything I've ever gotten used to. With every new tortured breath, with each excruciating throb in my groin, with the construction noises in my head, somehow I know that if they don't stop suddenly, they'll slowly fade and I'll be better.

And that's what happens. It takes longer than I wish it would. As my head begins to clear, the drumming becomes a background noise and the shrieking takes shape as a torrent of high-pitched Cantonese, English and Spanish obscenities from Lei Yue. Everything still hurts too much to get up. The paving stones don't seem so comfortable anymore, which is strangely comforting.

I open my eyes, rubber them around without moving my head. There are four small feet sheathed in delicate black velvet slippers, the bright blue hems of tight *cheongsams* skirting the ankles. They look nice, pretty porcelain doll feet.

I'm focusing on a small bow, outlined with sparkling stones, on one of the slippers, when something hard and heavy rolls onto my outstretched hand. I have to move my head to see the narrow, black rubber wheel crushing into my palm. It hurts, but not so much as moving my head.

One of the doll feet slides under my chin and lifts my face so I can look up. Bellevue is there in his chair, smiling down at me.

"Nice to see that Floss and Betty have kept up their chops, Sharp. I hope you are impressed. You'll find they haven't broken anything. They would have if I had asked them to. I considered having them practice on your little friend as well, but where's the challenge in that?" Lei Yue is still yelling in the background, something about leave him alone, and police and just plain old rage.

I want to talk back to Bellevue, but it's too much work.

"Maybe you weren't bullshitting me, Sharp. If so, well, I won't say I'm sorry. If you were, maybe you've learned your lesson and it won't be necessary to hurt you even worse next time. "

The foot pulls away from my chin, fast. My face bounces on the pavement. I must be recovering because I notice how much that hurts. Something warm, wet and smelling like something I don't want to think about is poured over my head. Bellevue barks out a few words. The wheel rolls off my hand and I can hear him whistling "You Are My Sunshine" as he and the girls fade down the alley. I never liked that song.

I HAD A HARD TIME CONVINCING ROOM SERVICE to send up ten buckets of ice. The guy who finally showed up with it was happy to dump it into the bathtub when he saw the two hundred-yuan notes. I didn't know what part of my body to ice, so I filled the tub with it and cold water then settled myself in.

Numb is good, but I'm not so sure about blue. It's getting hard to see where the bruises end and my skin begins.

There's a knock on the bathroom door. "Ray, you decent?" It's Lei Yue.

"I'm blue. If you can stomach that, come on in."

She does. She looks startled, blushes a little, but doesn't avert her eyes.

I don't think she can see much anyhow. Even if she can, I'm not in any mood to care.

"I've never pictured you naked before, Ray. But if I had, you wouldn't have been this color. It doesn't suit you. Maybe you should call a doctor, get checked out."

"Soon as I warm up I'll change back to my normal color."

"That's not what I meant."

"It'll be okay, just a lot of bruises, aches and pains. All a doctor would do is give me pain killers and tell me to take it easy."

"What's wrong with that?"

"What's the point? I don't need to pay an expert to tell me something I already know. Aspirin and booze will take care of the pain."

She shrugs. "It's your body."

Lei Yue sits on the edge of the tub, making sure to keep her eyes on my face. She dips a hand in the water and quickly takes it out. "*Chingada, cabron*, that's *mucho frio*, how can you stand it in there?"

"It's better than how it felt out there, a little. So, what happened? Are you okay?"

"You got beat up by a couple of girls, don't you remember?"

"I know that, but it all happened so fast, I can't get the whole thing straight in my head."

"We walked out of the club, no one gave us any trouble. We spent a minute or two on the sidewalk trying to work out what to do next."

"Did we?"

"Not unless you think deciding to go back to the hotel and have a drink was the solution to the thing."

"I guess not. What then?"

"We started walking toward the hotel. When we got to the back of the building, where the alley cuts through, I got shoved into Bellevue's lap. One of the girls kicked you in the head, the other pushed you into the alley and they started in on you. Bellevue pulled a gun and got me to hold still enough for him to tie my hands together behind my back with that plastic tie thing."

"Is that it? What'd that bastard do to you? Are you sure you're okay?"

"Yeah, I'm fine. He just held me there and enjoyed the show."

"How'd she manage to kick me in the head? I'm not tall, but I'm taller than either of those two."

"It was pretty cool. Like something out of a Bruce Lee movie. She's good."

"So you enjoyed the show, too. Shit, cool for you, maybe. How'd she kick so high in such a tight dress?"

"How do you think? She hiked up the dress. Nice legs."

"Please don't start developing crushes on women who are mean to me. I don't know if our friendship can put up with that."

She reaches out to touch my knee. When she takes her hand away it's obvious how blue I'm getting. "Sorry, Ray. I was trying to lighten things up. Let me get you a towel. You've got to get out of there before you have worse problems than being beat up."

"One more thing. What got dumped on my head?"

"You really don't want to know."

"I can take it."

"Bellevue's got a colostomy bag. I recommend a lot of shampoo and hot water."

I'M SHIVERING UNDER THE COVERS ON THE BED. Lei Yue is rummaging through the minibar. "They've got four of those little bottles of vodka. Maybe it's cheaper from room service."

"I don't care, Lei Yue. Bring me the vodka, help yourself to whatever you want."

She brings the bottles over, along with a bottle of brandy and a bag of peanuts for herself. She fluffs a couple of pillows up against the headboard and sits next to me. She picks up the TV remote and switches on CNN without any sound. Some demonstrators are being tear-gassed somewhere. It could be anywhere.

The first bottle of vodka goes straight down in one long, burning gulp. The warmth radiates out from my throat. I've got the second one open quick.

"Bellevue's got something to hide, that's for sure, Ray."

I finish the bottle and crack open the next before responding. "You think?"

"Sorry they didn't beat the sarcasm out of you, *cabron*."

I snake the frozen hand that doesn't have a bottle in it out from under the covers and put it on her knee. "It's been a shitty evening. Now I'm sorry, too. I'm glad you're here. You sure you're okay?"

"Don't get mushy on me, Ray." She pushes my hand away.

"Shit, but you're defensive. What is it with you?"

"You know. Leave me alone."

"Know what?"

"*Chinga cabrone*, let's just watch TV or something."

"No, really, Lei Yue, you're my friend. My best friend. I worry about you. You seem so angry a lot of the time, lonely."

"What, and you aren't? Can't you have a relationship with a woman who isn't a *puta*?"

"What about Irina?"

"She was a hooker, Ray. You liked that about her. You never had to worry she might get too close. And she broke your heart. Don't forget that."

Lei Yue's the only person I ever talked to about Irina. I tried to make her understand why I loved her so much, why it tore me up when she went back to Russia. I think I was trying to make myself understand all that, too.

"Okay, granted, I'm screwed up. But what about you? Don't you want someone, need someone? Hell, don't you ever just want to get laid?"

"Why? You offering? I'm not interested."

"You know what I mean."

She leans against me and I can see her eyes moistening. I try not to let her see I'm looking.

"I don't have a lot of friends, Ray. I never have. At the moment, you're it."

"You've had boyfriends before, haven't you? Lovers?"

"Yeah, a few. It didn't work out."

"Never?"

"Well, there was one guy in college. That was real *romantico*. We got each other hooked on dope. In the end we loved heroin more than each other. I kicked, but it was the hardest thing I've ever done. I still want it. I want some right now."

I put an arm around her and squeeze. I try not to let on how much it hurts to do that. Maybe we would be a good couple. Either that or we'd rip each other to shreds. She lets me keep my arm there for a little while, then pulls away.

"What do you think Bellevue's hiding, Ray?"

"I guess we're changing the subject."

"That's right."

"What you guessed earlier would be my guess. A little child labor, a little indentured labor, bad conditions; I'll bet you can throw in some environmental atrocities, cutting corners on health and safety regulations and a few other things and you wouldn't be far off the mark. Even in China you need to keep that sort of stuff under wraps, unless you're a government or military enterprise. Those bastards get away with whatever they want."

"You sure this room isn't bugged, Ray?"

"I don't know, they used to bug hotel rooms. Now I figure they don't care what anyone says unless it's in public."

"If you say so. Still…"

She picks up the TV remote again and cranks up the sound, loud. What's next?"

"Some proof would be nice."

"Of what?"

"Whatever it is that's going on in Bellevue's factory. The connection between him and BC. Tom Suwandi's role in it. Your Mexican guy confirmed some of it, but not enough. If we stick with the foreign, private companies and leave the Chinese government out of it, we'll probably be okay."

"You think the government's in on it?"

"Not as policy, but someone in a high place is getting their cut. Certainly the army. Better we leave that sleeping dog lie. No one's going to mind if we dig up any scandals involving foreigners. The Chinese can step in, take credit for it, make it look like they're doing something about corruption. Cracking down on foreigners always looks good to the nationalists. Hell, they might even give us medals."

"Or kick us out of the country and not let us back in."

"Well, yeah, that, too."

I'M STIFF, SORE AND PISSED OFF when I wake up. I don't remember falling asleep. Lei Yue's still here, on top of the covers, snoring lightly, one of her short legs thrown partially over me. CNN's still on. There's other demonstrators being tear-gassed by other cops in some other place. There's shooting. It's business as usual out there in the world.

The clock radio on the nightstand tells me it's late, a little after ten in the morning. At least I assume it's morning. I wasn't beat up so bad for it to be the next night yet. I figure I'll let Lei Yue sleep until I've taken a shower, got dressed. I slip carefully out of bed and pad into the bathroom.

What I see in the mirror isn't pretty. It never is, but it's worse than normal at the moment. There's a large swelling on the side of my head, a richly colored left black eye, a bruise shaped about like China itself over my kidneys. My groin is swollen, and not with thoughts of yesterday's barber shop. It's not the right color, either.

And the blister on my nose hasn't gone away. I fish around in the basket of toiletries on the counter, find a sewing kit, pull out a needle and pop it.

I turn on the shower and sit on the edge of the tub, waiting for it to warm up.

What do I know so far?

Bellevue has something to hide that's probably at his factory. That's it. And I can't even prove it, not yet. Maybe he had me beat up because he doesn't like my face. Everything else is rumor and speculation.

But I'm beginning to believe the rumors, and the speculation is looking on the money. That isn't enough. If the point of all this is to make it all public so as to bring down the bank, or force the authorities to do something about it, I need to come up with some facts, some proof. That, and I wouldn't mind taking Bellevue down a few notches while I'm at it. Tom Suwandi, too, if he's got anything to do with it. Garcia might be who ties them together. Lei Yue's going to have to work that angle.

The hotel's plumbing has been updated enough that the water pressure is good and I don't run out of hot water. I know I'm supposed to be icing bruises, but I had enough of that last night. The hard hot pounding of the shower's spray feels like what I need.

I can't stay in the shower all day. I get out, dry myself off and head back into the bedroom. Lei Yue's gone. There's a note on the bed. "Gone to change. Ordered breakfast. Back soon."

A minute or two later there's a knock on the door. Room service wheels in a cart with two pots of coffee and two steamers of *char siu bau*, barbecue pork buns. As the waiter leaves Lei Yue comes back, looking much too chipper.

She begins to say something and I put a finger to my lips. "I'm not talking until I've finished my first cup of coffee."

I perch on the edge of the bed to sip the coffee. It's awful, of course; this is China. It's both burnt and weak at the same time. But it's got caffeine, which begins to do its job about halfway through the first cup. Lei Yue ignores me, slowly eating a pork bun, looking out the window at the street below.

I pour a second coffee and take a bite of *char siu bau*. The pork is overly sweet, cloying. I put the bun back.

"Okay, sorry, I really needed that. I can talk now."

"So, what's our next move, Ray?"

"You tell me."

"We should talk to the workers at Bellevue's factory. They're not happy. I could see that. They might have something for us."

"Sure, but we can't show up, walk in and start talking to people."

"Why not? They live in dormitories at the factory. They're from the provinces, room and board are part of the deal. We just have to get into the dorms."

"Will they let us in?"

"I don't think it's a prison, Ray. But the factory's guarded."

"It might have more in common with a prison than you think. Did you see enough to get any idea of how we can sneak in?"

"Not really, but it isn't like there's layers of razor wire and guard towers or anything like that. Just a fence and a gatekeeper's post."

"Worth a try. When should we go?"

"Tonight. Any thoughts on what we should do today?"

"Why don't you call Tom Suwandi, thank him for the introduction and ask if he has any other contacts for you. Didn't he say he was going to show you around? At some point you need to talk more with Garcia, see if there's any way to connect him with Bellevue and Suwandi."

"Bellevue's probably told Suwandi about last night. That might be a problem."

"What? That he had his girls beat me up because he thinks something might be fishy? All we told him was what we already told Suwandi. He doesn't know if he really has something to worry about, or if he's just being paranoid. Either way, at this point Suwandi would just want him to keep an eye on us, not do anything more."

CHAPTER **FOURTEEN**

S ounds like he's trying to steer you toward Bellevue."

"I'll say. They drove me around in circles all day. Four factories, only one of them having anything to do with food. It makes those exotic teas that open up into flowers in your cup, nothing to do with what I'd asked about."

"What were the others?"

"One made plastic housings for some kind of electronic doodads, one made kid's toys, the other made sex toys. I had no idea there are so many kinds of vibrators."

"They at least give you a good lunch?"

"Nope, some box thing with a soggy cheese sandwich and an over-ripe pear."

"I won't torment you with what I had for lunch."

"Don't. So, other than fine dining, what'd you do all day?"

"Looked up friendly reporters, tried finding out what they've got on Bellevue and Suwandi without giving much in return."

"Any luck?"

"Nothing we don't already suspect and can't prove.

"Where's that leave us?"

"I also scouted Bellevue's factory. I don't think it will be too hard getting into the dorm area. At least for you. The fence has a lot of gaps and the place is open on the river side."

"Once again, I get to do all the dirty work."

"Which one of us do you think is more likely to draw attention?"

"You owe me."

"Put it on my account."

"It's growing fast. One of these days you're going to have to pay it off."

"What? It's not one of those things that all works out even in the end?"

"Not that I've seen so far."

"WHAT'S SO NORMAL about East China Normal University, anyhow?"

"I don't know, Ray."

We just passed the sign for the university. It's taken us almost an hour in a taxi to get no more than halfway.

"I'm getting tired of spending all this time in cars and taxis, Ray. They sure do put their factories on the edge of town."

"Wouldn't you? They're trying to clean up Suzhou Creek. It used to be China's most disgusting waterway. Since, well, forever, everyone's dumped whatever they want into it."

"It still looks pretty disgusting."

"It is, but apparently it doesn't smell as bad as it used to. It's now China's fifth or sixth most disgusting waterway. They've been moving a lot of the factories west, making them cut back on what they dump into it. Bellevue's is one of the new ones."

"It didn't look all that new to me."

WE EACH TURN AND LOOK OUT OUR WINDOW, quietly watching the city pass by through the glass. The farther out we go, the fewer high-rises there are. We're never too far from the creek, or the Wusong River as it's called on some maps. I catch more frequent glimpses of it as the density of the urban area decreases.

After a while there are as many open fields as there are buildings and the creek is a constant dark, snaking landmark to our right. A group of kids herd a small flock of geese in front of the decaying wall of an old warehouse. Oxcarts mingle with the trucks and few private cars on the roadway. We're not there yet, and we'll get to Bellevue's factory long before we would get there, but we're headed in the direction of old, rural China. The China that, to me, feels deceptively peaceful.

AMONG THE ADVANTAGES THE INVESTIGATING BIZ has over the journalism biz is that you rarely need absolute, incontrovertible proof of anything. When I was a reporter there were things that I knew were true, other reporters knew them, too.   But we couldn't write about them because we couldn't nail them down solidly enough to be lawsuit proof, or even to satisfy our ethics. Yeah, we had some.

I know Bellevue's up to no good. And I know he's tangled with Tom Suwandi. I can't prove that, but enough of what I've heard adds up to it being true. Once in a while DiDi's clients want hard evidence for a criminal or civil prosecution. But more often, what they want is leverage or simply an informed opinion. Still, it needs to be a lot of information.

All I've got to do now is come up with enough to get some dogged reporters interested. Then they can do the rest. That shouldn't be all that hard. Then Lei Yue and I can get out of here. We can go home. China loves to crow about its thousands of years of civilization. All too often, it doesn't seem all that civilized to me.

Too many new factories in China are little more than mechanized versions of the workhouses you read about in Dickens. The People's Republic is doing a great deal for some of its people, but it's doing much of it on the backs of the others.

And the people doing the heavy lifting to build the "new China," like people at the bottom of the heap anywhere, are happy to have someone to complain to. That's what Lei Yue and I are counting on.

WE HAVE THE TAXI DROP US OFF a few blocks away from the factory, at a small jumble of cafes, bars and beauty salons. It's the sort of commercial strip that springs up near any new factory, like camp followers chasing an army. The usual bevy of so-called hairdressers cluck enticingly as we walk past to a teahouse. It irritates Lei Yue.

"*Putas*. Why do they assume it's okay to solicit you when you're walking with me? *Chingada* whores think the big, handsome *gwailoh* can't possibly be serious about a dwarf?"

"Handsome? Cut 'em a break. They're blinded by desire for what's in my wallet. That's the only bulge in my pants they're really interested in."

"Go on, then. Don't let me stop you. What about that plump one across the street? She looks like she'd give you a good tumble. Well cushioned, anyhow. Want me to translate the negotiations?"

There's a note in her voice that I don't like. I'm not sure if it's judgemental or jealous or what. But she sounds irritated and I'm not sure why. I choose to ignore it.

"We're working. Let's get a pot of tea somewhere and scheme." I steer us into a small, dark teahouse in the middle of the block and immediately regret it. It's filled with more hairdressers, although in here they'd be called waitresses.

Our waitress leans close against me to take the order. She only talks to me, despite the fact that I don't speak Mandarin and it's Lei Yue who does all the talking. She goes toward the kitchen and I get shot a look of disgust.

"Hey, I didn't do anything. I even tried leaning away from her." Lei Yue doesn't answer. She keeps throwing me the evil eye.

The waitress comes back with our pot of strong red Yunnan tea and a plate of boiled peanuts. She pours my cup and walks away without pouring one for Lei Yue. I grab the teapot and pour her cup.

Lei Yue looks down at the steaming cup, picks it up and holds it to her nose. "Smells stale."

"Whatever happened to this place, Ray? What about 'women hold up half the sky,' all that sort of stuff?"

"You weren't a believer, were you? The great socialist proletarian revolution, all that?"

"No, not so much, but I always thought they had good intentions. How could it have gone so wrong?"

"It's better than it used to be, at least for a lot of people."

"I've never seen a place with so many *putas*, Ray, so many people for sale in one way or another. It's all about money. It's worse than America."

"Even with all the construction cranes and neon and fancy restaurants and nightclubs, it's still a helluva lot poorer than the U.S."

"You don't have to be rich to appreciate things other than money."

"Nope, sometimes being rich even gets in the way. But every single person who lives here has recent memories, or their family does, of incredible hardship, of famine, even."

"So they're insecure. What's that got to do with screwing over women?"

"And men, men get exploited here, too, don't forget them."

"But women get it worse."

"What else is new? Show me somewhere they don't."

"I'm just saying, it sucks, is all."

"It does. So's this tea, and what's with the cold, mushy peanuts?"

"What are we doing, Ray?"

"Investigation may be likened to the long months of pregnancy, and solving a problem to the day of birth. To investigate a problem is, indeed, to solve it."

"What the fuck is that, *cabron*? You read it in a fortune cookie?"

"It's a quote from Chairman Mao."

"I'm not going to ask. What do we do now?"

"We'll walk over to Bellevue's factory and split up before we get there. I'll go to the front gate and make like a crazy *gwailoh* to distract the guards. You walk along the fence looking for somewhere to get in and go to the dorm or the dining hall."

"Is that going to work?"

"I think so, other than the two guards at the front, I don't think they patrol the perimeter with dogs or anything like that."

"I don't like the sound of 'I don't think.' It'd be better if you knew."

"That's what I've got. So far as we know it's just a food processing plant. They don't have any industrial secrets to protect."

"I don't know, Ray. My family's pretty tight with its eggroll recipe."

"Guard dogs? Machine gun-toting-muscle? That tight?"

"You don't know my family. But, okay, what do I do if I need your help?"

"Scream, make a ruckus, I'll do what I can."

"That's not all that reassuring."

"Okay, so we'll figure out some other way to talk to the employees."

"No, I'll do it. But keep an eye on things, will you?"

She looks worried. I'm worried, too. This might not be the smartest way to go about this. But I try to look confident when I take her hand.

Lei Yue yanks it back and throws me a look. But I think deep down she appreciates my concern. I hope so.

THE FACTORY IS ALONGSIDE THE RIVER. The fence encloses three sides, the site's open at the riverbank. It's dusk and a few outside lights are on, but the areas around the four buildings are mostly in shadow. I know from my earlier visit that the biggest building is the factory itself. There's the workers' dorm with the dining hall attached, a storage unit and a shipping building with loading docks on two sides, one for trucks and one for river barges.

We split up about a block away. If Lei Yue can't find a hole in the fence, she'll slip around on the river side. I watch until I'm sure she's out of sight, then I walk toward the front gate and the guard house. Both guards come out when they see me approach. They're rent-a-cops in tattered uniforms with over-sized epaulettes and cans of pepper spray on their belts.

I wave, give them a big smile and loudly shout out what little Mandarin I know. "Hey fellas, *ni how ma. How bu how?*"

One of them looks bemused, the other irked. They're wondering what a crazy foreigner with a beat up face is doing out here in the industrial suburbs shouting, "Hello, how are you?"

Irked one puffs himself up. I don't understand a word he says, but he keeps yammering away anyhow. I walk up, close enough that if I get any closer I'll be standing on his feet. I smile as broad as I can, enough to make my mouth hurt.

"*May guan-shi.*" He looks at the bemused one as if to ask him what doesn't matter, even if I'm the one who said it.

I follow up with a shouted, "*Wu shiang huh.*"

That helps. If the crazy foreigner wants a drink, well, foreigners are like that, aren't they? It also helps explain why my face looks the way it does. They both look a little relieved at being able to pigeonhole me. Irked keeps talking.

I throw an arm around Bemused and start babbling in Cantonese. I can go on for a while in the language of southern China, and of course, it's as incomprehensible to my new pals as English or Urdu.

That irks Irked and bemuses Bemused even more.

So far neither of them has made any sort of move. It's not that it's hands off foreigners in China, like it is in some countries, but any sort of violence still requires a level of seriousness that we haven't got to yet. I don't need to keep them occupied all that long, anyhow. I lightly maneuver Bemused around so I can look over his shoulder, down the line of the fence. Lei Yue's had more than enough time and I can't see her. Maybe it's time to leave.

I take my arm off my new pal and step back. I wobble a little, trying to look like I'm already one or two sheets to the wind. "*Wu shiang huh. Gan bay!*" I clench my hand around an imaginary glass in the universal sign for "cheers" and mime taking a long drink. I smile and wave, turn and stagger away back toward the commercial district.

No doubt they're watching. Before long they'll get on the phone and report that there's a drunk foreigner stumbling around the neighborhood. With all the development and nightlife and easy access, you can get lulled into thinking China's a free country. It isn't. There's always someone keeping an eye on you, and someone else with an eye on them. If word gets out that an unreported, inebriated *yang gui-zi* —I think that's the impolite Mandarin for me—is wandering around an area that they don't normally wander around in, there'd be hell to pay. The best that Bemused and Irked could hope for would be to lose their jobs.

I need to stick close by in case Lei Yue needs my help and can manage to attract my attention, but I can't just stand around. There aren't a lot of people visible other than a few blocks away in the commercial area, but it doesn't matter, they're here. If I stand in the same place for long, I'll gather a crowd.

There's a light and a Coca Cola sign about halfway down the block to my right. The shopkeeper is putting up the shutters for the night, but I convince him to overcharge me for a couple of large bottles of cold beer and a pocket sized bottle of rotgut rice wine. Drunkenness is a good a cover for a foreigner. People expect us to be loud and obnoxious and are polite enough to try and ignore us when we are.

I make a show of using a bottle opener on the counter to open one of the beers and then dramatically swig from it as I leave and shuffle down the street. I stick close to the darker parts of the sidewalk and pass dusty, orderly prefab warehouses.

At the end of the third block I get to a small canal that drains into Suzhou Creek. It's choked with refuse and has a sharp chemical smell. If this is what floats downriver to downtown Shanghai, I don't see how they ever expect to clean the place up.

There isn't a lot to see walking along the canal toward where it meets the river at one corner of Bellevue's plant. A dozen or so small covered boats, *sampans*, are tied up to the bank. Lanterns flicker on board three of them. Through a paneless window I can see a man and a woman eating dinner on one. One boat is spitting water into the canal from the hose of a laboring pump driven by a coughing generator.

The other side of the canal is dark, agricultural. A rich loamy odor wafts off a newly turned field, fighting its way into my nose through the dense veil of industrial pollution. On my right the factory is mostly quiet, a little dim light filtering out through filthy windows, a faint chug of a generator from somewhere beyond.

I make my way onto a small outcropping of rocks where the canal meets the river. A long dark form, a barge riding low under a mound of dirt, a red lantern at the stern and a green one at the distant bow, chugs slowly upstream. An open *sampan* pitches and yaws in the barge's wake as it tries to cross the creek.

Looking downstream I can make out another barge tied up to the loading dock of the factory. There's a small tug alongside it, a bright beacon turning slowly at the top of a mast. The light doesn't quite reach where I'm standing, but if I'm to move any closer, I'll have to be careful to avoid being spotlighted.

The light reaches to the edge of the fence where it ends at a pole sticking out of the river. I wait until the beam swivels away, then work myself around the pole and onto the rocks on the other side. I move quickly to the shadows on the back side of the factory building.

I peek in through a window but can't make out much. I think it's the packing plant. I can see a large loading door open to the river where the barge is tied up at the far end. I can't see anyone in the building and I can push the window open enough to crawl into the place. So I do.

I hear scuttling and cheeps when I land on my feet inside. It's rats, scurrying to get out of my way. I move from the window, behind a tall stack of wood crates, and wait for my eyes to adjust.

Once they do, there isn't a lot to see. More wood crates, stacks of unfolded cardboard boxes, long tables, palates of boxes near the door, a fork lift. I move around the edges of the building over to the open loading bay. I peer carefully around the frame of the door, but there's no one on the barge, the dock or the tug.

I look out the windows along the side of the building away from the river. I think the factory itself is the building across from me. The hum of a generator and of refrigerator coils vibrate through a slightly cracked open window. The only light comes from a bare bulb over a metal door.

Light and soft voices come from the building next to the factory. I'm pretty sure that's the worker's dorm. Lei Yue should be there now. I think I can get closer without being seen.

I don't want to risk opening a door, so I climb back out the way I came in, then work my way around the packing building. It's not as dark as I'd like. I steal around to the far side of the factory, but there're lights along the street and I like that even less.

There's a window in the factory building that pushes open easily. Other than the humming there's no sign of anything going on inside. I clamber in through the window. A different set of rats scurries out of my way, voicing their displeasure at my intrusion.

Faint light from the dorm building filters in through small smeared windows at the far end. I move slow across the factory so as to avoid making any noise. The floor is greasy in spots and I almost lose my footing a couple of times, having to grab hold of a slick, metal table top to maintain my balance.

Two long steel work tables run almost the length of the place. They each have a trough down the middle. A fetid, sour stench of organic decay rises off every surface. At the far end I get to a wood cabinet, the door handles latched together with a padlocked chain. I can pull the doors ajar enough to see that it's filled with gleaming choppers. I wouldn't mind having some sort of weapon, but I can't squeeze my hand in far enough to clutch one of the cleavers.

The windows are coated with slime, more translucent than transparent. There's a hamper filled with oily rags nearby. I take one and wipe a window pane, but it only moves the grease around. I spit on the window and try that. It works a little better. I can make out some details, but there's not a lot to see.

The next building over is the dorm and the cafeteria. There's an upper story with curtains on the windows, a few vaguely outlined people in the light behind them. That must be the sleeping area. The ground floor is dark.

There's a door, also illuminated by one dim bulb. It opens and a man and a woman, dressed identically in blue pants and smocks, step outside. They light up cigarettes. They ignore each other for about five puffs, then drop their smokes, take hold of each other's hands and slip away into the shadows. I hope they're not coming in here, looking for privacy.

They are.

A door about halfway back down the length of the factory creaks open and they peer in. I hunker down behind the hamper full of rags. They glide to one of the tables about twenty feet away from me. They kiss, pressing themselves against each other.

They separate and wordlessly undo their belts, letting their pants drop to their ankles. The woman turns around and leans her front against the table. The man works her panties down, puts a couple of his fingers in his mouth and sucks on them, then brings them down to her, lubing her with his saliva. She laughs low and wiggles back against him.

Even when circumstances don't allow for much in the way of niceties, people still want sex. We're only animals, after all.

He enters her from behind, reaching a hand around and up underneath her smock to cup her breasts. She inhales sharply, then starts moaning softly. He brings his other hand up to her mouth, to quiet her. I can see her wrap her lips around his fingers. I can hear his breathing pick up speed as his thrusting increases. She moves around, raises a leg to let him get deeper. His breathing gets harder. I can't see clearly but I think she's clamping down with her mouth on his hand, I can see the strain in her jaw.

Then he grunts. She releases his hand from her mouth and groans. Their rhythm is disrupted, his knees go a bit slack, her whole body tenses, then shivers, then is still. They remain frozen for a moment. Then he falls forward against her and the table moves, scraping against the floor, making a sound that probably isn't as loud as I think it must be.

She turns around quick, kisses him. They both stoop to pull up their pants, then quickly slip back out the door. I hear someone yelling, someone running. The door bangs back open and the beam of a flashlight slices around the factory. There's a dull clunk. Someone's thrown a large, industrial switch. Bright, green-tinged flourescent lights flicker and pop on overhead.

CHAPTER **FIFTEEN**

I like dogs. But I'm not crazy about the one that's snarling, snapping and looking at me like I might make a tasty snack.

I don't like the look I'm getting from Irked, either. His mood's escalated to really pissed off. He's holding a nasty looking billy club, bouncing it against the palm of one hand.

He barks something at the beast. It backs away to his side and sits, but keeps its teeth bared. He motions me to come closer. I do, but try to keep out of range of his club. He steps toward me and raises it, though. Thinks he's being tricky, bringing it down fast and around to the side to whack me in the kidneys.

He's too slow. I turn and catch it against the palm of a hand. Despite the pain that shoots down my arm, I wrench it from him. He hadn't bothered putting his hand through the leather loop at one end.

Yanking it from him pulls him off balance and he begins falling toward me. The dog jumps, looking to make a meal of me. Instinct takes over and I kick and shove Irked away faster than I could have thought about it. He crashes back the other way, into the dog, sending the two of them sprawling. That confuses the beast and it starts attacking him. It buys me some time.

But for what?

Bemused is probably still at the front gate, but I don't want to stick around to find out, or to find out if Irked can get control of the dog. I sprint to the door and out, shutting it behind me, looking for something to prop against it to slow any pursuit. There's a trashcan. I manage to wedge the lip of it under the doorknob. Maybe that will accomplish something.

It's brighter outside than it was. Someone turned on the lights. I can't run off and leave Lei Yue behind. If they start searching the place for me, they'll find her.

It's still dark on the ground floor of the dormitory. The blinds have gone up on some of the upstairs windows, faces are peering out, wanting to see what's going on. Without any cover between here and there, the people looking out will see me if I try to get to it.

All I can do is hope they don't care. I run to the dorm building, keeping my head down, hoping I might not be immediately recognized as a foreigner.

It feels like it takes a lot longer than it does. I run around to the darker side of the building, find an open window and climb in. I was right. It is the dining hall. There are long, rough wood tables and another room at the far end, probably the kitchen. There are stairs in the middle of the room, faint light and a soft burble of voices easing down them.

I crouch underneath a table near the stairs and wait. The voices are all speaking Mandarin, of course, and I can't understand any of it. A couple of times I think I catch Lei Yue's voice, but it's hushed, quiet,

I can't be sure.

Maybe the dog's killed Irked and is happily eating him, but I doubt it. In which case I'd better do something before I'm found. I start to crawl out from under the table, but I bump into one of its legs and it scrapes on the floor.

The voices upstairs stop. I freeze, hold my breath and listen. Someone's coming down the stairs, softly, trying to not make any sound. I can see legs, backlit, about halfway down the stairs.

"Ray? If you're down there, get up here quick. We have to hide."

It's Lei Yue. I scramble out from hiding and go to the stairs, look up at her. She's standing about three steps down from the top, her hands on her hips, looking angry.

"What the hell are you doing? You're going to get us in deep shit, *pendejo*."

I whisper back. "Okay, so I'm an asshole, granted, what do we do now?"

"Get the hell up here."

"What about the women up there?"

"I've already told them about you. Soon as I heard the dog barking and the commotion, I told them it had to be you."

I walk up the stairs, following Lei Yue into a large women's dormitory. It looks like a prison. There are two facing rows of bunk beds with tall cabinets at the ends. The windows are covered with metal fencing. There's a brightly lit bathroom at the end of the building and I can hear water running. Fifty, maybe sixty women in varying states of dress stare at me like I'm a creature from another planet.

Which I guess I am.

Lei Yue tugs on my arm and leads me to a huddled group of five older women. They don't look happy.

"Ray, keep your mouth shut. Let me do all the talking." She launches into a torrent of Chinese, punctuated with rude gestures in my direction. After a short while the women nod what looks like yes, but it makes them look even less happy.

Lei Yue turns back to me. "They're going to hide us. They hate the assholes who run this place and they want to see them exposed. But they're taking a risk. We have to do what they say."

She tugs on my arm again, leading me toward the bathroom. Two of the older women run ahead of us and we wait near the entrance while they go in. They come out quickly with three younger women with wet hair, wrapped in towels. Two of them scowl at me. One smiles in a way that I might find encouraging in other circumstances. She looks a little familiar. I didn't get a good look at the face of the woman in the factory, but it could be her.

The older women come out and motion us in. They lead us to the far corner of the large communal shower. One of them points to the bare lightbulb above us. I can't reach it. I turn to Lei Yue.

"You're going to have to get on my shoulders, see if you can unscrew the bulb."

"*Chingate*, Ray. Am I some kind of circus act now?"

I look at her and shrug and hold out my hands, palms up, the fingers interlaced. She shakes her head but steps onto my hands and I boost her up to my shoulders, holding tight onto her legs while she wobbles up there.

She manages to unscrew the bulb, and though we aren't exactly plunged into darkness, it does darken considerably. Lei Yue climbs down.

One of the older women hands her a scarf and says something, pointing at me. Lei Yue smiles when she turns to me.

"I'm supposed to tie this scarf around your head to blindfold you."

"What?"

"The guards are all men and they aren't allowed in here when women are showering. Even the women supervisors are shy about it.

Some women are going to come in and take showers while we crouch down in this corner. Hopefully no one will look in here."

"Can't I face the wall, or promise to keep my eyes closed? What if something happens and I need to see?"

"Too bad, *cabron*, they don't trust you."

"They don't know me."

"If they did, they really wouldn't trust you. Shut up and bend down so I can tie this thing on."

MY KNEES ARE KILLING ME, my legs are shaking, but I'm not about to sit on the wet floor. I feel Lei Yue next to me, rocked back on her calves, barely breathing. I hear women showering, talking lightly to each other, the sounds slide around the tiles. When I roll my eyes down I can see a little beneath the blindfold, but I'm also facing the wall. If I turned around and lifted my head it would be obvious. I don't want to risk making anyone mad.

There's a ruckus in the dorm, men's voices, loud and insistent. There's banging and scraping sounds, furniture being moved around, cabinet doors opening and closing. Women are shouting. Two male voices are shouting back.

The sounds get closer, the voices louder, more demanding. A shrill piercing chorus of female voices rises to meet the male voices somewhere near the door to the shower room. I nudge Lei Yue, whisper.

"If they come in here, I'm taking off the blindfold."

She nudges me back, spits a soft "shssh" into my ear.

A loud shriek sirens from one of the showering women, shouts from the others. I don't have to see to know that one of the men peeked. A contrite male voice sounds like it's apologizing, backing away. I'm about to rip off the scarf and turn around. Lei Yue puts a hand on my shoulder.

"Hold it, he's not coming in. They're going away."

A long minute goes by. The showers turn off. I hear the pad of bare feet walking away. A low voice whispers in Mandarin. Lei Yue nudges me.

"You can take the blindfold off. We can get up."

My knees crack when I unbend them. My right foot's asleep. It's a good thing I don't have to run, or fight.

The older women are there, scowling. And a younger, smiling one fresh from the shower, a towel loosely wrapped around her. They're all talking at once, keeping their voices down, directing their words at Lei Yue.

Lei Yue takes it for a little while, then holds up a hand. It never ceases to astound me that someone so small can have such a commanding presence. The three women immediately stop talking and rivet their attention on her.

She speaks, softly but forcefully. I don't understand a word she's saying but it wipes the looks off the old women's faces and causes the younger one to chuckle.

The three of them walk out. I start to follow but Lei Yue puts a hand on my arm. "Wait here, they're going to get you some different clothes to change into."

"Why? What's wrong with what I've got on?" I'm wearing jeans and a long-sleeved shirt.

"No one else is wearing anything like that. You stand out. We've got to sneak out of here."

"What are they going to have that'll fit me?" I'm not big, but I'm bigger than anyone around here.

The young woman comes back dressed in a long, thin nightshirt. She holds up one of the women's work smocks, more of a dress really. It's dark blue, stained in places, ripped under the arms. She smiles and hands it to me. Our fingertips brush and she blushes lightly. I look at Lei Yue who's smirking, a laugh trying to crack out of her face.

"This is all they've got? No men's clothes? Is it even going to fit?"

"Only way's to try it on and see, Ray. If it's any consolation, I don't think you'll look very good in drag."

I hold the thing up. It might fit, but not over my shirt and pants. I motion for them to turn around. Lei Yue does. The young woman holds her ground, broadening her smile. I smile back and stare straight at her while I unbutton my shirt. She blushes again, but doesn't turn away. I think she might be the woman who'd been having sex in the factory. She's the right shape and size.

When I get my pants off she's still looking. I don't know what she's expecting to see, but I doubt that a slightly overweight, pale, hairy forty-seven year old *gwailoh* is the stuff of which her dreams are made. I hand her my pants and shirt to hold onto.

The smock's underarms rip a little more toward the back as I force it down. Once past my shoulders it frees up a bit and drops into place. It's about micro-mini length. My boxer shorts peek out from underneath the hem. My upper body feels like it's wrapped in duct tape. I move my arms, wiggle my shoulders, hoping to rip the seams a bit more. None of it helps much.

"Okay, Lei Yue. I'd tell you not to laugh, but I don't think it'll do any good."

She does, loud. And it's infectious. The young woman starts laughing. Several more women come in to see what's so funny and they laugh. I'd do it too if it wasn't for my chest being so constricted.

All I can do is stand there and take it. Eventually it dies down. I look at Lei Yue. "Glad I could help lighten the mood."

"We're not laughing with you, *cabron*, we're laughing at you."

The young woman hands me my clothes back and then continues to stand mutely, looking at me.

"Lei Yue, what's with her? Never seen a *gwailoh* before?"

The young woman pipes up something in Mandarin.

"She says we need to tie a scarf around your head, there aren't any women here with hair like yours."

The young woman goes away and comes back with a dull, black scarf that she wraps around my head, knotting it in the back. She reaches out and undoes the top button on the smock. It eases some of the pressure off my chest. She says something, smiles about something I don't understand. Then walks away.

"What'd she say?"

"She said she saw you. It excited her. What the hell does that mean?"

"I don't know." But I do.

CHAPTER **SIXTEEN**

The night's still young, unfortunately.

Lei Yue is in the smallest smock they could find. It fits her fine on top where she's pretty much regular-sized. But with her short legs she's had to tie a string around her waist and fold some of it over that to avoid dragging it along the ground like a bridal train. I'm hunched over, trying to look smaller, carrying my clothes in a canvas laundry bag. We make a silly looking pair, so the young woman and a couple of others are with us. The idea is that we're a group of girls out for a stroll in the fresh night air.

Not that the air is fresh. It's thick with pollution. The river is especially pungent where the canal runs into it. The smell of diesel and tar roil off passing barges. Dumpsters overflowing with rotting scraps from the factory add to the olfactory onslaught. Nice night for a stroll.

And for a cigarette. There's no rule against smoking in the dorm, but the women tend to go outside to feed their habit. So we've all lit up and are doing our best to look casual as we walk around. If we can get close to the corner where I snuck in without calling much attention to ourselves, Lei Yue and I can sneak out.

I'm not sure why the women are helping us. I whisper the question.

"They don't like their boss, Ray. Probably less than we do. I'll give you the details when we get out of here."

"If we get out of here." I raise a shoulder in the direction of a couple of guards who are coming our way.

Lei Yue nudges the young woman, says something to her. She and one of the other women walk toward the guards. The rest of us keep walking, slowly toward the deeper shadows. I risk a look back. The two women are standing in front of the guards, flirting, by the look of their body language. The guards are distracted, at least temporarily. We've got to get out of here quick.

The door to the packing plant's not too far away. At least we'll be out of sight in there, and can get closer to the back way out of the compound. We amble toward it, trying to look like three girls with no particular place to go.

I'm opening the door when I hear a shout. I turn around. The guards are coming, no longer distracted. Lei Yue says something to the woman we're with. She stays outside as we hurry in, closing the door behind us.

"Come on, Lei Yue, we'll have to run to the water. There are some *sampans*, maybe one will take us across the river."

It's not that far, which is good since Lei Yue doesn't run very fast and my motion's restricted by the tight smock and the aches and pains I've still got from last night's beating. We make it to the fence and get around and down behind some rocks when the guards come out of the loading bay and start looking for us. One heads our way, the other creeps onto the docked barge.

We scuttle down the rocks to the edge of the water, then slowly make our way up the stinking canal toward the small boats. The sound of domestic chit chat comes from one of them, a man and a woman. We creep to the bow, where it's tied with a tar-stained rope to the factory's fence.

I push down on the bow to make the boat dip, to get the attention of the people inside. The voices stop. Lei Yue softly calls out something. A canvas flap over the doorway on the boat is pulled back. A man's face appears, backlit, narrow, the eyes widened to catch some light, trying to see us. I stay in the shadows. I'm a lot more likely to scare someone off than Lei Yue.

"Mut yeh?" He's speaking Cantonese, wants to know what this is.

Lei Yue does all the talking. Low and fast.

When she's done, he tells us to wait. He ducks back into the small cabin and we can hear him whispering. In a moment he's back, climbing onto the deck and toward us. He's an old man, but spry, maybe in his seventies but looking a lot older than that. He eases himself off the boat and moves past us, up along the rope. As he passes us he looks me over and chuckles, then says something to Lei Yue.

"They'll help us, Ray. Get on the boat, go into the cabin."

We clamber aboard. I look back and the old man is untying the rope. An old woman, not much younger than the man, is standing in the entry holding back the canvas door. I thank her in Cantonese as we walk past and inside. She looks startled, then her mouth pops into a big, toothless grin. Lei Yue says something to her and she laughs, clapping me on the back with a bony hand.

The interior is tiny, no more than six feet long by six wide with a rough low wood ceiling. There's a platform along the far wall, about three feet deep and three high, a stained mattress rolled up at one end, a beat up blue metal trunk underneath. A red plastic crate is a table. It's set with the remnants of a sparse dinner, two cracked porcelain rice bowls, two sets of green plastic chopsticks and a small serving platter with a strand or two of leftover noodles in a greasy orange sauce. The only décor is a small framed photo of Chairman Mao and Zhou Enlai and a tacked up picture of a smiling young woman with a chubby, laughing baby in front of the Chinese theater in Hollywood. Other than that, there's some clothes and towels hung from nails sunk into the plank walls.

The small boat rocks as the old man makes his way around to the stern. His face appears in a window cut out of the back wall, above the sleeping platform. He hisses something at the woman, then his face drops from sight. I hear a tug of a cord, the sputter of an engine, the wood underneath me begins to hum.

The old woman whispers to Lei Yue who turns to me.

"She wants us to pull the trunk out from under the bed. We're supposed to hide under there."

I look at it again. "Under there?"

"Got any better ideas, *cabron?*"

I don't. The trunk isn't heavy, it slides out as if on rollers.

"You get in first, Ray. It'll be easier for me to find a place to fit after you."

The space is less than six feet long and I'm a little under that tall. I get down on the floor. It's damp and greasy and vibrating in a way that isn't going to make my bones happy. I roll into place on my left side, my back against the wall, my knees slightly bent. Lei Yue rolls in after me, facing out.

The old woman slides the trunk back up against the opening. I hear her unroll the mattress on the platform, then she gets up onto it. It sounds like she's sitting with her back against the wall, her legs out in front of her using the trunk as a footrest.

I FIND LEI YUE'S EAR and whisper into it. "Why are they helping us?"

"It's China, Ray. If people don't help each other all hell breaks loose."

"Yeah, but it's risky."

"They don't like Bellevue's factory, either. They're charging them too much to tie their boat up here and the factory dumps a lot of bad stuff into the river. There aren't any fish left."

"Why not move?"

"It's not so easy. And it won't be much better anywhere else."

I'll never understand China.

I sense the boat backing away from the water's edge and out into the canal. I feel it turning, hear the small engine straining against the thick, black industrial water.

I take a deep breath and my nose fills with the odor of tar and diesel and a slight sour vegetable stench from the old, waterlogged wood. I bury it into Lei Yue's hair in front of me. That smells faintly of shampoo, sweat and fear. It's an improvement.

"Ray, what're you doing? Get your nose out of my hair." I can hardly hear her over the burbling of the motor, the rattling of every loose everything on the boat.

"It smells nice."

"No it doesn't. And this really isn't the time. If you start getting *hahm sahp* I swear I'll figure out some way to kick you in the *cojones*. I don't care how much noise you'll make."

"I'm not getting horny. Just trying to keep myself from sneezing."

"If you sneeze in my hair, I'm still going to kick you in the *cojones*."

She means it. I fight back an itch in my nose.

"Do we know where they're taking us?"

"Not exactly. All they said is that they'd help us get back to the city."

"Why are they speaking Cantonese?"

"Something about it being cheaper to retire here than in Hong Kong and they want money to send to their daughter and grandson in California."

"If this is where they live, I can see that it's cheaper. I don't think the poorest person in Hong Kong lives like this."

"You seen the poorest person in Hong Kong?"

"Isn't it that woman who lives on the hill above the *Shau Kei Wan* market?" It's a lame attempt to lighten the mood.

She elbows me hard, in the ribs. "Shut up."

I try to come up with another wisecrack, it helps keep my mind off what's going on. Before I can, I hear shouting, a voice that sounds loud across the water even muffled by the metal chest in front of us.

The old woman slaps a warning hand on the mattress. We don't need to be told. The boat's still moving at the same slow pace down the canal toward the river. The yelling keeps coming from the direction of the shore. One of the old woman's feet is nervously drumming against the chest. The old man doesn't seem to be shouting anything in response.

I can tell when we get to the river. The boat is yanked hard, by the current, to the right, in the direction of downtown Shanghai. The small motor revs up, trying to keep us moving out from the rocks, to the safety of the flowing center. I can still hear the shouting, but fainter over the high cake-beater whine of the struggling engine. Both the old woman's feet are drumming on the metal trunk, out of sync with the sounds being torn from the rough planks and aged equipment around us.

"Who's yelling? What?" I whisper into Lei Yue's ear but I'm not sure she can hear me over the racket.

She doesn't respond. I don't repeat it, keeping quiet for a very long time. My joints ache from the damp and the vibration and the hard wood. I'm getting a headache from the noise and the smells. When I was a kid my family had a housekeeper who'd been smuggled across the border from Tijuana to San Diego, with an aunt and a cousin, in the trunk of a 1964 Chevy Impala. That must've been something like this. Only I'm not hoping for a whole new better life when I get out, or even a job. I'm hoping no one's going to beat me up. Or worse.

I'm squirming, flexing, doing isometrics. I don't know how Lei Yue manages to hold so still. There's no way I can stay in here all the way back to the center of the city.

She twists her body, turns her head in my direction. "Stop your fidgeting. You're making me *loca*."

"When do we get the hell out of here?"

"I don't know. Helping us is dangerous for these people. They probably want to get rid of us as soon as they can."

"I still don't get why they're helping us."

"It's China, Ray. There must be dozens of reasons. I don't think anyone here is all that happy. It doesn't hurt that I gave them money."

"How much?"

"Not much, a hundred *yuan*."

"Now I really am confused. Why would they help us for that little? They've got a picture of Mao, they're patriots."

"Maybe. Or maybe Mao's just a sort of god to them, a replacement Buddha. Maybe they figure it looks good if any of the authorities bother them about anything. And a hundred isn't so little to them."

"What would someone want to bother them about?"

"How should I know? Their bourgeois, capitalist-roader, imperialist-lackey tendencies. The fact that they come from Hong Kong. The government here is always sticking its nose into people's business.

And most people resent that. They're people who are helping us. Haven't you ever heard of not looking a gift horse in the mouth? They've got their reasons."

Didn't the gift horse in the mouth thing come from the Trojan Horse? Isn't the point of that that sometimes you ought to look into the mouth of the horse? My mind's wandering, trying to distract itself. There's a solid thump against the front of the boat. Something's banging against the hull as we move over it. Then there's a terrible clanking, a clatter. I smell smoke. The old man is yelling. The old woman gets off the bed and rolls the trunk out of the way, saying something low and fast.

Lei Yue claws her way out and looks up at the old woman. "*Mei tse-ah?*" She wants to know what's the matter.

I don't understand the answer but it's clear I've got to wiggle my way out of the hiding place. I do. It takes some stretching and bending so that I've got control of my limbs. Lei Yue and the woman are talking in hushed tones.

The old man sticks his face through the window and spits out a rush of words. Lei Yue nods, then turns to me.

"The rudder's been knocked out by something. We're in the middle of the river, but the current is slow. He's going to try and pole us over to the other side and let us off."

I step to the small doorway and look out. It's mostly dark, a few dim lights from a highway on the other side of a field. There are rocks along the shore. Looking back in the direction we've come from I can see a lot of lights around the factory. There're people on the loading dock and on the barge and tug tied to it. I can't tell if they can see us. They've got the lights on. We don't.

Keeping low, I crawl out to the bow. I see a bend in the river ahead. If the current keeps us moving and the old man keeps us at the right angle, we should hit shore in a minute or two.

"Lei Yue, get up here, we'll have to jump soon." She crawls up to my side. The old woman walks up, ignoring us, carrying a bamboo pole. It will help keep us from smashing against the rocks. Lei Yue looks up at her and says something that makes her laugh.

"What'd you say?"

"Nothing, just a joke."

I'd ask what it was, but there's no time. We're within feet of the rocks. The old lady jams the pole into the sediment below and the boat slows, swinging around. I get up and call out my thanks, *"Doh jeh,"* as I leap for land. I turn around and almost slip into the water, but catch myself, stretching out my arms to help Lei Yue.

She almost knocks me over, barreling into my chest. I hold onto her and step back. The boat's already spun around, the old lady sending us a short wave as it curves around the bend, then out of sight.

"WHERE THE HELL ARE WE?" Lei Yue's looking around, but it's too dark to see much of anything.

"At the edge of a field. We should get off these rocks, someone might be able to see us."

"It smells like shit."

"Yeah, I know, fertilizer." It's probably "night soil," human fertilizer, but I don't think I'll mention that. Looking back across the river I see the tug pulling away from the docked barge, heading into the current, a spotlight on its prow scanning over the water.

"Try to ignore it. We need to get out of sight."

Lei Yue's scrambled up the rocks. "There's a path up here."

I pick my way up to her side, take a look. "We're still pretty exposed. Let's get around the bend quick." There's some low bushes ahead, where the river curves to the left. They'll give us some cover.

We get into the bushes just before the tug passes, its hot beam of light searing into our eyes.

"Think they can see us?"

"I hope not. Find out anything interesting at the factory?"

"Yeah, I was doing fine until you showed up."

"I wanted to be nearby in case you needed help."

"I didn't."

"Not yet, at any rate. But you never know."

"Okay, Mr. Knight in Shining Armor, what do we do now?"

"Get back to town."

"How? Hitchhike? I think there's a road on the other side of the field."

"If we can find someone with a *sampan* to take us down the river, they're more likely to keep their mouths shut."

"Why's that?"

"Poor people are less likely to have any love for the local bigshots. Anyone with a car's going to have more of a stake in the way things are and might not want to take a chance helping out a couple of foreigners in the wrong place."

"Welcome to the workers' paradise. *Viva la revolucion.*"

"There'll be time for counter-revolutionary sarcasm later. Let's change back into our own clothes. Then let's find a boat."

A CLOYING PUNGENCE OF LICHEN AND MANURE is the reason I'm taking only shallow breaths through my mouth. Lei Yue, too.

The barge had pulled over to offload some crates at a floating dock near a huddle of restaurants about a half mile east of the bend in the river. We'd negotiated a ride all the way down to where the Suzhou spills into the Huangpu, a few blocks from our hotel, although I'm not sure it's a good idea to go back there. We've got some time to figure out what to do next, where to go.

The barge pilot didn't ask any questions. Two hundred *yuan* was more than enough to make him happy and keep him quiet.

The hairy crabs are quiet, too. They're stuffed into the boxes we're sitting up against, trussed with narrow strips of bamboo pith. There's a thousand crabs, maybe more. They'll sell for as much as forty bucks each at restaurants in Shanghai and Hong Kong. There's not a lot of meat on them, but what there is, is delicious—if it doesn't kill you.

A few years ago there was a cholera outbreak here, and in Hong Kong. Someone had transported a few barges of hairy crabs downriver in holds that had recently been used to transport human shit upriver for fertilizer. They hadn't bothered to wash the tanks in between. You eat your crab, you take your chances.

At least cholera can kill you quick. Hairy crabs are happy to eat almost anything. A lot of them are raised in ponds and lakes near some of China's heaviest polluters. I wouldn't be surprised if you could pick out your crab with a magnet.

"Ray, I'm hungry."

How can she be hungry, with this stench? "I don't think one of these would make very good sushi."

"Sashimi. We don't have any rice."

"Well, not that either. I'd be hungry, too, if it wasn't for the smell. There's nothing we can do about it until we get back to the city. Tell me what you found out. It'll take your mind off your stomach."

"It's enough to give me an upset stomach. The people who work there, they're like slaves."

"In what way?"

"They all come from small villages, far away. Recruiters showed up and promised them forty *yuan* a day to come here and work. It sounds good, I guess, five dollars a day, about five times what they'd make on the farm if the crops didn't fail."

"Okay, so far so good."

"Now's when it gets bad. They put them on buses to bring them to Shanghai. They told them not to pack anything because there isn't any room and they won't need anything anyhow, everything will be provided.

"So they get here and there *is* all that stuff, but they have to pay for it. And the bus ride, and their food, and something for the bed they sleep on, and the water and electricity they use, and a commission for the guy who brought them here, and a bus ride into town if they ever manage to get a day off and aren't too dead tired to go into town, and there's a lot of things they get fined for if they don't do them exactly the way the foremen tell them to."

"Why don't they leave?"

"They can't, not until they pay back all the money they owe."

"After that, then?"

"It's a one-year contract and they're only paid at the end, when all the money has been taken out of their wages and the bus takes them back to their villages."

"Why don't they go to the police, the authorities?"

"Whose police? What authorities? They signed contracts. None of this is illegal. The recruiters work in the countryside, they know where their families live. They've all heard of someone who did go to the cops, then disappeared, or whose family got kicked off their farm.

"They're scared. They're tired. They think that no matter how bad it is, there's probably still more money in it for them at the end of the year than they'd have made at home, at least if they keep their mouths shut and do what they're told. That enough reasons for you?"

"Too many. Where are the communists when you need them?"

"In Beijing, bragging about the growth in the economy. And eating, probably. I'm still hungry, Ray."

"I'm not. I'm mad."

"Can't you be both?"

"Are they?"

"Who?"

"The women who work in Bellevue's food factory."

"Sure they are, Ray. Plenty mad. But they're too hungry to do anything about it."

"What're we going to do about it? What can we do?"

"I was afraid you were going to ask that."

I wish to hell I knew. If Bellevue wasn't around to exploit these people, someone else would step in to take his place. That's what he'd say.

And he'd be right. But it's got to stop somewhere. And I don't like him.

"We're going to crush the crip."

"I thought we're not supposed to use words like that, Ray."

"Okay. We're going to crush the kid-killing, motherfucking, handicapped bastard. That better?"

"Can we duct tape him to his wheelchair and push him into one of these night-soil toting barges?"

I put my arm around my friend. She doesn't shrug it off for a change. I look out and down at the dark, slimy water oozing past. The lights of a passing truck on the highway to the north judder on the potholed road. There's the low thrumming of the engine pushing this stuttering barge. A soft yellow glow filters into the eastern sky, shed by the enormous metropolis we're creeping toward.

It would all seem so peaceful if it wasn't for the rising high-pitched whine of a speedboat upriver. The sound slices through the thick air, coming up fast.

CHAPTER **SEVENTEEN**

It didn't take long for the speedboat to pull up alongside the barge, for the factory guards to find us and bundle us onto their boat. There wasn't any sense in fighting with guns pointed at our chests. It was too short a ride back to the factory.

Now my head's ringing like an old-fashioned wall phone in a college dormitory with an angry parent on the other end. I don't know whose foot it was that made it that way, Floss's or Betty's.

Bellevue, or someone, dresses them funny. At the moment they look like a matched set of counterfeit Chinese girl scouts; in forest green *cheongsams* with red sashes decorated with what look like merit badges. One of those badges has got to be for knot tying. The one who roped me to the wheelchair did an excellent job. Only my head can move, but it doesn't want to.

My chin is flopped down on my chest, a bobblehead with a sprung spring. I think I'd like to lift my face, but I'm not sure why. I doubt that will make it hurt any less, or put a stop to the clanging.

I don't have any choice. There's a sudden flash of beautiful pedicured pomegranate-tinged toes and my chin snaps up. My head whips back so hard and fast that I'm afraid my throat will tear. My eyes open and through the haze of tears there's a smear of green fluorescence.

"Enough. I want him alert."

Bellevue rolls up, grabs my fast swelling jaw and wrenches it around.

"I warned you to keep your nose out of my business, Sharp. You wanna look around? Here, have a look."

He rolls back a little, and with a hard tug, spins me in a tight, rapid circle. The wheelchair I'm tied to almost topples over. He spins me again, and again. I start heaving. Not much comes up. There isn't much.

He stops my spinning, leans in close. "Don't worry, Sharp, I'm not going to let you pass out. Betty and Floss want to play with you some more."

I'm catching my breath. If I concentrate on where I hurt it helps me focus.

I haven't seen Lei Yue since they tied me to the chair. Bemused and Irked threw a cloth bag over her head and dragged her away.

"What've you done to Lei Yue?"

He laughs. It's one of the ugliest sounds I've heard in a very long time. "I'll have some fun with her. It's a shame you won't be around to watch. You might find it amusing. But I'm sorry, I've had enough of you."

"No need to apologize, Bellevue. The feeling's mutual."

"I think I'll go visit the shrimp, Sharp. I'll leave you to Betty and Floss for a little while. Maybe you can channel your inner masochist. You might even like what they do to you. At first."

His chair whirs as he works its joystick and moves away. The girls head toward me, one from each side. Is it better to brace myself or to relax? Whichever I do, it's going to be involuntary pretty quick. A nice looking hand whips a long strip of shiny gray duct tape across my mouth and around the back of my head. They don't want to hear me shouting—or screaming.

A commanding voice calls out something in Mandarin. The girls freeze. Then English. "Mr. Bellevue, stop. We are not barbarians."

It's Suwandi. I never thought I'd be happy to hear him. Bellevue puts on the brakes as his boss steps out of the shadows.

"Mr. Suwandi, I found this asshole and his midget snooping around, talking to the workers."

The banker doesn't say anything, just makes a hand gesture and nods in my direction. It's meant for one of the girls. Floss, or Betty, bounds to Bellevue's chair, shoots out an arm with the palm of her hand flat, and chops the vet across the neck. The gurgling noise chudders out of him after he's already unconscious, or dead. I can't tell which.

"I tolerate failure even less than I do interference, Mr. Sharp. You and Mr. Bellevue are minor irritants, but the smallest mosquito can prove deadly if it is not swatted. I would apologize for what I have to do, except that if it was not me, it would not be long before you irritated someone else of power who would do the same thing." Suwandi makes another gesture. I instinctively lower my chin to cover the front of my neck as he fades back out of sight.

But I'm not chopped. Hands grasp the handles at the back of the chair and turn it to face the loading bay leading out to the river. I hear the motor of Bellevue's chair and I look to my left as it passes me. The girl who hit him is seated on his lap, driving.

We wheel outside the building, a light *thud thud thud* across the loose planks of the dock. There's no boat out there and we're not turning left or right. I'd struggle against the ropes, but they're so tight I can't even do that. I can only sit and tense my muscles and watch and listen and smell the foul air and feel the bite in my wrists and ankles. Floss and Betty, the deadly girl scout twins, take us to the edge of the dock.

The one driving Bellevue's chair springs from his lap. She's graceful, a study in the economy of motion. She glides behind him and with little effort pushes him into the water. He sinks immediately, a short spark from the electric motor and he's gone.

I'm shouting something into the tape. I don't know what. I can't think. My life isn't flashing before my eyes. Time isn't slowing down. I hit the water head first. It's black. It's cold. I fight against it, try to hold my breath but it's hopeless. I stop fighting. Everything slows. The water enfolds me like a warm, comfortable blanket. Then, nothing.

CHAPTER **EIGHTEEN**

It's *chingada fria* in here. And dark. And I'm getting itchy and my stomach's got that bad feeling. If only *el Gordo* would come back soon and pump me with some more of that sweet juice. I know it's not doing me any good. But I don't care. It's all I've got. There's nothing else. It makes me feel so good. It lets me not think. What's wrong with that? I got over it back in college. Maybe I can do that again. Or maybe I won't want to. Right now, I just want it.

El Gordo's good with the needle. Gentle. Makes me warm inside, tingly. Makes me feel like someone's turned on some lights.

Where's Ray? *Do lei loh moh*, where's Ray? The motherfucker. No Bellevue yet. I was sure he'd be at me by now. I wonder what's keeping him. I hope they dope me up big time before he shows.

Where the hell am I, anyhow? The *cabrones* have moved me a few times, but always with a bag over my head, burlap. With too much of that stuff, what do they call it? That stuff from wool that makes me sneeze.

It's bigger than a closet. Takes me seven steps one way from wall to wall, a dozen the other. I can't see the ceiling, but it's up there somewhere, out of reach. There's two buckets. One with water. I hope they come and empty the other one soon.

THEY GRABBED US OFF THE BARGE. A speedboat came alongside, the guys Ray was calling Bemused and Irked pointed guns at us and we did what they told us to do. They took us back to the warehouse. Bellevue was there with his *putas*, Floss and Betty. They tied my hands behind my back. They tied Ray to a wheelchair. I guess that was Bellevue's idea of a joke. Then they threw the bag over my head. I could hear Ray yelling, telling them to leave me out of it. For all the good that did. The last thing I remember about any of it was being jabbed with a needle in the crook of my left elbow, going woozy, going out and then waking up with the worst *chingada* headache of my life in a place like this one.

It's been some time. I try to keep track but it isn't easy. Maybe a few days. Maybe a week. Maybe a month. It couldn't be more than that. Could it? The only light I see is when the fat guy, *el Gordo*, comes in with the dope. He holds a small flashlight in his teeth so he can find a vein. I think he's Chinese. His body smells of acrid, sweaty garlic and ginger. His breath stinks of cheap rice wine, the kind they mix with snake bile.

There's someone else, a woman. Maybe one of the *putas*. She has a strong scent like a cut flower that has about a day left in the vase before it needs to be thrown out. She comes in first, in the dark, and grabs me with long, delicate, vicegrip strong fingers, holds me still until he's done and I've gone limp with bright, happy explosions inside.

She doesn't really need to do that anymore. I like the *fan*, the powder, the heroin. I think that's what it is. I like its *beso*. It kisses me so good. It's like it's making *sopa*, stirring the ingredients all up inside me like a talented tongue in my pussy. My *dona blanca,* my white lady lover. I've tried to tell them that. Tried to tell them they don't need to force me anymore. But my voice isn't working. I can croak some sounds, but I don't think they can understand me. They never say anything.

When are they coming back? Isn't it time? I'm so thirsty. The water's out. I splashed my face, rubbed down my arms with the last of it. I'm breathing through my mouth. It helps shut out the stink from the other bucket. Where's my *puta*? Where's my flower whore? *El Gordo*, I want you. I want the prick of your needle. I want your *broca*, your drillbit, your stinging prick.

Maybe I can sleep. But if I do I'll dream and I don't like my dreams. Not lately. Not the ones I've had in here. *Los monstruos*, they're so big and I'm so small. And I don't like being small, not when it makes me help-less. And sometimes Ray shows up and saves me, shakes me awake, gets me away from *los chingada monstruos*. But sometimes he doesn't and they swallow me and I wake up and it's so dark and I think I'm inside them.

Where is Ray? What are they doing to him? He always gets out of these things. He's no superman but he always gets away. Why hasn't he come for me yet?

I sit on the thin mattress, my back against the cold stone wall. I don't even have to feel my way there. My body knows where it is. I hug my arms around me, try not to scratch myself. All I can do is wait and try not to think.

I don't want to go home. I don't want to be here. If I go home I'm just another *enana,* a dwarf stuck in her parents' business. I can hear my father, "let the dwarf work in our *Casa de Chop Suey* in Mexicali. They'll come in to see the *monstruo*." *Pinche cabron, do lei loh moh, chingada chancho.*

I won't go back there. Even here is better. When *el Gordo* visits. Where the fuck is he? Where's she? I want my *fan*. I want the good kiss. I want the white lady to make the soup in my insides.

THERE'S THE RAP ON THE DOOR. The panel slides open at the bottom. It's big enough to push the buckets out. Then someone else who doesn't say anything pushes them back in, one emptied, the other refilled.

The water's good. Dirty, tepid, but so good it takes effort not to drink it all at once, not to dump it over my head. They'll push in food next. Rice, vegetables, maybe a little stringy meat or bony fish. I'm hungry enough to eat it. And not long after that, *el Gordo* comes with my sweet.

He knocks on the door as if asking permission to enter. He's got a light tap, like the back of one knuckle. As soon as I hear it I move to the middle of the room and turn around, waiting for the *Puta's* embrace. Waiting for her slender, tapered fingers to wrap around my arms, to hold me like a strong but gentle lover. Showing me that I'm all hers. She raises one of my arms, last time the left, this time it will be the right, and holds it out for *el Gordo.*

I wish I could watch him prepare my sweet. I don't know what he does. Does he ease the needle into a rubber gasket at the top of a small glass vial? Does he cook the *fan* with a butane lighter under a spoon, then draw it slowly up and into the syringe? Does he hold the works upright, tapping it lightly with that casual knuckle of his, slightly pushing the plunger to ejaculate the air bubbles? I want to watch. I want to savor the anticipation, to lick my lips, to taste it with knowing what's coming.

But *el Gordo* always comes prepared. The *Puta* grips my right bicep. The penlight beams from his mouth into the angle of my elbow. I've got strong veins. The big one throws a slight shadow and my eyes lock in on the needlepoint as it zeroes in, shiny, glistening, metallic, right under the small scab that's formed further up along the faint blue line.

My thin silver lover slides into me. A light fluffy cloud of bright red blood blooms into the syringe, strings out into curlicues, entwines itself with the clear sweet liquid, turning it the girly pink of my child-hood bedroom.

When it's the right mix *el Gordo* soundlessly eases my sweet back into me, pumping it into me. No endearments are needed, no whispered words of love.

For a moment it burns, sizzles in my arm, then smoothes out. I don't notice when the needle withdraws, spent. I'm busy. The warmth spreads out from the puncture in my skin to my gut, to my loins. It finds its way to my head where every warm, beautiful sunrise and sunset I've ever seen blossoms.

The *Puta* oh so gently lowers me to the thin, lumpy *cama*. She strokes the top of my head and it's like a kiss. I pucker my lips, lightly wet them with my tongue. The warmth of her floral scent adds to the heat building inside me. I want to take her hand and hold it to my lips, to sup on those delicate fingers.

But she takes her hand away and I don't mind. Everything is good, so good. And right now I'm wanting for nothing. I lie on the thin mattress and I know there's a reason I shouldn't like this. There must be. I don't know what it is.

AFTER THEY LEAVE I DRIFT, wrapped in the softest blanket imaginable, satisfied. Then I fall asleep and I don't dream. Or if I do they're good dreams, dreams of friends, of shared good meals, of the family I always wanted. When I wake up I keep my eyes closed as long as I can. Hanging on to the good part of what's inside me.

I wake up and it's dark, and still and I'm alone and I long to get back what I had a few moments before. Sometimes I think about Winnie Park, the woman Ray called Big Breasted Korean Housewife. I don't know why. Thinking about her makes me smile, even laugh. I wish she was here. I talk with her in my head but I don't really know what she'd say. I know she wouldn't want to be here.

It's not the dark. Or the cold even. It's the quiet. When I was first here I tried singing, reciting poems, making speeches. But now I can't remember any of those things. I'm not sure I can remember how to talk. What would I say? How could I say it? Does my mouth still work? My tongue? Am I only left with all this chatter in my head? I hate it. *El Gordo* can shut it up. But not for long, not long enough.

How many more days have gone by? I can't even remember how many times they've come with my sweet. And that's the most important thing, the most important thing there is.

This time when they come for me I drop my hand, my right hand, and touch the flower *Puta's* thigh. I stroke along the muscle. It's strong, and smooth under her dress. And the dress is cool and satiny. And she brings her lips to my ear and whispers something. And her whisper is like spun sugar, almost as sweet as my lover melting into me from the needle.

I don't know what she says. I can't hear the words. I can only feel the moist, delicious breeze in my ear. The brush of her lips against my finest hairs. The flower smell wafting into me, slipping into my brain. A wraith making gentle love to my soul.

I moan, I think. And when the *Puta* begins to lower me to the mattress I cling to her, try to bring her down with me, to wrap myself within her. She can protect me. I know she can.

And she lingers for a moment, an eternal moment. And brushes my ear with her lips and words again. And I could have understood her this time. I know I could have. But the sweet is bubbling in my veins, in my head, gently pulsating along my spine and somewhere as deep as it's possible to get inside me. And that's all that matters. All I understand. All I need. And the wraith leaves me with a long, light, loving stroke across my face. I want to hold her hand there, against my lips, feel the healing brush of her fingertips. But I can't raise my own to keep it there. And it's gone.

CHAPTER **NINETEEN**

There's someone in here. I hear breathing. I smell baby powder, a faint wisp of cheap perfume, sharp, sour fear. I can almost hear a heart beating. It's a different rhythm than mine, faster, more frightened. I lift myself up on the mattress. I try to do it silently.

"*Qui es? Who's there?*" Did I say it? Or did I think it? I wish I knew if my mouth was working.

"*Lei bingo-ah?*" No answer. I still don't know who she is. Perfume, baby powder, it's got to be a woman.

"*Shei?* Who are you? Can you hear me?"

She's whimpering, then crying, coming from the back corner of the cell. I push myself up, stand. I'd go to her but I don't want to scare her more. I wish I knew what to say, or if she can hear me at all.

I must still be in China. How would they have got me out of it? I don't think they've moved me that far. My Cantonese is harsh sounding. That's how I grew up speaking. If she's Chinese from the Mainland she might not speak it anyhow. I need to speak gently to her, reassuringly. I'll use Mandarin or English.

"*Wo jiao Wen Lei Yue. Dong bu dong?*

"I am Lei Yue. Do you understand me? Do you speak English or *Putonghua?* What's your name? *Ni jiao shen me ming zi?*"

Her crying has devolved back into whimpers and sniffles. She still doesn't answer.

"I'm going to come and take your hand. We can talk. Is that okay?"

She sniffles hard and follows it up with something that might be "yes."

I could find my way around this cell with my eyes closed. Some joke that is. I know right where she is.

Do lei loh moh, Ray. Where are you? We could get out of here. Or maybe you'd like the sweet, too. You are a friend, a good friend, and that's what I want from you. But if you were here, instead of her, *el Gordo* could sweeten us both and we'd hold each other and it would be almost like we were lovers. Better, maybe.

She starts when I find her, when I reach out and touch her. She hits her head against the stone wall and lets out a small grunt. I run my fingers down to her hand, clasp it with mine.

"*Ni yao zuo ma?* Do you want to sit?" I give a gentle pull. She resists briefly but then lets her hand go limp in mine. She reaches out her other hand to put on my shoulder, to let me guide her.

Her first word is one of surprise when she has to reach down to me.

"*Xiao.*"

"Yeah, I'm small." I clutch her hand firmer and pull her the few quick steps to the bed. I sit and tug her down next to me. She scoots back, putting her back against the wall.

"*Ni jiao?* What's your name?"

It's so soft I can hardly hear it. "Mei Lin."

My voice must be working. But my Mandarin isn't. I learned it in school. I grew up speaking Spanish, English and Cantonese. It's enough work just to talk. I don't want to struggle for words.

"Mei Lin, do you speak English?"

"Speak little." A soft hissing sound accompanies her words, like she's got a small speech impediment. I can't place the accent. It's not from Shanghai or Beijing, not the south. It's a country voice.

"How long have you been here?"

"Not know. I working salon. Man come give me drink. I go sleep, wake up here. Where here?"

I wish to *chingate* I knew. I reach out a hand and put it on her ankle. She pulls the ankle away, but I leave my hand there and in a few heartbeats she puts it back. She wants the contact as much as I do.

"I don't know Mei Lin. I was working with my friend Ray. Some bad men caught us and put me here. They've been giving me drugs."

"Ray? Mister Ray? He is *mei guo?*"

"Yes, yes. Mei Lin, did you see him? Is he here?" My brain won't listen to the part of it that's saying there must be a lot of Americans named Ray.

"No see him again. Same man come salon, give me drink, ask many question about *mei guo* Ray. I see him before. Good man, good heart, strong. He pay me good money. But man tell me bad thing."

I can't see her, but I'd bet real dollars she's cute. I have a good idea what she was doing in that salon and it wasn't haircuts. Ray's one *chingada ham sahp loh.* That must be why she's here. Someone saw the horny fucker with her, and Suwandi and Bellevue don't want to leave any loose ends.

I feel bad for her. She fucks a guy for money and ends up here. Maybe they'll give her the sweet, too. Then maybe it'll be okay.

But it's not. I don't hurt at the moment. I'm not sweating or itching or feeling bad in any way other than angry. That's how I get sometimes. For a little while. I can almost keep track of time that way. *El Gordo* and the *Puta* come for their visit and everything is beautiful. Then I sleep and I wake up feeling like this. Then I get tired again. I've tried to count the minutes, the heartbeats, but I lose track. Then I sleep again and I dream, wild dreams, mostly bad. Then the itching wakes me up. Then food comes. I don't want it but I force myself to eat. Then after that, some interminable time, there's the soft knock on the door again and it all starts over.

How can I explain all this to Mei Lin? Should I bother? Does it matter? They'll do with us what they want. Won't they?

Mei Lin describes her Ray and there's no doubt he's mine, too. He's always had a weakness for *putas*. I try not to resent Mei Lin for it. It's not her fault he can be so *menso,* so *stupido.*

"What's the bad thing the man told you?"

"I sorry. You liking Mister Ray. I like, too. Bad thing happen."

"What bad thing, Mei Lin? Did something happen to Ray?"

She's crying again, really racked with sobs. It makes me want to cry. I move back to sit next to her, give her some human contact, comfort. Maybe it's for me. I throw an arm around her and she nestles into it.

Hard, warm tears fall on my shoulder and I fight back my own. I had too much to cry over when I was growing up. I don't do it often. If I start doing it now, I don't know if I'll ever stop.

I pat her on the head, whisper soothing words. What does she know about Ray? I need to calm her down so I can find out.

"Tell me, Mei Lin, tell me about Ray."

She takes her head off my shoulder and sniffles a few times, harder.

"Mister Ray, he husband? Boyfriend?"

"No, he's my friend. I work with him."

"He killed, dead. In river. Find body."

I freeze, a chill so deep I can't even shiver. My voice comes out slow, flat as a cold slab of marble.

"What? How do you know? Maybe the man was lying."

"Man come to salon and ask question. He show me newspaper with picture. I sorry your friend, dead. He is nice man."

She takes one of my hands and holds it. "I so sorry."

I MUST HAVE BLACKED OUT. My head felt like it was going to explode and I can't recall much after that.

Screaming? I'm pretty sure I did some of that. Crying? A lot of that, too. I pounded my fists against something hard. I know because they're sore and swollen. *El Gordo* has come for me. How many times? I barely even noticed.

Mei Lin tried wrapping me in her arms. I remember pushing her away, speaking harshly. Where is she now? If she is in this cell I can't hear her. She's not here, or the terrible drum beat in my chest and my temples is masking any other sound.

Ray? Dead? That's what it was. It can't be. The stupid *puta* told me that. Saw some picture in the paper.

"Mei Lin, Mei Lin, are you here?"

A tentative hand touches my foot. "I here. Okay?"

I reach out one of my hands, searching for her. I find her hand and hold on tight.

"How long has it been?"

"Long? How long? Do not know."

"How many times has *el Gordo* come?"

"Go-doh?"

"The big man, the woman, with the *fan*."

"They come five time."

Five times. Twice a day, maybe. I don't know. They must have come a few hours ago. I'm in the lucid state. Too lucid. Ray, dead. Can they come with my sweet again, now?

"Mei Lin, are you sure it was Ray's picture in the newspaper? What paper?"

"*Renmin Ribao*, big news. Picture on front."

That's the *People's Daily*, the official newspaper of the country. It is very careful about what it reports, especially if it's something that might not look good for China. A foreigner being murdered in Shanghai is not something it would report on lightly.

I shuddered and shook and when I ran out of tears my body kept crying without them. *El Gordo* and the flower *Puta* came and they shot Mei Lin up, too. And we clung together as the sweet took us away, each separately, but she felt like a lifeline.

I COME TO WITH HER FACE NEAR MINE, her legs wrapped around me. Her breath is impossibly sour. Mine probably is, too. I can't even remember the last time I brushed my teeth. She's sleeping. I pull away as gently as I can.

I'm all cried out and waking into the phase when I can think. And I've got to think. Got to figure out something to do other than simply exist here in the dark waiting for my treat. Ray wouldn't want me to. He'd do something. He'd be driving me *loca* but he might get us out of here.

Mei Lin and I could probably beat *el Gordo*. He's fat, slow, his breath wheezes. The two of us could take him.

But the flower *Puta*, she's strong, *muy fuerte*. I can sense it. And she's fast and she's always alert.

Is there anything we can use as a weapon? The buckets. They're plastic, but they've got metal handles with a plastic tube over the middle. Maybe that's it. If I can take off the handle I can scrape it on the stone floor and sharpen one end. It might not work. But it's something to do.

The shit bucket's in one corner, the water in another. I don't want to risk spilling any water, so I crabwalk my way over to the other.

Breathing through my mouth, keeping my face as far away from the bucket as possible, I feel around where the handle is attached. The metal is a little heavier than a wire coat hanger. It pokes through small holes in plastic tabs that stick up from the sides and is bent to keep it in place.

It might take a while to bend the crooked metal back and forth enough to break off the tip, then sharpen that. I'll have to wait until I know I've got enough time. If I put the handle back on without bending it back fully into place, I'll be able to get it off easily next time. Hopefully they won't notice anything when they take it to empty it.

Mei Lin doesn't like it. She doesn't think we've got a chance. The dark, the not knowing, the stench, the dope, it's all getting to her.

She's curled on the mattress, her face turned away from the rest of the cell. I move up against her, curl around her, stroke her hair, along her shoulders, down her arms. I put an arm around her and she clasps it tight.

We drift off. But it's the restless sleep, the one with dreams. They aren't too bad this time. Ray's in one and I'm happy to see him. He's worried about me and I keep telling him not to worry. Mei Lin's in there somewhere, I think. I keep getting her mixed up with Winnie, the woman in Hong Kong. And they both smell like my flower *Puta*. And at some point it turns sexy. There's a warm, moist pressure between my legs.

I wake up that way. I lie still, calming myself. Mei Lin has twisted around in her sleep. She's facing me, her breasts pressed against my chest. One of her thighs snugged hard up against my crotch. It feels good. If only I could lose myself in it.

But the gnawing inside has started. The itching is crackling out of my pores. I can't clear my head. All I can think about is *el Gordo* and my sweet and how much better it is going to make me feel.

CHAPTER **TWENTY**

There's the hard rap for the buckets. I push them out, hoping they don't notice what I've done. I hear sloshing, the sound of water pouring, They're pushed back in.

A little while later the food. Rice, an overcooked vegetable, a gristly, fatty piece of barely warm pork. I don't want it but I have to eat. I need strength. I bring the two bowls over to the mattress, find Mei Lin's hands by touch and give her one. She wolfs hers down like always. I guess it's not much worse than what she ate on the farm, or in the factory or the salon.

I chew mine slow, deliberate, thinking of it as nourishment, not food, trying to squeeze every last vitamin, every calorie I can out of the repulsive meal. I couldn't eat it fast anyway. I'd just throw it up, now, or later, when I get my sweet.

El Gordo's all I can think of. I try to work my brain around to something else, anything else, and I can't. I try not thinking at all and I can't do that, either. He fills me.

Mei Lin wants to talk. I'm not sure I can do that. Maybe it will take my mind off what's coming.

"What you do with bucket?"

"Something. Maybe. I might be able to hurt them, so we can escape."

"What do they do to you, me?"

Chingate if I know. She was already working in a brothel. There's got to be worse ones they can send her to. As for me, I don't want to find out.

"I don't know, Mei Lin. We'll try not to let them do anything bad." I put my arm around her. She lays her head on my shoulder. We sit, me waiting for my sweet. I don't know what she's waiting for.

THE GENTLE KNOCK COMES and I try to stay alert, try to notice everything. It's hard to concentrate. I don't want to be aware of anything other than my lover, the needle. But I've got to focus.

The door opens and the flower *Puta* comes in first. This time I'm not standing, waiting for her. I want to see what she does. She makes a surprised noise, then spits something low and fast out in Mandarin. I hear Mei Lin get up from the mattress. I begin to get up also, but a slippered foot stretches out and pushes me back down. She must have heard me, she couldn't have seen me.

"Wait your turn, shrimp," barks out the mouth of the *Puta*. It's guttural and ugly and not at all the dreamy voice I'd conjured in my head. It's the harshest Mandarin I've ever heard. They're the first words she's spoken, and they make me mad.

Mad is good. It helps me focus. Helps me take my mind off of what I most want. There's a very faint light, more a lighter shade of black, spilling from around the silhouette of *el Gordo* in the open doorway. Most people wouldn't notice it, but my eyes are sensitive from all the time in the dark.

The *Puta* is standing near me, holding on to Mei Lin. She says something and *el Gordo* steps in with his needle, his penlight spotting the target. He misses her vein on the first try. She groans as he yanks it back out to try again. The second time he hits his mark and she sighs as she's guided back down to the mattress.

A hand fishes around searching for me. I can't see it, but I can sense its movement easily enough. I let it find me and I'm hoisted to my feet, ready to be taken by my lover. And he finds my vein. I think I should try to fight it, not let myself soar with it. But I can't. Why should I? You give in to the one you love. Don't you?

ANOTHER CYCLE GOES BY and the routine is the same. After they leave and I've drifted and I've slept, I make some headway with the bucket handle, bending it back and forth against the cold stone floor.

Mei Lin and I talk. She hasn't been here long enough to crave the sweet the way I do. It feels good, gives her comfort in this place, she wants it but she doesn't have to have it. I try to make her understand how hard it's going to be for me to fight, feeling the way I do. She doesn't get it, how I almost want my sweet even more than to get out of here.

She doesn't say much, but there's something about the way she holds my hand. It's like she knows I'm the weak one. She's strong, with the grip of someone who's done a lot of hard manual labor. The more we do talk, the firmer the tone of her voice gets, it's regaining something it had lost. She's a lot stronger than I thought she was. The life she's led, I guess she's had to be.

Another cycle goes by. The bucket handle is getting closer to the breaking point. I've got to be careful not to break it until I'm ready. Until after they've returned the emptied and refilled buckets. And by then my whole body is screaming for *fan, caballo*, my white powder lover.

I'm feeling that way now. Ready as I'm going to be, which isn't much. Forcing myself to lean against the handle on the floor, turn it and lean against it the other way. Back and forth, back and forth. Finally it snaps, the metal stressing past its breaking point.

I feel the point with my thumb. It's sharp, but I want it sharper. I hone it on the stone, trying to get it as fine as the needle I long for. If we get out of here it might be some time before I can get more of what I need. Maybe just the needle will do, my lover sliding into my flesh. Maybe it can feed my hunger by tricking me, for a little while.

I work the metal against the stone, twisting it in my hands. I work along its side also, trying to make a cutting edge. When I touch it again it's hot. I feel a drop of blood forming where it stuck me in the finger. I squeeze the cut onto my lips. It's salty and rich and tastes of life. It gives me strength.

IT'S TIME. I don't want to do this. I want to succumb. I want to hold out my arm and surrender. But I clench my teeth and grasp the sharpened bucket handle.

We have a plan. Mei Lin moves to the corner by the door. I stay on the mattress, hoping to make the *Puta* bend down to get me. I'll stab her, try to take her out somehow. Mei Lin will trip *el Gordo*, then follow through trying to knock him out against the hard floor. It's not much. It won't work.

The door opens. My flower *Puta* comes in. I make a weak noise so she knows where to find me. She bends down to grab me, to bring me to what I want so much that I almost drop the wire and let her. But I don't.

I snake a hand up and onto the back of her neck, as if helping her bring me to my feet. My thumb finds the pulse in the side of her neck. It's slow, steady, beating counterpoint to the thunderous drumming in my chest. Is my heartbeat as loud as I think it is? Will the sound warn her? I've got to do this fast, before I think too much or feel my longing too much.

There's a scuffling and a surprised grunt and a thud from the door. Mei Lin has started. I whip my other hand around fast and sink the wire deep into the *Puta's* neck, right where my thumb had felt her lifeblood flowing. I like it when my sharp metal sinks into my veins. It feels like life flowing into me. So does this.

Her shriek cuts through me. She throws me off but I hold onto the wire and wiggle it as I pull it out. I feel the hot, thick viscous spray of her blood. I hear it splatter on the wall behind me. I taste it on my lips and I lick them. I don't know why it helps, but it does.

The *Puta* is scrabbling around on the floor, grabbing for me. I kick at her, but then she gets my ankle and clenches it. I feel her hand flexing, weakening then strengthening then weakening again, following the beat of her heart that's pumping the life out of her. Finally it relaxes, and her other hand brushes against me as it drops limp.

I'm covered with thick, cooling, sticky blood and my stomach is turning inside out with fear and disgust and wanting my *fan* and my ears are pounding and I've got to shove all of it deep down inside me so that I can do what else needs to be done.

I listen. Some of the pounding isn't coming from inside me. It sounds like a melon cracking open on a sidewalk.

It stops. There's a deep, fast exclamation of a breath, then a hiccup, then the sound of someone moving back toward the wall next to the door.

I crawl over to Mei Lin, feeling my way around the pooling blood. My fingers come into contact with what feels like the mashed skull of *el Gordo*. Mei Lin got lucky when she tripped him, he must have fallen flat on his head. The pounding I heard was her finishing the job.

I find her seated upright, stiff against the wall. I wrap my arms around her and squeeze her as tight as I can. I'm not sure if that's for me or for her.

She whispers. "Kill him? I kill the fat one?"

"Mei Lin, we need to find his light, then we've got to get out of here. If I need you to help me I'll tell you." I'm not sure we really need the light. I know I need what else he was carrying. It's better if just one of us is moving around, looking for it.

I crawl all around *el Gordo's* body but can't find anything. Sweeping the floor in front of me with my hands, I crawl toward the back wall. I find a few small shards of glass and a needle sunk into the blood pool. Something kicks me inside and I want to lie there and mourn, but I can't. I prick my finger with the needle and that small point of pain helps me keep moving.

I feel around the *Puta's* drained body. I feel under her right thigh, the thigh I remember stroking and it felt so cool and smooth and strong under the fine silk of her dress, and I don't want to remember that. So I remember her calling me a "shrimp" and how much I hated that. I'm glad she's dead. And under that unmoving, cooling thigh I find the penlight.

It's one of those small metal ones that you twist the head to turn on and widen or narrow the beam. When I've watched the spotlight on my needle, my lover entering me, it's nearly seared my eyeballs. I can't blind myself, or Mei Lin, now.

"Mei Lin. I found the light. I'm going to turn it on. Close your eyes. You don't want to be blinded. It's better to let your eyes adjust slowly. I'll let you know when to open them and where to look."

My own eyes are closed as I twist the head and turn on the light. I pass it in front of my shut lids a few times, enjoying the faint glow through them. I point it toward the corner of the cell, then slowly open my eyes. The beam is at its narrowest and just slightly pools against the dark, non-reflective concrete of the wall. I look at it for a while, trying to keep patient, trying to keep from reveling in having light at last, light I control.

I slowly widen the beam, carefully sweeping it along the wall, trying to avoid hitting the blood pool that might reflect back at me. At first I can only make out rough shapes, my eyes have fallen out of the habit of definition. It seems like a long time before I start adjusting.

There's a slight glint from on top of the mattress, at the end away from Mei Lin. I look closer and it's the other syringe. It's intact, loaded. I go to it, pick it up, fondle it. I want it so much. I want it more than I've ever wanted anything. I want it even more than I want to get out of here.

I've never done it myself, not even back in college. What's his name? I can't remember it and I'm glad for that, always took care of the needles. But I think I can, I know I can. I start flexing my arm and clenching my fist to bring my veins to the surface. And I rub my thumb lightly over the top of the plunger and my breathing picks up speed. And it's all I can think of. It's all that matters.

"Lei Yue." She's never called me by name before. I didn't even know she remembered it.

"Yes." I can wait another moment if I have to, but not much more than that.

"I open eyes now. Okay?"

I run the light along the wall to look at her. She's pretty, like I thought she'd be. Older than I thought, but not by much. She's almost at attention, a good solider waiting for me to tell her what to do. And *chingada burra* that I am, it gets to me. I put my lover gently down. I'll take him with me when we go.

"Slowly, open them slowly and don't look at the light when you do. Look to your right, at the wall." I move the light away from her. I tell her to move her head to look around the room, trying to see what she can without looking into the beam of light. I move up the mattress to sit beside her and guide her eyes. Mine have adjusted enough that I wish they hadn't.

I want to spare Mei Lin the sight of what she's done. No need. She takes my hand, directs the beam of light at the gray and red mulch of *el Gordo's* head. She gasps, leans against me. But she doesn't seem nearly as upset as I thought she'd be, as she ought to be, as I am.

"On farm, before I come to Shanghai, I kill many pigs."

I never killed anything bigger than a bug before. I can't let myself think about that now.

El Gordo keeps a wallet in his back pocket. I take the cash, three hundred Renminbi and a business card with a phone number scrawled on the back of it. The card is for a vice president of a shipping company, BajaChina, with offices in Shanghai, Hong Kong and Ensenada, Mexico. The name on it is Eduardo Garcia. The name's familiar, but my memory's hazy. I can't quite place it. *El Gordo's* identification card says his name was Chao Huojin.

I stand up. With the beam on full width and our sensitive eyes, it's light enough to see. But I don't want to. Not until we're out of this cell. I move to the end of the mattress and pick up the syringe. I cast the beam around until I find the sharpened wire. It's the only weapon we've got. I pick it up and wipe the blood off it on the *Puta's* fine silk. I hold it and the syringe in one hand and hold out my other to Mei Lin. She takes it and I pull her up and off the mattress. We step around *El Gordo* and out the door.

CHAPTER **TWENTY-ONE**

We're in a basement. There are several low windows covered with cardboard. I might be able to see out of one if Mei Lin gives me a boost. I demonstrate clasping my hands together and holding them palms up so as to create a step. She does and I can reach the bottom of one of the windows. I peel away a corner of the cardboard and look out.

It's dark outside, but there's a faint glow from streetlights. The window is at ground level. It looks across a small patch of dirt, a sidewalk, across a small street at what looks like an old, dull apartment block. It must be late. I don't see any people or lights in apartment windows.

I step down and we move as quietly as we can to the rough wood stairs at the far end of the basement. There's a door at the top, no light leaking from behind it. We can't hear any sounds other than our own breathing.

The stairs are solid, long settled into place. They don't make any noise as we creep up them. I'm ahead and I stop at the door to listen. I don't hear anything on the other side other than a low hum from what sounds like a refrigerator. I slowly turn the knob. It isn't locked and the door cracks open without a sound.

It's a typical, small Shanghai neighborhood house, a room for sitting and eating with a small two burner and sink kitchen area along one wall. There will be a tiny bathroom and another room for sleeping. The front door should open directly onto an alley or a street.

It does. And we're outside. In spite of the stench of rotting vegetables and a nearby open sewer and the dank, industrial pollution, the fresh air is wonderful, magnificent. It fills my lungs and makes my head swoon and for a moment I can forget the fast growing gnawing pains in my gut.

Mei Lin squeezes my hand. She's got tears in her eyes. "Where we go now?"

I don't know. Away. Away from here. Far and fast. I pull on her hand and we head to the right. There's no reason why. We need to move some way, any way.

We walk to the end of the block and turn left. To the end of that block, then right. Then a block and to the left, then the right, zig-zagging our way out of the sleeping neighborhood. Mei Lin doesn't recognize our surroundings. We keep walking.

I catch a faint sour breeze that feels like it's coming off of water. We follow it to its source and there it is. Suzhou Creek flows past, looking like our way out of here. Shanghai's to the right, to the east, I can tell from the current.

There are small boats tied up along the bank. Most of them have people sleeping on them. We could wake someone up, they'd be happy for three hundred RMB to take us to the city. Or they might not. Or the bad guys might have a faster boat and they'd catch us again.

How long before someone discovers the bodies of *El Gordo* and the *Puta?* How much time do we have? What time is it? What day is it? There's so much I want to know.

My gut's on fire. My head is splitting, *delor de cabeza.* I'm shaking like there's an earthquake rumbling up from my feet. I'm itching like a swarm of maggots is trying to bust out of my skin. I know what will fix me. But I can't have it yet. I've got to hang on and get us out of here.

Mei Lin looks at me like she wants to know what we're going to do. I don't know. I don't *chingada* know. Don't look at me like that. Shut the fuck up. Leave me alone. I want to scream at her, at the world, at everything. And I can't even scream.

She takes my hand. The one I'm holding my lover in. She pries my fingers apart and takes the syringe and needle from me. She waves it in front of my face, back and forth, in slow time. My eyes follow it, wanting it, wanting to grab it from her and stick myself.

Please let me have it. I'll do anything, anything you want. I'll be your slave, your lover, whatever you need.

She leads me and I follow her hand and my lover to the side of a large crate on the bank of the river. She sits me down, sits down with me, holds my arm across her chest. She takes the penlight from my other hand and spots it on the crook in my elbow, like *El Gordo* did. And there's warmth there, something healing in the light and I relax and sigh and breathe deep and steady. And she pierces my skin with the needle and a puff of relieved air spills from my mouth. And slowly she presses it home and we both watch as my blood mingles with my sweet. And then even more slowly she eases the plunger down, easing into me, pressing into me. And it's so good, so much what I need.

And then she pulls it out, fast, half-done. I reach for it, wanting to slide it back in, finish myself. But my reflexes are slow. I feel warm, tingly, safe, all the good things. Just not enough of them.

Mei Lin stands up, holds her hand out for mine. "Finish later. Now go."

It takes me a little while but I get up. I feel steady. The gnawing inside me has stopped, the *perros* have stopped barking, they're back in their *casa*. How'd she know to do that? She got me straight. And straight's what we need right now.

Tension flows out of me and I relax. I've got a friend, a companion, someone who can help take care of me. I pull her head down, approach her stinking mouth with mine, flatten my open lips against hers and press the flat of my tongue up against her. She tastes salty and sour and rank and I swear I can catch a hint of my dead flower *puta's* mineral-rich blood as well and she opens her mouth a little and the tips of our tongues flirt for a moment before I pull my head back and look straight into her eyes.

"Thank you. *Xie xie ni.*" And she smiles and she's got a beautiful smile. And we hold hands down to the river.

But I don't want to be on the river. That's how Ray and I got caught. And Ray, *chingada* hell, Ray. Why? I don't want to be on this river. I don't want to see it ever again.

There's a road on the other side. A few cars and trucks cruise by. I point to it.

"It will be faster if we get a ride."

Mei Lin looks up and down the river. There's not a bridge in sight. "How go other side?"

We can't swim. Not across this foul water. I won't touch where Ray died. I scan the bank on our side. There's one boat that has a faint light glowing inside its cabin. I tug Mei Lin toward it.

It's tied up about a hundred yards downriver from the rest of the boats. As we approach, I can hear why. Deep, bass and drum heavy rock and roll thump out of the small shack built onto a slightly less small barge. We walk up to its side and knock hard on the wooden deck.

The boat shifts as whoever is inside gets up and moves. The music cranks down low. A voice with a thick, gravelly accent shouts out, "sorry."

Mei Lin knocks again, shouts, "we need help," in Mandarin.

The boat shifts again and the door to the cabin opens a crack. A silhouetted shaggy head sticks out. "The fuck? What? Who?"

The accent is so thick, the voice so full of marbles that I have to struggle to understand it. I can't understand why it's speaking English, when it's so obviously not its native language. Mei Lin and I look at each other, not sure what to do, what to say, or in what language.

Sometimes you have to take a chance. "I'm Lei Yue. My friend is Mei Lin. We were kidnapped. We've escaped. We need help. Can we come on board?"

"Wait a minute." The head is withdrawn, the door closes. The boat shifts again and there's the sound of things being moved around. Then the door opens again and a strong beam of light fires out of it, pinning us where we stand, blinding us.

I hold my hand up to shield my eyes. I can't imagine what we look like. I haven't seen a mirror in however long I've been gone. I don't know what I look like anymore.

"The fuck? You two are nasty. The fuck that is on you, short one, blood? Looks bad, man."

I'm about to turn around and start running. I grip Mei Lin's hand tight and get ready to pull her along with me.

"Okay, okay. I help you. Get on the boat, stay out of my cabin. Don't want you stinking my place up."

Mei Lin climbs on board, then helps me up. We huddle together on the wet planks at the front of the boat.

He's standing in the fully open door now, watching us. He's hung a kerosene lantern from a peg next to the entrance to the cabin. It casts enough light to see him. He's tall, rail thin, wearing a baggy pair of what look like army pants and no shirt. He's got long, shiny black hair that hangs straight down past his chest and one of those wispy beards that Chinese scholars always have in kung fu movies. His features are more Mongolian than Han. He's got a friendly smile, but his bright, large eyes look wary behind it.

"So ladies, what is it I can do to help you?"

Since he's speaking English, I figure I'll do the talking.

"We escaped from a cell, not far from here. Can you take us to the other side of the river, to the road? We need to get a ride to Shanghai. We can pay you."

He nods his head in a way that I can't tell if it means yes or no, then holds up a hand. He disappears back into the cabin and I hear rummaging around again. He comes back out holding a bundle, then sidesteps along the side of the cabin to the back of the boat.

In a little he's back, with the bundle cradled in one arm and a sloshing bucket of water in his other hand. He sets the bucket down near where I'm sitting on the deck and drops the bundle by it.

"Okay. There's soap, a towel and two long shirts. That is what I can do. You wash. I take us to Shanghai. Okay?"

Not okay, but I don't know what to say. I don't know how long it will be before *el Gordo* and the *Puta's* bodies are found, and who will come after us then. I don't know how long I'll last on only half my sweet. I can't be on this river for a long time. I don't want to be on it at all.

"Thanks. But could you please just take us across the river to the road? We need to get back to the city fast. And the men who kidnapped us might be after us. It could be dangerous for you. They have speedboats."

He squats down to the level of our eyes. He looks as comfortable on his haunches as if he were reclining in a La-Z-Boy. He sticks out a hand. "Rong Guowei."

I put mine in it. "Wen Lei Yue. I meant what I said. We should be going and you should just take us across the river."

He shakes his head. "If you do find a ride Miss Wen, there is a police stop twenty minutes to the east. Shanghai is far. The police here are not good. It is best if I take you and your friend past that place. Now, I will leave you two to wash and I will take us downriver."

What's the point in arguing? I don't have a better idea.

The small boat shudders, then sputters, then settles into a surprisingly deep, powerful vibration as it pulls out into the Suzhou's current. Mei Lin and I wash as best we can with the one bucket of water, wetting the towel and scrubbing ourselves raw with it. I could still use a long, hot soak in a tub and a skin stinging needlepoint shower, but it's as good as anything's felt other than my sweet for a long time.

And I want my sweet now. But I don't feel bad yet. I'll wait until I need it.

THE BOAT MOTORS DOWNRIVER with a lot more speed than I would have thought it had in it. Everything on it rattles and shakes with the deep thrum of the engine. Pots and pans bang around in the cabin, an anchor chain rattles like a *Dia de los Muertos* skeleton. Mister Rong has cranked back up his rock and roll. It sounds like a frightening hybrid between Tuvan throat singing and death metal played through a blown speaker.

The shirt of his that I'm wearing comes down to halfway between my knees and my feet. It's baggy, but could pass for a dress. Mei Lin's is very short. It might pass for a dress on a sleazy bar hostess. I guess that's not too far off base. She's very pretty. I can see why Ray picked her. The sibilance in her voice is because her tongue is pierced. That must have hurt.

We make our way along the narrow walk to the back of the boat, where Mister Rong is steering. He gestures to the large bamboo mat that he's seated on. I sit, tucking the shirt underneath me. It's almost funny watching Mei Lin try to be demure sitting down in her shirt. It's impossible, and after circling a little she gives up the effort and just sits down, leaning her back against the cabin, stretching her legs out in front of her.

At the back of the boat we're protected from the chill coming off the water. The air is fresh, crisp, rich. I fill my lungs with it and start coughing. I'm not used to it. It's been a long time since I've had a deep breath of anything that wasn't stale or rank.

Mister Rong puts a hand on Mei Lin's outstretched foot and a look of concerned interest on his face. "What happened?"

Mei Lin starts to answer him in Mandarin and he holds up a hand to stop her. "I am sorry. I want only to speak English."

She looks perplexed. I'm confused. "But you are Chinese, Mister Rong."

He smiles at me. "And so, too, are you, Miss Wen. But you have an odd accent. I think you are not from China, or even Taiwan or Hong Kong, but somewhere else. Am I right?"

"Yes, from Mexico."

"And you are more comfortable speaking in English? Why not Spanish? Why not Chinese?"

"I went to school in California. I worked for many years in English. Most of my friends speak English. My Mandarin is not very good. I don't know."

"For me, Miss Wen, it is a matter of principal. I am Chinese, but by my choice no longer am I a man of China."

His English is good, but it is so heavily accented, and what he said, does it make sense?

"I'm not sure I know what you mean, Mister Rong."

"Do you recall my full name, Miss Wen? And do you know its meaning?"

"Rong Guowei. Rong is 'martial,' like the military. Guowei, 'preserving the state'?"

"Very good, Miss Wen. Your Mandarin is not so bad after all. Yes, I am Mister the Military Preserves the State. I was born during the Cultural Revolution. My father was in the army and wanted his son to have an appropriately patriotic name."

"Okay, what does that have to do with your not speaking Chinese?"

"Not long after I was born, my father was killed in an artillery battle between his army unit and a faction of Red Guards. Because he was on 'the wrong side of history' as they said in those times, they came and burned our house with my mother inside it. I was an infant. They took me away and raised me in their revolutionary barrack. It was as if I was raised by wolves, Miss Wen."

"But things have changed since then, Mister Rong. The government punished the Gang of Four. There has been progress, reform. It is a different country than it was when you were a child."

A look of terrible sadness washes over his face. He looks down at the ground for a moment, then up at the sky. When he looks back at me it is with a blank stare.

"Perhaps, but not enough. When I was old enough I went into the army. The new People's Liberation Army, but there were still the same old factions. There was still the wrong and the right side of history. And there was corruption everywhere. The army served itself, not the people.

"One day I walked away. I will never go back. China is a large country filled with many people. In the old China, even the China of ten years ago it was not so easy to get lost. Everyone knew who you were, where you were. But now, all people look after only themselves. Now I keep my name to remind myself of my bitterness. But I reject my mother tongue. To speak Chinese is to be one with China. I will no longer be of China. Do you understand, Miss Wen?"

The Chinese way of looking at the world has always been a mystery. Whenever my mother or father wanted to teach me anything, or scold me, they'd start each sentence, "We Chinese..." Nothing ever made me feel so un-Chinese as that. I'm a mutt. I like it that way. Maybe I do understand him. That doesn't make him any less *loco*.

"How do you live, Mister Rong?"

"Rong, only Rong. I live on my boat. I stay with friends. I fish sometimes. I find junk to sell sometimes. I do favors or small jobs for people. I live simply, it is not so hard. Maybe a little lonely." He looks at Mei Lin. His eyes soften with attraction and so do hers. That was fast.

"Where did you learn your English? It's very good."

"Thank you. But I do have this accent. I would like to rid myself of it, but I fear that is impossible. I was a good student. When I decided to renounce the language of my birth, I became an even better student. I have also spent much time with American movies and rock and roll."

Mei Lin nudges me with a foot. She's been trying to follow our conversation, but her English isn't up to it. Especially not with Rong's voice. I do my best to translate. She only looks more confused.

"I no understand."

I look at Rong. He smiles at me and shakes his head "no." He's not going to help.

I try again and I can see her concentrating. When I finish she bows her head for a moment. Then she leans forward and puts a hand high up on Rong's thigh. It's meant to be comforting, but there's something sexual in it, too. I can see that in both their expressions.

"China hurt Mister Rong, hurt family. Mister Rong no want be Chinese people because hurt. Want be only people, only be Mister Rong. I think I understand. China hurt me, too."

If Ray was here he'd tell me to drop the whole subject. This isn't the time for philosophy. Later he'd remind me of the first trip he took to Vietnam. He met a woman who was the only survivor in her village after it had been vaporized by American bombs. He apologized to her. As an American he felt guilty. She took his hand and told him that she knew it was his government that had destroyed her village and killed her family, not him, not the American people.

That let him off the hook, but he'd never fully bought into it. The government was the people, wasn't it? The culture, the society, "to be American is to be America," he once told me. Whatever that meant. I've never felt especially Chinese, or Mexican, or even like a dwarf. It seems like a waste of time worrying about it.

I want Ray here. I want to punch him on the shoulder, call him *cabron*, tell him he is the most *gringo* man I've ever met. And then I want to laugh with him. And now I want to cry. And I do, lowering my head to hide my tears from Mei Lin and Rong who are talking.

They notice, but let me cry. I'm glad for that. I don't want to explain anything. Mei Lin rests a reassuring hand at the top of my back, underneath my neck, and they keep talking.

When I'm done I take a couple of deep, painful, hiccupping gulps of air. I wipe my eyes on the sleeve of the shirt I'm wearing. I'm tired, so tired. And it's the kind of tired I get before the bad sleep, the one I wake up from with the gnawing and itching and craving. We've got to get somewhere soon.

"Rong, where are we going? Shouldn't we go to shore?"

"I will take you to Shanghai. No one is chasing us. It is only three or four hours more. We can go to the house of my friend."

I'm too tired to argue. Too depressed. "Okay. I need to sleep. Can I go into your cabin?"

He doesn't even have a mattress. I lie down on the well worn woven bamboo mat, close my eyes and hope that whatever demons visit me will be kind.

CHAPTER **TWENTY-TWO**

I wake up screaming. Mei Lin's arms are wrapped tight around me, shaking me, wringing me out of it and calming me down at the same time. I'm bathed in sweat. I was drowning, crying for help but no one could hear me. Every time I opened my mouth to yell it filled with gelatinous, acrid goo. Or was it Ray who was drowning?

My teeth are chattering. Mei Lin forces her hand into my mouth to stop them. I breathe through my nose, deep. I can smell her, salty, a little sour, a faint wisp of soap. Her scent helps slow my pounding heart, level out my breathing. I open my eyes wide to look at her, open my mouth to release her hand.

She smiles at me, smoothes my wet hair back off my forehead. "Bad dreaming. No be frighten. Okay, now."

As my senses return I realize I don't feel the vibration of the boat. We've stopped. Rong is standing in the doorway to the cabin.

"Where are we?"

"Shanghai. I tied the boat up next to the Henan Road bridge over the Creek."

"Close to my salon."

"We can't go there, Rong. That's where they picked up Mei Lin. Ray and I were staying at the Peace Hotel. It's nearby. This is where they'd come to look for us."

"Don't worry, I have a good friend, he lives nearby. We will go to his apartment. Are you ready? We should go now. It's still dark."

I'm not ready. Once my body woke up, so did my craving. I need my sweet. I can't think of anything else, can't do anything else.

I put a shaking hand on Mei Lin's arm. "Mei Lin, I need..."

She stands up, whispers something to Rong. He looks sad, hurt. He turns away.

"I will wait outside. Come when you can."

Mei Lin steps to the table and returns with my lover in hand. It is so beautiful, so warm looking. She approaches me with it, gleaming in the faint yellow light of the kerosene lantern, erect, strong, straight, ready.

I hold up my arm, twist the short sleeve of the shirt tight around my bicep, clench my fist. I have such good veins, such receptive veins. They await the slight sting and welcome punch of my sweetheart. I don't watch this time. I want to let him surprise me, sneak up on me, take me from behind and sweep me up.

And he does. And again it's not enough. It's more like the satisfaction you get when your ears are clogged and you hold your nose and blow and they clear up. It's good. You're back to normal. But normal's not what I want.

Mei Lin slides the needle out of me. She holds the syringe up for me to see. "All finish."

I take it from her hand, gently, oh so gently. I look around the room for something to cap the needle, to protect it. I tear a softened piece of bamboo from the mat and carefully slide my lover into it, then put it in the shirt pocket. I reach out for Mei Lin's hand, to have her help me up. I'm clear now, good, for a little while.

RONG'S FRIEND LIVES ON THE FIFTH FLOOR of a crumbling building in the Chinese Islamic neighborhood near Mei Lin's salon. The early morning smells of sesame bread baking, chunks of lamb sizzling on skewers over hot coals, apple, and cardamom-infused smoke rolling from the mouths of white bearded old men in cafes, strong and sweet coffee, seep into the apartment through the cracked windows. For the first time in a long time, I'm hungry.

Lei Jingguo, Rong's pal, is sleeping when we walk into his place without knocking. Rong walks to the side of his bed and bends down to wake him up, whispering in his ear. Jingguo bounds out of bed dressed in nothing other than bright red briefs. He's huge, as tall as a basketball player but round like a sumo wrestler. He squats in front of Mei Lin and me and thrusts out a hand for us to shake. It's the size of a large Hunan province ham, but flabbier. I wrap my fist around his thumb and squeeze gently. In a booming voice, in a rough dialect I can't place, he introduces himself to us.

Rong walks over and puts a hand on one of his friend's mountainous shoulders.

"Jingguo is a very good, old friend. We have known each other since we were boys. His name means "administering the state with thunder." His father was in the Red Guards. He was in charge of the artillery that killed my father. We were raised by the same wolves. Now, we are as brothers."

The big man stands up, towering over all of us, a broad grin pasted across his winter-melon-sized head. He says something else in the odd dialect and looks at me as if expecting an answer.

"I'm sorry, I don't understand. *Dui bu qui. Wo bu dong.*"

He says it again, slower, but that doesn't help.

"Rong, what's he saying?"

"I'm sorry Miss Wen, I don't know either. Jingguo only speaks a dialect from Guizhou province. I don't speak it."

"I thought you were as if brothers?"

"Jingguo does not speak English. Should we choose to do so, we are both capable of speaking Mandarin Chinese. But we choose to not do so."

I want to say that's as stupid a thing as I've heard in a long time, but I don't. It's not really all that more *loco* than anything else.

"Does he have a phone? I need to call Hong Kong. My boss will be able to help us."

Rong taps his friend on the arm to get his attention, then mimes using a telephone and points at me. Jingguo holds up a hand and walks out the door. I hear a light rapping on a door across the hall. A woman's voice answers. In short order he's back with a heavy, black, old dial phone trailing a long cord that stretches a foot or two into his apartment.

It's still early, but I can't wait to call. It takes a lot of convincing, but the operator finally agrees to reverse the charges. I can hear Bill Warner's groggy voice on the other end. He repeats my name twice, once waking up, the second time alert, wary. He accepts the charges.

"Who is this?"

"Mister Warner, it's me, Lei Yue."

"You're not dead?"

"No, not yet. But, Ray? What about Ray?"

"Is this really you? It sounds like you."

"It's me, Mister Warner. Say hello to Ringo our receptionist for me. You met Ray in the coffee shop at the Hotel Lisboa in Macau. You hired me when you were investigating the Cambodian art. I was shot in Phnom Penh. It's me."

"It is you. I'm so glad. I was sure you were dead." He does sound glad, although it's hard to tell. Warner has a flat way of speaking.

"What about Ray, Mister Warner?"

"Lei Yue, I'm sorry. I'm really sorry. Ray's dead."

I was ready for this, waiting for it. It doesn't help. Hearing it from Warner sounds final, more real, whatever little hope I have that it might not be true, might be a mistake, drains right out of me.

I drop the phone and break down sobbing, my whole body heaving, my gut churning even worse than it does when it's been too long since I've been with my lover.

I'm vaguely aware of Rong picking up the phone. He speaks in soft tones, turned away from me, while I convulse on the dirty, pealing linoleum squares. Mei Lin sits down, cradles my head in her lap, strokes my hair.

It takes a while before I'm done, but then I am. I wipe my nose and eyes, breathe deep, then hold my hand out for the phone. Rong finishes what he's saying and hands it over.

"Mister Warner, I'm sorry, I just…"

"No problem, Lei Yue. I know how much you liked Ray."

More than that, really. I loved him. As a friend, probably the best friend I ever had. I wouldn't have fucked the *cabron* to save my life. I loved him too much for that. I smile when I think of it, regain my voice.

"What happened?"

"First, what happened to you? When's the last time you saw Ray?"

I give him the short version, leaving out that I'm a *drogadita*. I'll deal with that myself, and it won't be long before I need to. What am I going to do?

"Where are you now, Lei Yue?"

"Ray? Are you sure it really was Ray? What happened? When?"

"I'm sorry, Lei Yue. It was definitely Ray. I saw his body. There's no doubt. He was pushed into the Suzhou in the wheelchair they tied him to. He drowned. It was about six weeks ago, give or take a day or two."

I've been gone six weeks? It feels longer, or shorter. I don't know what it feels like.

"What about Bellevue? He did it."

"Someone did it to him, too. Right around the same time. They found his body in the same place."

"Suwandi?"

"Nothing. No one can connect him to any of this. His bank loaned money to the factory where you were, but they don't own it. Neither did Bellevue. It's owned by a shipping company."

I remember the card from *el Gordo's* wallet. "BajaChina?"

"Yeah, that's right. What'd you and Ray find out about them be-fore …well, before?"

"Nothing. I found a card from one of their vice presidents in the wallet of the man I left in the cell."

"When you get back here I'm going to want to hear it all, in detail."

"How am I going to get back, Mister Warner? I don't have my passport, clothes, money. I'm afraid to go out of this apartment. It's in an area that Suwandi's people will be looking for me."

"Are you sure they're Suwandi's?"

"I'm sure. I'm going to find a way to get those *chingada cabrones.*"

"First things first. I have connections in Shanghai. Sit tight and I'll send someone to get you."

"What about my friend, Mei Lin? I can't leave her for them to find." I look around. She's sitting on the bed next to Rong. Their hands are on each others legs, above the knee. They're sitting close together, deep in conversation. As deep as they can get with her lim-ited English.

"I'll see what I can do. Put your friend Rong back on the phone. He can tell me how to find you."

WHILE I WAS ON THE PHONE Jingguo put on clothes and went out. While Rong talks with Warner I get up off the floor, sit on the bed next to Mei Lin and look around. There's a plastic dresser with a small, cheap radio and cassette player on it. Some clothes and a coat are hung on a standing rack. There's a small folding card table with four folding chairs. A two-burner gas cooker, a greasy charred wall behind it and a large black wok on one of the burners, sits on top of a small refrigerator. Across the room is a sink, next to a door that I guess is the toilet.

I take one of Mei Lin's hands and hold it up to my face. "Mei Lin, I talked with my boss in Hong Kong. He's going to help us."

She breaks out in a big smile. I'm not sure what there is to be so happy about.

"No problem, Lei Yue. Rong, he is good man. He ask me to go with him. We go on boat."

"Where? What will you do?"

"Not know. He is good man. I not work in salon anymore. Stay with Rong, make happy life."

I don't know if she's gone *loca* or if it's a good idea. I don't know much about her, but we've been through a lot together. And I don't know much about him other than the strange life story he told me. Maybe it will work. I hope so. I wish it was that easy for me.

Rong gets off the phone, comes over and sits on the other side of Mei Lin, draping a protective arm around her.

"I will take good care of this woman. We will be safe, happy. We will be poor, but this is China, we shall have much company in our poverty. And the way that people become rich here, they are poorer in many ways than we shall ever be."

I could argue with him, but why? And if I don't have to worry about Mei Lin, so much the better. I can concentrate on getting home, then figuring out how to get the *cabrones* who killed Ray.

And finding my lover. What am I going to do without him? I'll need him, soon.

I tell them congratulations. Then fall back on the bed. I'm so tired, and wanting.

Maybe I slept. I didn't dream and it feels like I'm waking up when Jingguo comes back into the apartment. He's carrying a stack of Styrofoam food containers. I'm sure they'd smell delicious if my stomach wasn't beginning to churn. I know I have to eat something. I'm not sure I can.

Jingguo puts the takeaway boxes down on the table, then crooks a finger at Rong who gets up and walks into a corner of the room with him. They turn their backs to us. The big man shows something to Rong who swivels his head to scowl at me and Mei Lin.

He motions Mei Lin over to him and hands her something. She clutches it in her hand and goes to the toilet. Rong turns to me.

"My friend says that there are men on the street asking about you and Mei Lin. They are not the kind of men you want to meet. You must stay here until the man your boss sends comes for you."

"Okay, thanks. I hope your friend doesn't mind having us here."

"He wants to help. Now, go and see Mei Lin in the toilet. She has something for you, something you need. But there is not a lot. You will have to find something more before long."

MEI LIN AND MY LOVER are waiting in the bathroom. It's no more than a closet. If we both stand, we're pushed up against each other. I gently move Mei Lin to sit so that I can stand in front of her.

"Lei Yue, I sorry I go with Rong. I no want to leave you if you no want."

What'd she say? I can only concentrate on the folded paper in her hand and my lover in her other hand.

"*Que?* What?"

"You be sad? I no go with Rong."

It takes a lot of effort to do anything at all other than what I want, but I put my hands on her shoulders. I'm careful not to jar her arms. I don't want her dropping anything.

"No, no Mei Lin. I'm happy for you. It's good. My boss will help me. I'll go back to Hong Kong. You go with Rong."

She looks at me, her eyes moistening with tears. I stroke her head. She'd better snap out of it soon before I go crazy.

I take the packet from her and carefully open it. I think there's enough for four or five really good times, maybe ten times if I just get myself straight and don't get high. I don't know how long it's going to be before I can get some more, so I fight back against what my whole body is telling me to do.

The problem is, it's powder. How do I turn it into liquid and get it into my lover? I used to watch what's his name do it in college. I was fascinated by it. I need a spoon and matches.

I fold the packet closed again and hand it back to Mei Lin. "Wait."

Jingguo does have a metal spoon and a lighter. He looks at me, sadness in his gigantic, heavily lidded eyes. I don't care.

Back in the bathroom Mei Lin stands up to let me sit on the toilet. I estimate a tenth of the powder, put it in the spoon, put in a few drops of water, then fumble with the lighter. Mei Lin reaches out to help, her hands are steadier. I offer her some and she says no. "No good, Lei Yue. You stop."

She's right. I know that. I don't want to hear it. Later. I watch the powder bubble into liquid in the spoon. I ease the needle into the small puddle and suck my sweet up into my lover. I shake it around a little, letting it cool. I flick a finger against the syringe to get the bubbles to the top, then give it a small squeeze to pop them out. I ball my fist but there's a scab where the vein pops up. I move the point down, to an unblemished patch of skin. I hope it's thin, that my blood flows close to the surface beneath.

It's harder than I thought it would be. The skin resists and my lover lingers on the surface, not sinking in. I close my eyes and push and I feel the hot steel slide into place. I can almost hear my skin sigh with relief and the sigh spreads through me, warming my whole body.

It's stronger than I thought it was going to be. It's good. I lean back against the tank, put my head back and let my eyes go out of focus somewhere between here and the distant liquid ceiling. Mei Lin is saying something, but she sounds far away, her voice slowed by the distance, by the soup in the air between us.

Mei Lin opens the door and walks out into the room. I sit there feeling good, so good. Nothing bothers me. I'm not sad, not scared. There's the burble of voices, soft, comforting voices. I don't know the words they're speaking, but they wash over me, soothe me.

After a while, I don't know how long, I don't have a sense of time anymore, only events, I get up and go out to join the others. They're sitting at the table, eating the food from the Styrofoam boxes.

They want me to eat. I know I should, but I can't. The smell of the food makes me want to throw up. Maybe I can eat later. I sit on the bed and drift, relaxing into how good I feel, bathing in the light that filters in through the window.

THERE'S A HARD KNOCK AT THE DOOR. I must have dozed off because I startle awake. Rong grabs Mei Lin by the hand and motions me to get up. He moves us into the bathroom, closes the door. Mei Lin and I huddle together, straining to hear what's going on at the door, holding our breath.

It's an American voice, speaking college perfect Mandarin. I hear the name "Bill Warner" and let my breath out.

Footsteps enter the apartment and the door closes behind them. A gentle rap comes at the bathroom door. "Come out, it's okay."

We open the door. Rong reaches in to take Mei Lin's hand. He looks at me. "He is from the U.S. consulate. Your boss has sent him."

He looks like the student body president of a large, state university, all tousled blonde hair, sparkly blue eyes, square jaw and broad flat shoulders. He's in a cheap, dark blue suit with a white shirt and dull red tie. He strides up with a businesslike expression set on his face and sticks out a hand.

"Bill Fraley, Ms. Wen. I'm from the consulate's trade office. Mr. Warner has asked me to escort you to the airport. I have your ticket and the necessary paperwork."

I don't give him one of my hands. I put them on my hips. "I'm sorry, Mister Fraley, but I'm a little nervous at the moment. Do you have identification?"

"Yes, of course, Ma'am." His hand slides into his jacket's inside pocket and comes out with a thin leather case. He flips it open in front of me, as if he was a policeman trying to get my attention. There's a business card in the top window that says he is who he says he is and works for the U.S. trade commission in Shanghai. The bottom window has an ID card with his picture, some sort of government seal and a bunch of numbers that don't mean anything to me. None of it looks like anything anyone couldn't get printed up, cheap, almost anywhere in China.

"What do you know about Mister Warner, Mister Fraley?"

He puts his ID folder back in his pocket and smiles. His body relaxes. "Bill and I go back a few years, before he started DiDi. He was my senior in the Ag Department in the Hong Kong consulate."

That means he was a spy, C.I.A. Ray told me about that.

"What did you work on with Mister Warner, Mister Fraley? Do you know anything about eggs?"

He laughs and his body goes even more informal.

"Oh, so Bill told you about that. Well, yes, I went with him on an egg promotion trip to Pakistan. I think that was before he met your colleague, Ray Sharp, in Macau. I'm sorry about Mister Sharp, Ms. Wen."

"Is your department doing anything about Ray?"

"I can promise you, it is being looked into."

I don't know if that really means anything or not. But he isn't going to tell me.

"How are you getting us out of here, Mister Fraley? I have heard there are people looking for us in the neighborhood."

"Us?"

I sweep my arm to indicate Mei Lin and Rong. "My friends are in trouble, too. I won't leave them until I know they're safe."

He doesn't take his eyes off my arm. He reaches out, takes my left wrist and holds it up. He stiffens again, looks stern. "Have you got a problem, Ms. Wen?" It is obvious. The insides of my elbows are bruised, they've got small scabs, red dots.

I look him straight in the eye, try not to get upset or angry. I feel both. "They injected me with drugs, heroin I think."

He lets my arm drop and he turns to look at Mei Lin, Rong and Jingguo. "Who? These people? Your friends?"

I pull on his jacket to get him to turn around again and look at me. "No, these people helped me. It was *el Gordo* and the *Puta*. They were the only ones I saw."

"The fat man and the whore? Huh?"

"They kept me in a dark cell, injected me with drugs. It was horrible." I can barely get out the word "horrible." It was that, but it also feels like I'm betraying my lover. I want to tell him it's okay, I'm happy now. I only need to be left alone with my white lady. But I know better than that.

"Who were these people? Do you know?"

"I think *el Gordo's* name was Chao Huojin. I saw it on his ID card. I don't know the *Puta's* name. It might have been Betty or Floss."

"Her name was Da Ehuang. The bodies were found. Did you have something to do with that?"

"How? Where?"

"Someone did a bad job of disposing of them in the river. What do you know about it, Ms. Wen?"

"They kept me in a cell near the river. Mei Lin, too. They put her in with me. I don't know how long ago. Not as long as I was there. We escaped."

"Mei Lin?"

I nod my head in her direction. "My friend. That's why you have to help her. She helped me."

"Okay. I'm not going to ask what you know about the death of Da and Chao. They were bad people, connected to the Sun Yee On triad. They were going to turn up dead or disappear, sooner or later anyhow."

"Da has a sister, a twin. They were both with Bellevue. They were his bodyguards or something. They were with Ray and me when they brought us back to the factory. The last time I saw Ray, they were hitting him. All I know is that their English names are Floss and Betty. I don't know who's who."

"Yeah, we know about the sister, Nuying. The Shanghai police are looking for her. They figure she knows something about Bellevue and your friend Ray."

"What do you think they wanted with me, Mister Fraley? Were they going to keep me locked up forever? Why the drugs?"

"These people are into a lot of bad things, Ms. Wen. Obviously they wanted you out of the way, but they also wanted to keep you alive. I think the drugs were because they wanted you compliant for something. It could be anything. I don't want to sound rude, but maybe they had a special order from a brothel somewhere, or a rich man who buys slaves. That's possible. Or they had some way they thought they could use you as a spy for them. Two of the people who could answer that question are dead."

CHAPTER **TWENTY-THREE**

Row seven, business class, China Eastern Airlines from Shanghai to Hong Kong is the non-smoking section. It's not doing me much good. The people in the rows in front of and behind me are puffing away like the factories we flew over on takeoff.

I don't mind too much. How could I? My lover and I, we had a little *fiesta* in the ladies room of the airport lounge before boarding. Then I had to say goodbye. I left her there. I took a small amount of the sweet with me. I can sniff it in the plane's bathroom before we land.

I'm poured into this big seat. No one's next to me. The stewardess keeps coming by to ask what I want. I want to sit here, maybe drink something sweet and cold. I don't want to watch the movie, or read anything, or talk to anyone or think about anything. I want to sit here and feel the warmth from my lover and know that no one is trying to hurt me.

FRALEY CALLED HIS OFFICE and we waited in the apartment until a couple more men in suits showed up. Jingguo said goodbye and went to sit on the roof of the building. All these people made him nervous.

The new men went downstairs to wait by the front door. When they called upstairs, Fraley herded me and Mei Lin and Rong down and into a van with the name of a plumbing company on the side. They drove us all over the city. It would have been like a tour if there had been bigger windows. After a while we were at Rong's boat.

Mei Lin cried and clung to me when we said goodbye. I clung back. I tried to work up some tears but I don't have any left. Maybe I'll never have any again. I liked the feel of her arms around me, the warm wash from her eyes on my neck. It was like my lover, but in a small way. I'll miss her. But now she's one less thing to worry about.

Rong went first. He walked up and onto his boat like it was any other day. He moved to the back and I could hear the engine start through the open window in the front of the van. When he was ready to cast off, the new men in suits bundled Mei Lin onto the boat. They disappeared into the cabin with her. I watched from a small darkened window in the van as Rong pointed the prow into the current and headed downstream toward the Huangpu river.

We stopped at the consulate on the way to the airport. I took a shower, managed to hold down some noodle soup. Fraley's secretary got my sizes and ran down the street to get me a change of clothes. She came back apologizing about the color, pink. I used to hate pink. Now I don't care.

I'VE GOT MY EYES CLOSED when we land in Hong Kong. Not sleeping, not dreaming, not anything other than floating inside myself, empty, content.

A few minutes before the pilot turned on the seatbelt sign, the stewardess told me that if I wanted to use the bathroom, I should do it now.

Did she know? I went in, locked the door, opened the packet of my sweet and poured some on my hand, more than I share with my lover. I poured the rest down the toilet. I didn't want to go through customs with it.

I put my nose down and sniffed hard. It burned a little and at first felt like it might give me a headache. I felt it build behind my eyes.

But that didn't last long. Then I felt relaxed, calm, good. It wasn't like making love. There wasn't the excitement, the power, the release. It wasn't like coming. It was more like afterwards, and now my sugar had me wrapped in her arms and we were warm, sated, melded into each other, at peace.

I'm feeling all that, unconsciously, not aware of anything around me, when there's a hand on my shoulder. My eyes take a moment to focus. Then out of the fog comes Bill Warner.

"Lei Yue, you're in Hong Kong. I've come to take you home. They let me come on the plane to get you."

"Home?" Do I have a home? I have a 350-square-foot apartment on the thirty-second floor of a twenty-year-old building in Western District. There's a bed in it, a chair, a small table. Anything more and it would feel too crowded. Is that home? Is that where he wants to take me?

I used to spend more time at Ray's apartment. We'd be drinking at the Foreign Correspondents Club and he lived nearby. I didn't want to be alone. I'd want to sleep on his couch but he never let me. He'd sleep on it, give me his bed. I'd make us coffee in the morning.

I do still have tears. A lot of them. And no words. I can't talk. I can only cry all the way into town.

Warner has the car pull up in front of my building. I have to talk now. I can't get out here. This isn't home. It's not what I want, what I need. I start sniffling, hard, trying to find words.

"Mister Warner I, I don't know where to go."

He puts a hand on my shoulder again. He's not very good at being comforting. Or I'm not so good at being comforted. I leave it there, but it isn't doing anything. I think he wants to do something to help me. But he doesn't have any idea what to do. I don't know what he can do, either. I don't want him to do anything.

"I've got to go, Lei Yue. We've checked out your apartment. It's fine. I've got security people who will come by to make sure everything's okay. Go upstairs, get some rest. Come to the office tomorrow whenever you feel like it, and we'll talk. You can help me figure out what to do about Ray's apartment, about his stuff."

I don't know if I'm ever going to feel like it. But I don't tell him that.

He gets out his wallet. "Let me give you some cash to get you through the next few days."

I take it and don't say anything, just nod my head in thanks.

We get out of the car. He goes with me to my front door. He's had a new lock put in, gives me the new keys. I don't want to go in. But he wants me to. He needs to go. I unlock the door, put a hand on the knob and tell him goodbye. I watch him down the hall and into the elevator.

The new lock is a lot better than the old one. It relocks smoothly, easily. I take the stairs down to the parking garage. Warner's security guys might be in the lobby and I don't want them to see me.

Where can I go? What do I need, want? I'll need my sweet, a new lover. I know people at the Foreign Correspondent's Club, and they'll want to help me. But it won't be the kind of help I want. They'll be concerned. They'll want to fix me. Maybe I'll want that later, not now. I can't face it now.

Winnie, Winnie Park, the Big Breasted Korean Housewife. She might give me the help I want. I liked her. I don't know why but I did. And I'm pretty sure she liked me. In any case I need to be moving and she's a place to go.

THERE'S GRUNTING COMING FROM INSIDE HER ROOM. And a deep male voice calling out some name I don't recognize. I sit on the filthy stairs waiting for her to finish, for her customer to leave.

It's not long before he does. He's short and very fat, a large roll of flab hanging below his waist under his oversized Manchester United shirt. She says goodbye to him at the door and he simply grunts in reply. I stand up quick, getting out of his way so he can waddle down the stairs. I turn to face Winnie who is still standing in the doorway. She looks surprised, and pleased.

"Lei Yue? It's been a while. I thought...I tried calling you but you never answered, never called back. I thought...Come in. Please, come in."

I go to her, wrap my arms around her and burst into tears, those *chingada* tears. Now that they've started again will I ever stop crying?

She doesn't say anything, puts her arms around me, closes the door, takes me to her bed and lies us both down. My face is buried between her breasts, the salt water flowing from my eyes soaking the two of us. I'm almost hyperventilating and she squeezes me rhythmically as if helping me to breathe.

My crying goes on and on and when I dry out I'm still crying, even though there's no tears. And then I'm hiccupping and shivering and then exhausted, so *chingada* tired. And I can't keep my eyes open and Winnie's arms feel so good wrapped around me and I ease into warm, lovely blackness.

There's stars, and I'm floating among them. There's voices, friendly voices, people I know and trust. I don't know what they're saying but I feel pampered by their words. There's a dim, pulsing red sphere and it makes a sound like a heartbeat and warmth radiates from it. And I'm just there, happy to be there, nothing to think about, to worry about, to do or say.

And then the knocking wakes me up. It's loud and sharp, metal on metal, slicing into my ears. I start. Where am I? Whose arms are these wrapped around me? My heart's pounding, a shrill warning pops off in my brain. I start squirming to get up, get away. The arms wrap tighter.

"Shhh, Lei Yue, it's me, it's Winnie. You were sleeping. Don't worry." Her words slip into my ear and her breath is cool and refreshing and I remember where I am, how I got here, why I'm here. I stop struggling.

"Stay here. I've got to get up and get the door. I'll send him away. Stay here. Don't make a sound."

I don't want her to get up. I don't want her to leave me. I clutch to her hand and try to hold her down. She gently slides it out from mine. "I'll be right back. Don't worry. It will only be a moment."

She gets up, dressed in panties and a t-shirt. When she moves I can smell her, a light tickle of perfume, woman and a faint wisp of garlic that is homey, comforting. I inhale deeply and the scent of her calms me and is a little unnerving at the same time.

She pulls a white envelope out from between some books on one of her shelves and takes it with her to the door. She cracks open the inner door. She speaks low, as low as it's possible to speak in Cantonese, and hands the envelope to someone through the grate of the outer metal door. She closes the door softly and comes back to sit by me on the bed, taking my hand.

"I'm so glad you are here. But you're in trouble. What can I do to help?"

I look up at her, my eyes crusted over with dried tears. I rub them with a corner of a sheet on her bed. I shove myself up to sit close to her.

"My friend, Ray, he's dead. And I'm, I'm a *drogadita*." In case she doesn't understand, I push up the sleeves of the shirt I'm wearing and hold my arms out for her to see.

She takes both my hands and looks deep into me. Her eyes are beginning to well up, turn a little puffy and red. I can see her fighting it back.

"I'm so sorry about your friend. I could see how much you cared for him. And he cared for you, too. Is that why?" She tilts her chin and eyes down toward my pitted and bruised looking arms.

I want to cry again, but I'm finished for now. I need her help. I feel safe with her. I have to tell her. I can hardly talk, my mouth is so dry.

She has a small refrigerator. She opens a beer for herself, I want something sweet. She has an orange soda for me. I take a sip, then a gulp. I can see that she's waiting for me to talk, but she's not going to push it. She's waiting for me to do it in my own way, my own time. I scoot back so that I can lean against the wall at the other side of the bed. I gesture for her to sit next to me. I need the contact.

It takes a long time to tell the whole story. I have to figure out some of it as I go along. She asks a couple of questions. And they're good, they help me make sense of some of it. We're interrupted twice by knocks on the door, men looking for sex. She sends them away, tells them she's busy. How am I going to pay her back?

When I'm done she doesn't say anything, just puts her arms around me and pulls me to her chest. She kisses the top of my head, my forehead, and I turn my face up to her because I don't want her to stop. She brushes my lips lightly with hers. I open my mouth, barely enough to poke my tongue a small way out and brush her lips with it. She opens her lips, gently urging my tongue into her mouth, lightly stroking it with hers. Her mouth is soft, fleshy, moist and warm and suddenly I want to be consumed by it, to fall all the way into it.

My tongue snakes as far into her mouth as I can get it. It tangles with hers. It scrapes along her teeth and laps hungrily at the textured palate at the top. I cling to her, one of my hands finding its way up and under her t-shirt and onto her breast. I feel her nipple hardening under my fingers.

I can feel my own breasts pushed up against her. I take one of her hands and put it on me under my skirt, onto my panties, rubbing the back of it with my hand, trying to get her to put her fingers inside me.

I want this so bad I don't know where to start, what to do first. I've never done this with a woman before. Not much with men, either. But I need it. I need it like I need my lover. I want her to be my lover. To make me forget my other lover. I want her lips, her breasts, her pussy to be my new sweet. I want to lose myself in her.

But she pushes back, holds me away, takes her mouth from me, her hand off me and gives me a look I can't figure out. She's smiling, happy, her lips pursed in a way that I know wants more. But she's also set, holding back. I can feel tears coming to my eyes again. I almost start hiccupping again with the sudden taking away of what my body so much wants.

"You, you don't want me."

She looks horrified, startled. "No, that's not it at all."

"What then? When I first met you, with Ray, you said you don't do couples, or women. I'm sorry I, I, I just couldn't help it. I need you. I need someone."

She strokes my face, looks sad. "No, Lei Yue, no. That's not it. I only make love with women, the rest is, it's just fucking. With you, I want you, too. But I won't do it with a woman for money. That's all."

"But this isn't for money, is it?"

"Oh hon." She kisses me quickly on the lips, a nice, slightly open mouthed kiss that she pulls away before I can start anything again. "It's that, I haven't had a chance to take a shower since that fat pig was here before you came. I can't do this, not with the feel, the stink, the taste of him still on me. I can't do it. I want to be fresh for you. I want to be me, only me. I'm sorry."

I kiss her quick on the lips, relieved, understanding. I've never done what she does, but I know what she's feeling. I look around the room.

"Where can we take a shower?"

She laughs and strokes my arm. "I usually go to the women's sauna on Mongkok Road after I finish working."

"What do you do between customers?"

"There's a bathroom on the ninth floor. I go there and rinse up. I don't care if I'm not too clean for them."

I look around again. "You live here?"

She laughs again. I love the way her throat ripples and she shows her teeth.

"I'm saving money. I don't want to spend anything on another apartment."

"I have an apartment. We can go there. But it's on the island. You'll miss your work."

"I don't care. Let's go."

Winnie begins to get up, pulling me with her. But my other lover yells at me from somewhere deep inside my stomach.

I pull back on Winnie's arm. "I've got a problem."

"I know. You told me. What do you want to do?"

"I want you to help me. But I need something before you can. I'll need something soon. Do you know anywhere I can…"

"There's a girl on the fourth floor, Mouth Like Vacuum Cleaner, some stupid name like that." Winnie blushes, then laughs. "I should talk. She's a junkie. We can probably buy some from her."

CHAPTER **TWENTY-FOUR**

I'm feeling fine. Mouth had made a big score and let me buy half of it a for little more than she'd paid. She didn't have an extra syringe and needle, though. And I'm not so far gone that I'll borrow a lover from a Mongkok *puta*. I want short, sweet, temporary oblivion, not a long hard death from AIDS or Hepatitis C. I sniffed it, and that worked well enough.

It's nearing rush hour and I can't face the crush on the subway. It's taking longer, but we're in a taxi. The driver's eyes keep appearing in the rearview mirror but I don't care. Let him look. I'm balancing myself on the seat with a hand high up on Winnie's thigh, almost under her skirt. I don't care what the driver thinks. There's warmth radiating from inside me, and more entering me through my hand, up my arm, from Winnie.

We're going to my apartment, but not for long. I can't stand the thought of it, small, impersonal, there's nothing I love there, nothing I want.

Ray's place feels more like home, comfortable. I need to go there sometime. I need to work out who to tell what, what to do with his stuff. I need to face him. I have a key to his place in my apartment. I tell Winnie that's where we're going.

"You sure? Are you going to feel okay about that?"

"I don't know. I really don't. I don't believe in ghosts, but I think I'll feel Ray there. I might want that. We'll see."

While I go into the bathroom where I keep Ray's key, Winnie stands in the middle of the only other room and makes a slow turn to look at all of it.

I come out of the bathroom holding Ray's key and a small bag I filled with things I might want: a toothbrush, brush, shampoo. Everything else will be at Ray's. He let me keep things there. Winnie is still standing in the middle of the room, facing me. She looks confused.

"You live here? There's nothing here, nothing of you. I have that horrible small room, but I've got my books, some pictures, some CDs. Lei Yue, where's your stuff?"

She's right. There's almost nothing of mine here, nothing I care about, anyhow. That's how I like it. Like a hotel room.

"I travel light. I never spent much time here. I didn't want it to feel like home."

I take a small suitcase out of the closet and throw some clothes into it, some jeans, a couple of blouses, a simple skirt, t-shirts, socks, a few pair of panties. I don't worry about matching anything up. I'm not a colorful dresser. It's pretty much all brown, black, a little dull green and some white.

I want to change before leaving, but I'm feeling shy. It's one thing when we're already all tangled up together at the same height on a bed, but I don't know what Winnie is going to think when she sees me. I'm normal sized from the waist up, and I've been told I've got a nice figure. But my legs, they're ugly, misshapen little things. Winnie's got beautiful long legs, the kind you want wrapped around yours.

Chingate. She likes me for who I am, or not at all. I face her and pull off my dress, the ugly pink thing they'd bought me at the consulate in Shanghai. I step out of my panties and stand naked in front of her. A grown woman who wants her from the crotch up, a short, squat, stubby-legged kid below that. She doesn't pretend not to look, doesn't stare into my face. She runs her eyes up and down my body. And she smiles.

"You've got a nice body, Lei Yue. Very sexy."

"From the waist up."

She reaches out to cup one of my breasts and I almost fall to the floor at her touch.

"You have beautiful breasts. Just the right size. Mine are too big. When I was younger I really hated them."

I want to reach out and touch hers, to bury my face into them, to inhale her deep. But I've got to get out of here, now. I pull on a pair of jeans, a t-shirt that has an illustration of a pair of chopsticks picking up Hong Kong Island and a caption saying, "1997 – The Great Chinese Takeaway," and lace up a counterfeit pair of Nikes that I'd bought cheap a year ago at Stanley Market.

"Let's go."

IN THE TAXI SHE HOLDS TIGHT ON TO MY HAND. "Are you sure this is where you want to go?"

I nod my head. "If I change my mind, we'll leave."

"Are you sure you want me there with you? Maybe you want to be alone with the memory of your friend, with his things."

Is she crazy? I give her a look that is meant to ask that. I take her hand and bring it up to me, opening and flattening my lips with her fingers. I push my tongue flat against her and coax one of her fingers into my mouth. I suck on it, soaking it. I partly close my mouth and pull my head back, scraping it over my teeth.

"Yes, I want you there. You can't leave me, not now."

Winnie nods and smiles and flicks her tongue out at me. I squeeze her hand tighter in reply.

Ray's apartment is a fourth floor walk up. He got it cheap because four is an unlucky number in Cantonese. It sounds too much like "death." It's about three times the size of mine. Enough to have a living room, a bedroom, a kitchen and a bathroom. It's about a quarter of the way up The Peak, in Midlevels. It's got a sliver of a view of the harbor that used to be wider before a local trading tycoon blocked most of it with a new, fancy apartment building across the street.

It looks the same as ever. No one's done anything to it. I'm glad for that. I don't know why they haven't cleaned it out. Winnie stands at the window, looking at the slice of harbor. She's standing next to a carved wood totem pole of ten heads. I'm hit with a wave of sadness. Those heads, from Indonesia, led to Ray's investigating stolen Cambodian art. That's when we met. It wasn't that long ago, not really, a little less than two years. It was a lifetime.

I go to Winnie, put an arm around her, lead her to Ray's couch. He and I sat here so often. Not even talking a lot of the time, lost in our own thoughts, comfortable with the silence.

Winnie leans over to kiss me and I let her brush my lips with hers, then I gently ease her away.

"Winnie, I have to kick."

"Kick?"

"The *fan*. I have to get off the heroin."

She rests a hand on one of mine. "Can you?"

"I don't know. It's hard. I did it before, when I was in college, but it wasn't as bad as this time."

"Can I help?"

"Why? Why do you want to help me? You don't know me."

She takes my chin in her hand and brings my face close to hers, close enough that she goes out of focus. Maybe it's easier for her to say what she has to say that way.

"I've had a shitty life, Lei Yue. I'm saving money so that I can get away, maybe go to America. But in Hong Kong, it's been lousy. And yours isn't so great, either. I can see that. You're so sad. Like me. I liked you when I first met you. I don't know why but I did. And I wanted you then, too. There's that, and there's something else. You've come to me and you need my help and you're the first person who's needed me for anything other than a quick fuck for a long time. And I feel like I need you, too. I'm not sure why, yet, but I do. It's like we are long lost sisters."

I know how she feels. But I can't talk seriously about it anymore. I pull back from her and put a mock look of horror on my face.

"Sisters? I never wanted to make love with my sister before." And I'm a little shocked that I want to now. I'm not a virgin, but sex has never been all that important. Maybe that's it. Maybe there's something else going on, too. I need someone to hold me, someone to feel anchored with. And a woman seems easier, simpler, more natural. And especially Winnie.

She smiles, kisses me on the cheek, gets up. "I'm going to take a shower. You can join me if you want."

I want too, so very much. But I need to make a phone call first.

WARNER ANSWERS as I'm getting ready to hang up.

"Due Diligence International, Bill Warner speaking. Sorry it took so long to get the phone. The office is closed and I was almost out the door."

"Mister Warner, it's Lei Yue."

"Lei Yue, where are you? The security men went to check on you and you weren't home."

"I couldn't stay there. It doesn't feel like home. I went to stay with a friend."

"Is that where you are now? I can send the security guys over there."

"No, that's okay, I'm okay. Mister Warner, what's going to happen with Ray's apartment, with his things?"

"I don't know yet Lei Yue. I've been busy and I guess I haven't wanted to think about it. Maybe you and I can figure it out together. You knew Ray a lot better than I did."

"That's where I am now. I had a key. I used to stay here sometimes."

"I didn't know you and Ray were…"

"We weren't. Just friends. But I felt more at home here than at my place."

"Okay, so what are you calling about, Lei Yue? I thought you were coming in to the office tomorrow. We can talk then."

"No, it might be a week, Mister Warner. I'll come in when I'm ready."

"Is it…? Fraley told me about the drugs."

"Yes, that's it. I've got to get off these things before I do anything else. My friend is going to help me."

"I can get you a room in a hospital, Lei Yue. A rehab place. Somewhere you'll be more comfortable."

"Thanks, but no thanks. I need to do this myself."

"Ray always said you were a 'tough broad.'"

"He called me a 'broad?'"

"Well, no, I threw that word in myself."

"Thanks. I like it."

"Are you going to stay at Ray's while you…"

"If you don't mind, that's what I was thinking I'd do."

"No, it's fine. I'll send someone around every day to see if you need anything."

"That's a nice offer, Mister Warner, but please don't. My friend will take care of me. Really, don't worry."

"Ray's dead. You've come back from the dead. You're addicted to what…heroin? You're going cold turkey with some mysterious friend. What? Me worry?"

"Ray always said you were a softie underneath it all."

"That, I don't like. Promise me you'll call if you need anything that your friend can't do for you."

"You got it, *hombre*."

WINNIE'S ABOUT TO GET OUT OF THE SHOWER, her skin glistening, beaded with water. The bathroom is thick, warm and wet. The steam curls around my naked skin, chasing the chill from me. It feels good. I need it to feel good. I want to feel the best I've ever felt, at least for a little while. I'll feel so bad, too soon.

I press against her, my breasts pushing on her belly. I back her into the stall, reach around her and turn on the water. It's hot, and it needles into us. I pick up the soap and turn her around so I can wash her back. I run the frothy bar in outline around her contours, tracing her shoulder blades, down along the bumps of her spine, out to the smooth, slightly fleshy gentle rolls along the side of her stomach, in circular motions around the protruding tail of her backbone. She leans against the tiles in front of her, her arms and legs splayed as if she was being frisked by the cops. But it's for balance. I can feel her gently squirming under my hands, her flesh tensing then relaxing. A long, lazy sigh escapes from her lips.

My hands run the soap out onto the rounded swell of her butt, along its sides, down to the crease where it meets the top of her legs. I drop the bar of soap and rub the lather onto her with my fingers, brushing circles from the top to the bottom of her crack.

Other than myself, I've never felt a woman before, and I'm not sure what to do. I skim the surface at the very top of her thighs, lightly trace soapy fingers along the inside curves of her ass. I ease my hand between her legs, gently combing the tuft of thin, coarse hair.

She reaches a hand down and takes mine, thrusts it hard up against her. I can feel her lower lips as they swell, then part and some of the liquid I'm feeling isn't coming from the shower. Her sex softly suckles on my fingers as she holds me up against her. Winnie presses down on my hand above her clit. I can feel it slowly growing, filling with blood, insistent against my fingertips.

She takes away her hand, props it back up against the wall and I lean against her, my breasts filling, the nipples hardening against the small of her back. I explore more with my hand, dip into her with a finger, trace her outlines.

I reach down with my other hand to feel myself. I can't be this swollen down there, can I? I can't be this wet, this wide open, this wanting. I lightly tap my own clit and almost fall to the tile floor screaming with the searing bolt of electricity that snaps inside me.

I press harder against her, taking my hand away from myself so my lower lips can crawl along her leg, open, swelling, wanting to clamp down on her, looking for something to hold on to, my clit rubbing against a taut cable of muscle. My hand stretches up to cup one of her breasts, the hard nipple poking between my fingers.

Winnie moans and pushes harder back against my hand, impaling herself on two of my fingers. My thumb moves up to make small circles around her clit, pressing down around its base, not quite touching it. Her knees are shaking and it's oh so slippery and I don't want to fall but I don't want to stop.

She bends down and turns off the water. Bends her knees and lowers into a squat, pushing more of my fingers deeper inside her. I cling to her back, bend around her butt, pounding my clit against her thigh, near frantic with what I want.

She pulls away and I gasp, start forward, begin to thrust myself back on to her. But she's only turning around to face me. Her body's flushed red from the hot water and the excitement. She hugs me back to her, kisses me deep and long, eases the both of us down to sit facing each other. She leans down and licks one of my nipples, takes a hand and puts it on me, a finger slips right in and I push hard against it, lifting my hips, straining to get it deeper into me, rubbing hard against the top of me right under my clit.

Her head moves back, away from me. She's watching me and my breath is coming harder and harder and I'm trying to watch her, my fingers, almost my whole small hand inside her. And her breath matches mine and our bodies are shaking and quivering. And I'm trying to watch her. I want to see her come. I want to see her lips, her eyes when I feel the spasms inside her. But it's hard, my eyes want to roll up into their sockets. Everything's a blur when I open them, a pulsating bright red when they're closed.

It's all building inside me like a gigantic wave headed for shore, rising and filling and broadening and blocking out the horizon. And little flecks of foam begin to appear at the crest and my breath comes in short, shallow puffs. And all there is, is Winnie's fingers inside me and the giant wave spreading out from there.

And when it happens it's like a massive stroke might be, a strong jolt like lightning crackling along all my nerves, snapping at every place on my body. It's so good that I think it has to kill me. But I don't think that because I can't think anything. I sizzle and pop and wave after wave after wave floods through me, washing every part of me out ahead of it.

And I don't know what happened then. I don't know anything until now, my face buried deep between Winnie's breasts. One of her hands on the back of my head, pushing my face into her. The other on my belly, my hands holding it there, pressing it against me, not wanting it to move but needing it there.

CHAPTER **TWENTY-FIVE**

Why waste it?" I unfold the packet and look at the *fan*. It looks so good. It looks like those steak dinners must have looked to those *chingada* monks at the start of all this. I spill it on one of Ray's plates on the kitchen table, start making lines with a knife.

"I wish I had my lover. My sweet is so much better with my lover."

Winnie looks a little startled, a little hurt. "What lover?"

Maybe I hadn't called it that out loud before. Maybe I'd just thought it. I reach a hand out to her.

"You're my lover, Winnie. I meant something else."

She looks so sad, and a little jealous, maybe angry. "What else?"

"I'm sorry, really, that's what I call my needle, my syringe. It's like a joke because it feels so good and it's inside me." It's not really a joke, but I can't tell her that.

She takes up my hands and looks me hard in the eyes. Her eyes are moist.

"Don't. Lei Yue, please don't."

I know what she's saying. She's right, but I do not want to hear it.

"Don't what?"

She nods her head at the plate. "If you're going to stop, stop, now. No more. I'll throw it away for you, down the toilet."

"But we already bought it. I'm going to pay you back."

"I don't want the money. I want you."

We both start to cry. She sits down on the chair, still holding my hands. We kiss. She tastes salty, wet from tears.

I murmur "okay" into her mouth. It vibrates her lips.

We pull back and stand up, both reaching for the plate at the same time. "I should do it, Winnie. But stay with me."

We walk into the bathroom together, still holding hands, me holding the plate in the other hand. I stand over the toilet and look down into the white bowl and it's so deep, so far away, so cold looking. Before I can change my mind I turn the plate upside down over it and I shake it. The *fan*, my sweet, lingers for a moment on the surface of the water before it's absorbed. I flush the toilet and stare transfixed as the water spirals down and out.

Winnie puts an arm around me, takes the plate from me, steps to the sink and rinses it off. I'm trying not to be mad, or frightened. My two lovers, one now gone.

Ray never believed in monogamy. He thought it was stupid, a denial of human nature. He once told me, "I've got too much love to lavish on only one person. I've got to spread it around." I told him he was full of shit and was only saying that because he'd had his heart broken by the Russian in Indonesia.

But I knew what he meant and it's hurting me now. Why can't I have both my lovers? Do I have to choose? I stand there and listen to the toilet's tank refill with water. Okay, I've made my choice. I'm going to regret it for the next few days, maybe a week. Then I'll see.

THERE'S NO FOOD IN THE APARTMENT, nothing to drink other than tap water, one half-full and one unopened big bottle of Russian vodka in the freezer. I don't want to eat. I don't think I'm going to want to for a while. But Winnie decides to go to the Park 'N Shop at the end of Macdonnell Road.

"Come with me, Lei Yue."

I'm sitting on the sofa, wrapped in a blanket even though I'm not cold, yet.

"No thanks."

"Come on, it will be good for you to get out of the apartment. Maybe you'll see something you want to eat."

The thought of eating anything makes me want to gag. I know I'm going to have to sooner or later, but later. I don't feel sick yet, but I know it's there, waiting. I don't want to be anywhere else when it hits me.

"No, please, Winnie I'm sorry, I can't go out now. Get whatever you want. I trust you."

She comes over and puts a hand on my forehead like someone's mom feeling for a fever. "Are you getting sick already?"

"No, not yet. I don't know when it's going to happen, but I just want to sit here now. Think about things. Okay?" What I really want to do, is not think about anything.

She wants to know if there's anything she can get for me that will make it easier — aspirin, stomach ache medicine, what?

Sure there is, *fan*, my sweet. Bring me some of that, and a new lover, too. That will make it easier. I shake my head "no."

Winnie leaves and I look around the familiar room. I'm jumpy, I need something to do. I get up and move around. There's a couple of small red lights glowing on Ray's stereo. One of them means it's turned off, the other that there are CDs loaded. I turn it on and open the tray. What was he listening to?

There's Bob Dylan, *Highway 61 Revisited*, of course. He kept trying to convince me how great that record is. It just sounds like a whiny old windbag. There's Charles Mingus, Irma Thomas, some noisy old L.A. punk band called The Plugz and Cui Jian, the Chinese rocker. And he's got the thing set on shuffle. There's a whole lot of things I'm going to miss about Ray, even some of his music. But the way he mixed it up was awful, ear-splitting. I'm not going to miss that. I close the tray and turn off the machine.

I run my eyes over his bookshelves, but I've done that so many times before. He read a lot. Mysteries, but only hard-boiled ones, history, biography. Sometimes he'd read books on economic theory or way out there *loco* science. He loved telling me about those books and either he didn't explain them very well, or they really didn't make much sense. But I liked it when he told me about them. He'd get so excited. I tried reading one once, on black holes. It made my head hurt, just like his *chingada* shuffle setting on his stereo.

His cabinets are jam packed and not well ordered. One of them is stuffed with photos and negatives and slides, loose, crammed into envelopes, spilling out onto the floor the times that I opened the door.

One time when he was out of town and I was staying here, I spent a night drinking his vodka and looking at his pictures. He knew a lot of women. And to hear him talk, and to look at the photos, I guess he was right, he did have a lot of love to spread around. He had really long, scraggly hair in the late 1960s and early '70s and he went to anti-Vietnam War demonstrations and rock concerts. In the pictures where they were separate, his parents looked sweet, loving, friendly. In those pictures where they were together they looked wary and stiff. They got divorced when Ray was seventeen. He was an only child. Sometimes I used to tease him that he acted like one. He never talked about his parents. I got the impression they were both dead.

I don't bother opening the picture cabinet. I'm not sure I can stand to look in it. I open the one next to it though. He kept a lot of junk in here that he picked up traveling. One of his favorite things was a ceramic sculpture from the Cultural Revolution in China. It's a Red Star rocket with a boy and a girl Red Guard riding on it. He said it made him laugh, reminded him of the final scene in the movie *Dr. Strangelove*. We watched a video of the movie once when we were stuck inside during a Typhoon Eight signal. Ray said if I hadn't grown up having something called "drop drills" in school, it probably wouldn't make as much sense to me as it did to him. He was right.

There's a red box with a gaudy black and gold ribbon that I don't recognize in the closet. It's about the size of a shoebox, but square. The lid is taped shut. There's an unsealed envelope being held in place by the ribbon, like a card on a gift. I take it off the shelf, carry it over to the coffee table and sit down on the sofa.

Ray's death certificate is in the envelope, along with a letter from a mortuary certifying that the contents of the box is something called his "cremains." If he was here, we'd laugh at the word. I don't want to laugh. I can't cry, either. I'm stunned, immobile. This small box? That's it?

For a few minutes I curl up on the sofa, hugging myself tight, staring at the box. I can't will it to not be Ray. I tell myself it isn't Ray. It's only a box filled with something with a stupid name. Ray was so much more than that. He couldn't fit in a box. *Chingate, chingate, chingate. Do lei loh moh*, Ray. *Do lei loh moh*.

I'm itchy and I can't sit still for long. When Winnie comes back I'm pacing from the coffee table to the kitchen, to the window, to the bookshelves. I'm trying not to scratch but my arms are already red in streaks. It's not so bad though. I knew this was coming and found nail clippers in Ray's bathroom. I cut my nails to the quick and dulled them down.

She sets three bags of groceries on the kitchen table then wraps me in a hug, pins my arms to my sides.

"Has it started? Lei Yue, what can I do for you?"

She plants kisses on the top of my head, squeezes me and it feels good to be held still, but I can feel a humming inside me, like a bee-hive under my skin.

I enjoy it for a moment, then break away, walk over to the coffee table. I stand over the box, open my hand and gesture at it like a game show hostess showing off a prize.

"What's that?"

"Ray."

"What do you mean?"

"His ashes. Something called cremains. Warner must have left them here when he couldn't figure out what else to do with them."

She looks stricken, puts a hand up to her mouth, comes over to stand by me. She puts an arm around me but doesn't try to wrap me up this time.

"Lei Yue, I'm, I'm so sorry. Where'd you find them? Let me put it away. What can I do?" She starts reaching for the box. I grab her hand and pull it away.

"No, I've got to see. I didn't want to do it alone." I sit down and pull the box closer so that I can open it.

"Lei Yue, wait. I'm going to need a drink if we're going to do this."

"Ray drank vodka. There's some in the freezer."

"I saw it. How do you want it?"

"I hate the stuff. I don't know how he drank it."

"I bought some juice, V8, orange juice, cranberry juice. You need something good for you. Which one of those do you want me to mix a little vodka with?"

I'm not sure what's the point. I'm probably going to throw it up in a little while. But the vodka with cranberry tastes good, cold. I'm thirstier than I thought I was and I finish off a glass before we even begin to open the box. Winnie makes me another one and slowly sips hers.

There's a sealed, black plastic bag inside the box. I lift it out, bounce it on my palms. It isn't heavy, maybe five or six pounds. I let it fall to the coffee table with a *thunk*. I tilt my glass back and drain the second one while looking at it.

"Winnie, could you get me another one. No cranberry juice this time. Ray always drank this *mierda* straight and if I'm going to toast him, that's how I'll do it."

She goes into the kitchen and brings the bottle back to the sofa. She downs the rest of her glass, then pours us both large slugs from the bottle.

I lean over and put my glass down next to the plastic bag. It's twisted at the top, tied with one of those thin wires they use for bread bags. I unwind it, let the bag unwind itself, then hold back the edges so I can look inside.

It's a light gray powder, not grainy, not quite as fine as talc. I reach in and rub some between my fingers. It feels a little like my sweet. When I take my hand out, my fingertips are dusted with it. I wrap them around the glass, soaking them in the condensation from the cold vodka.

I'm getting teary again. I know if I look at Winnie, at my new lover, my new friend, maybe the new most important person in my life, I'll bust out sobbing again. And I don't want to. I want to toast Ray dry-eyed.

I wipe my eyes on my sleeve, look directly at the plastic bag and lift my glass.

"Ray. *Cabron*. I loved you, *mi amigo*. I'm going to miss you. *Do lei loh moh*."

I don't look at her, but I hold up my glass in the direction of Winnie so that she knows I want her to clink hers to mine. She does. And I relax. It feels like a torch has been passed.

I toss mine back and the *chingada* vodka burns like that *chingada* torch all the way down. My head's getting a little light with it, woozy, not a bad feeling. But the burn finds its way to my stomach and focuses my attention down there and I know it won't be long before things feel very very bad.

CHAPTER **TWENTY-SIX**

They say withdrawal won't kill you. But I wish it would. If there's any part of me that isn't aching, churning, itching, sweating, burning, shivering and spewing, I'd sure like to find it, crawl into that small safe spot, curl up and go away.

"Winnie, I can't stand this. I can't *chingada* do it. Please, please, go get me my sweet, get me some *fan*. I'm going to die, please."

She's got her arms wrapped around me again, soaking in all the *mierda* that's pouring out of me. She thinks it makes me feel good. It doesn't. Everywhere she touches me feels like someone's working me over with brass knuckles. I can't stand it, but I can't squirm out of it. I don't have the energy. My insides are moving in all directions faster than I've ever moved before. But I can't make the outside move.

"Please, please, I'll do anything, anything you want, just get me my sweet."

She's crying and holding me tighter and not saying anything, not answering me. And she can get me what I want, what I need, but she won't. She's making me feel worse. Is she a sadist?

"You *chingada puta*, listen to me, listen damnit. Get me my *fan*. I'll fucking kill you."

She lets me go, a look so hurt and startled on her face that you'd think someone slugged her in the stomach. I roll away from her on the bed. I curl up, my own arms wrapped around me and I can't tell where they begin or end because it all hurts so *chingada* much that it all feels the same. Like I've melted into one big puddle of pain and nausea, my skin crawling on the surface and percolating underneath.

Winnie puts herself together, sniffles her tears back inside, wipes her eyes and her nose on a corner of the bed sheet. She looks at me again, mad this time, but the kind of mad I used to see in the eyes of my mother when she'd yell at me.

"That's what you think? That's what you think of me? You think I don't understand, but I know some words of Spanish. You think I'm a whore. A fucking whore. That's all you think I am? Yes, I'm a whore, with other people. Not with you. You want me to be your whore, okay, I'll be your whore. I'll go get you your fucking drugs, your *fan*."

Her words explode into my brain. She said she'll go get my sweet. She'll save me, fix me. It will all be better. I begin to relax. Then the need kicks me hard inside with pointy-toed boots, trying to break out. The pain's so sharp it almost splits me in half. It hacks into my head and is so searing and bright that for a moment I can focus. Ray used to say that there are some kinds of pain that smarten you up, that help you see better. It's something else I thought he was full of *mierda* about. But maybe he wasn't.

Winnie starts to roll away to the edge of the bed, about to get up. To get me what I want. But I can't let her.

It's the hardest thing I've ever done, but I uncoil myself, reach out and put a burning hand on her arm. I've got to do this quick before my whole being tells me to shut up, stop being such a fool, let her go get my sweet.

"Don't go. Winnie, don't go. I'm sorry. It's the *fan* talking, making me crazy. I can do this. I can if I have you to do it with. I want you. I want you here with me. That might be the only true thing I say in the next few days. Believe that, but don't believe the other things, the things the *fan* makes me say."

She puts a hand on mine and smiles, relieved. "You're hot. I'll go get a wet towel."

I fall back onto the bed, trying not to shrivel up this time, trying to lie flat, telling my arms and legs and fingers and toes that curling and clenching isn't going to make them feel better. I'm so tired with the effort that I'm nearly asleep when Winnie comes back from the bathroom.

The cool damp cloth on my forehead settles me, refreshes me. I ask Winnie if she can wet a whole towel, cover my body with it. She smiles and goes back to the bathroom. I try taking off the oversized t-shirt I took from Ray's drawers, but I can hardly lift my arms.

Winnie helps me undress when she comes back. She's so gentle, so kind. She rubs me lightly all over with the wet towel, but as the water evaporates I get chilled and start shivering. She puts me under the covers, gets an extra blanket and puts it on me. She takes off her clothes and gets into bed with me, holding me, her mouth near my ear but not saying anything. I relax and drift away on the pillow of her warm, steady, soft breath.

I DREAMT ABOUT SOMETHING. I can almost remember it in spite of this damn itching. It's like someone's stroking the inside of my skin with a coarse wire brush. I try scratching and can't get to it. I'd have to break the skin to get to it, and even then it might not be deep enough. I know that, so I try not to scratch. But I do anyhow.

My legs are twitching like a dog running in its dreams. Running from what? To what? What was I dreaming about? Was I running in my dream? Trying to kick something?

Ray was in it, I think. And the flower *Puta*. And knives, a lot of sharp, gleaming knives. I was happy to see Ray, and sad for the *Puta*. I wanted to tell her I was sorry, so sorry. I had to do what I did. She didn't give me any choice. But I couldn't tell her, she kept turning away. And I wanted Ray to kiss me, but he wouldn't. And the knives made a terrible noise, clanging against each other, sparks flying off them. And Ray was trying to tell me something. And I was trying to tell Ray about Winnie, about how I love her. And how I understood now, understood why he was such a sucker for whores. How there's something damaged inside them that's a lot like what's fucked up inside me. How attractive that is. How comforting. But we couldn't hear each other over the clamor of the knives.

And I'm awake now and it's not knives that are stabbing me in the gut. And the pain and the nausea and the heat and cold and sweating and shivering all start up again. And my nose is oozing and my mouth awash with saliva and my bowels are clenched hard against what I know will happen if I let them loose and there's anything still inside me to come out.

And it wakes up Winnie. And she sees what's happening and wraps her arms and legs tight around me again. And that hurts so *chingada* much, too much. And it will hurt too much if she doesn't. And I lie here hating her, loving her, hating myself mostly. And I can't do anything about anything other than suffer.

Days have gone by that way. I think it's been days. I don't know. Time is meaningless. I've long lost track of the beats of my heart, my breath, the arrhythmic pounding in my belly. The light hurts my eyes so I keep the room dark.

Sometimes I'm so restless I have to get up and pace, back and forth, around and around Ray's small bedroom, hardly able to keep up with the spasms in my legs. There's no room in here and I go up and over the bed and into the closet and over to the shut tight window and sometimes I pull myself up onto the dresser and sit there until I'm too antsy and have to jump off again. My legs are bruised from banging into things, from thrashing against the hard edges of the bed frame, the closet door.

It's not constant. It comes and goes in waves, leaving me spent, near paralyzed in between. Then Winnie wipes me down with the damp cloth. Sometimes I want cold water, sometimes water so hot it feels like it might scald the pain out of me. She comes with soup, noodles, fruit juice and insists I take it. And I do, but I'm not sure why. I just vomit it all back up again not much later.

ON THE SIXTH DAY after I watched the last of my sweet spiral out of my life, I know it's that because Winnie tells me so, I'm beginning to feel a little better. It's still bad, but not so terrible that I think I can't endure. I might even want to live.

When Winnie comes with the warm towel, it feels good, oh so very good. When she lies down with me I want her touching me. I want her breasts crushed up against mine, our lips lightly attached, our tongues gently playing. I want to give her pleasure and I put a hand down between us, lightly circling on her skin, brushing just so against her lower lips until I can feel her begin to move with some urgency against me. Then my fingers inside her, my thumb maintaining light pressure on the hood above her clit, I keep it slow, gentle, consistent until she starts pushing herself hard against my hand and I increase the pressure, the tempo. Then she stiffens, lets out a deep "*unhh*" and pushes my hand away as she throbs against my thigh.

When she recovers she covers my face with wet kisses, slides her hand down on me, starts to trail kisses along behind it, dipping her head toward my crotch. I reach down and stop her. I can't, not yet. I wanted to make her feel good, to do something for her. I'm not ready to feel that good myself. Later, maybe. Now I don't deserve it.

She turns her head to look at me, resting it on my stomach, silently mouths "why?"

I brush a lock of hair off her forehead, away from her eyes, run a finger along the ridges of her lips.

"I can't now. It still hurts too much. Soon, I promise."

She smiles and moves her face up to rest on the pillow next to mine. Our breath mingles, we look at each other, too close to focus, not saying anything, until we drift away, back to sleep.

TWO DAYS LATER I'M EVEN BETTER. I ask Winnie to bring me a pair of sunglasses. I put them on and go out into the living room. It's daylight, but the shadow of the building across the street is keeping it from being too bright. I drink a lot of water, some cranberry juice. There's a pot of chicken egg-drop soup on the stove and it actually smells good. For the first time in a very long time I feel hungry, very hungry.

I sit down at the table and she puts a steaming bowl in front of me. I take too greedy a spoonful too fast and burn the roof of my mouth. But it feels good going down, soft, warm. I finish the first bowl, ask for another. But I only manage a spoonful. I'm full already. My stomach has shrunk. I smile at Winnie, crook my finger to get her to lower her head, kiss her gently on the lips, then on the neck. I get up and go to the living room, sit on the sofa. Winnie follows, sits on the coffee table facing me.

"What did you do with Ray's ashes?"

"Put them back in the closet. I didn't know what you wanted. Is that okay?"

"Yeah, that's fine. I'll have to think about what he'd want me to do with them. We can't leave them here."

"What do you think?"

"I don't know. He once said he didn't care what happened to his body when he was done with it. But I do. I'll feel better if we take his ashes to some places that he loved."

"We?"

"You don't have to help me if you don't want, Winnie. You've done more than enough. He wasn't your friend."

She moves over to sit next to me, to hold my hands in hers. She doesn't say anything. She doesn't have to.

CHAPTER **TWENTY-SEVEN**

What about Suwandi?"

"Tom Suwandi, in Shanghai? He's dead." Warner tosses me a three-day-old *South China Morning Post* from a pile on his desk.

"What the…how?"

"Heart attack."

"What do you mean, heart attack? That's it?"

"These things happen, Lei Yue. People have heart attacks and die all the time."

"But not the people I want to, want to…"

"What? Bring to justice? Take revenge on? Sorry, you'll just have to learn to live with it."

"How do you know it was a heart attack? Maybe someone killed him, made it look that way. There had to be a lot of people who wanted the *chingada puerco* dead."

"I know people in Shanghai, Lei Yue. I've seen the medical report. It wasn't anything tricky."

"It's not good enough, Mister Warner. What about his bank? What about the other people he hurt?"

"The bank's gone under. There's nothing more we can do."

"What about Floss, or Betty, the one I didn't kill?"

"The police have been looking for her since Ray was killed. She's disappeared. Her name's Da Nuying, but there's nothing we can do about her, either. She's irrelevant anyhow, just a bit player."

"Not to me, she isn't. She killed Ray."

"That's why the Chinese are looking for her. If you know anything that might help them, I know some honest cops I can pass it to. Otherwise…"

"No, not yet. But I can go back there, look for her, see what I can find out."

"No you can't. I won't let you. I don't know that the Chinese will let you back in the country, anyhow. The whole thing's been an embarrassment to them, and they don't take well to that.

"Besides, there's no point. Suwandi and Bellevue are dead. The bank's gone and some of the companies that depended on it are gone with it. You're not going to bring Ray back. The monks aren't happy, but they found out what they wanted to know."

"You don't think Suwandi's dying is a little fishy? Maybe someone got him out of the way and took over his business."

"The medical report, Lei Yue. It wasn't faked. Believe me, it was a heart attack. A lifetime of fatty food, booze and no exercise caught up to him."

"Ray wouldn't have let it drop."

Warner drops his head and doesn't say anything at first. He's got a pained expression. He's a tough guy but I can see some regret in there. He wishes we'd never taken the job. He might even feel guilty that Ray's dead. Might even think it's partially his fault. I don't think it's me projecting anything. I can sense it in him.

When he looks back up and talks, he still looks sad. His voice is dulled down, soft. I should cut him a break.

"No, he wouldn't, Lei Yue. It drove me crazy and it was one of the things I liked and respected about him. But I've got to tell you what I told Ray all too often. We're in business. We do what we can for our clients and if there's anything else, we turn it over to the proper authorities."

I lower my voice, try to take the upset out of it.

"Who are the proper authorities in Shanghai, Mister Warner? Suwandi and his bank, Bellevue and his factory, they were only a small part of it. They're practically using slave labor in China. They're involved in people smuggling. The Mexican trade guy told me he could get me whatever workers I wanted. If they're doing that, and they're tied to the triads, which they seem to be, they're probably into drugs, guns, counterfeits, you name it. They killed Ray. We can't let it go. I can't."

Warner looks like he can't make up his mind between giving me a stern look or a sad one. He settles for something in between. If I hadn't watched him working it out on his face, I wouldn't know what it is.

"We are. You are. That's it."

I'm not going to argue with him, but this isn't the end of it. I can't let it be. I struggle to stick a look of resignation on my face and change the subject.

"By the way, Mister Warner, what should we do with Ray's ashes?"

"I don't know. I hadn't thought about it. I didn't want to think about it. That's why I put them in his apartment for the time being. I guess I'll send them to his family, if I can find them."

"He was an only child. I think his parents are dead. If you don't mind, I'm thinking of taking some of his ashes and scattering them around places he loved."

"Like where?"

"He talked a lot about Indonesia, about a valley in Bali. He loved the Star Ferry. He had a weird thing for Mongkok on a Saturday night, he used to go there and walk around when he wanted to think about things. He called it 'crowd surfing.'"

"Yeah, I remember him telling me that. It was something else I never quite got about the guy."

"And Macau. He loved walking around Macau. In the old Portuguese parts. That Russian woman, Irina, the one who broke his heart, she used to work there."

He considers it for a moment and looks relieved when he nods his head yes.

"Let me know if you need any help."

"What about his apartment?"

"The lease is paid in advance through the end of the year. DiDi paid it. You can stay there if you want. After that, let's see. When are you coming back to work?"

"I don't know yet. I'm still weak, Mister Warner. Fucked up in the head. Can I have a couple of weeks?"

"Lei Yue, I gave Ray the name of a shrink once. I don't imagine you want it any more than he did. But if you do…"

It is a good idea. I've started to think about killing the flower *Puta* a couple of times and I've fought it back. I can't think about that. I don't know why. I had to do it. She was always with Bellevue. She was with him the last time I saw Ray. Maybe she's the one who killed Ray. What would have happened if I hadn't killed her? Still, I'm afraid sometimes when I close my eyes that I'll see her. I killed her. I had to. But I don't want to see her. I don't want to look at what I did. And a shrink would make me do that.

"Thanks. I'll let you know." I get up to get out of there and he walks me to the door. As I turn to face him and say goodbye, he puts a hand on my shoulder, gives me a look that isn't ambiguous, it's definitely stern this time.

"Let it go, Lei Yue. For your own good, for everyone's, let it go. Ray's dead, you can't bring him back. The people who killed him are dead. Scatter his ashes, take care of yourself, come back to work when you can and move on with your life. That's all you can do."

He's right. But no *chingada* way I'm letting it go.

"SHOULDN'T WE SAY SOMETHING?"

I drop a cupful of Ray off the lower deck of the Morning Star into the dark, oily, stinking chop of Victoria Harbor.

"I don't think Ray would want us to. He was a strange guy that way, really sentimental, but he hated sentiment."

"A prayer? Something?"

I laugh at the thought and put an arm around Winnie to make sure she doesn't think I'm laughing at her.

"Ray hated religion, all religion. If I believed in ghosts, saying a prayer over his ashes would be the surest way to make sure he'd haunt us until we died."

"What would he want?"

"I think he'd want us to do what we're doing. He'd want to get on his white horse and fuck up the bad guys, fuck up their operations. But he'd try to protect me, us, try to keep us out of it."

"So, what are we going to do?"

"Scatter Ray. Then do what he would do. You don't have to do it with me. It might be dangerous."

"You really are taking over from him, aren't you? Maybe you should believe in ghosts."

"What do you mean?"

"We'll protect each other. I'm with you." Her hand squeezes my shoulder so hard it almost hurts.

I smile, thinking to myself, that's something Ray would have liked to hear.

I'm also a little uneasy. "Taking over from Ray." Am I? In what ways? I loved the guy, but he had his faults. I don't want to be like him, not much. But here I am, deciding what I'm going to do on the basis of what he would do.

And doing it with Winnie, a prostitute. That's something he'd do, too. But I love her. Or I'm falling in love with her. Or something. Why? Why'd Ray do it? Why am I? Or maybe I'm not. Maybe it's just her. She is who she is, no matter what she does for a living.

I'd read a book once called *Prostitution, Politics and the Dynamics of Power Relationships*. Or something like that. It was the kind of book that a lot of women read in college. Men, especially insecure ones, are attracted to women who make them feel powerful, in control. Why not women, too? I don't really think Ray was that way. I don't think I am, either. I hope.

It's something else I don't want to think about. They're adding up. Maybe I am more like Ray than I'd like to think.

HONG KONG'S A STRANGE PLACE. The water is disgusting, the air is foul, people are as rude and unpleasant to each other as it's possible for people to be, but the streets are clean. Fines for littering are heavy and enforced. Ray would have enjoyed watching Winnie and me trying to discreetly drop some of his ashes at the four corners of his favorite crowd surfing spot—Nathan Road and Mongkok Road.

The tightly pressed crowds help. Ray used to say that you could get away with almost anything in the middle of the pack trying to make its way around one of these corners. It's the anonymity of the masses. You have to plan ahead because you can't do anything at your own pace. If you don't fall into step, you'll be trampled underfoot.

I'd thought of that ahead of time and decanted some of Ray into four plastic film canisters I found in his apartment. They're in my pocket. I can pop the lids off of them with one hand. My other hand is firmly gripped in one of Winnie's. If nothing else, Ray would have appreciated what I'm going through. I'm too short. Crowds like this terrify me. But I take deep breaths and control my terror until we've circled the intersection and I've dumped some of the ashes at each corner.

Mongkok is full of quiet coffee houses. When we're done, I pull Winnie to the stairs leading up to one and find us a window table overlooking the fray on the street a floor below. The first conversation I ever had with Ray was in a place like this. I liked him right away. There was something about him. I knew from the start we were going to be close.

When I was a kid my father used to complain that I was like a puppy dog; I'd follow anyone home who was even a little nice to me. I don't think it's that. I hope not. I sense things about people. I sense them when I first meet them. It was like that with Ray. It was like that with Winnie.

We don't talk until after our coffees come. I'm drinking a double espresso, as strong and bitter as they can make it, and then I wreck it with enough sugar to turn it into sludge. Winnie orders one of those girly drinks, something with a lot of stiff whipped cream and shaved chocolate.

"Lei Yue, how are you feeling?"

"About Ray? Mad, mostly, at the moment."

"No. You? Mad?" She smiles and reaches for my hand.

"Every day it's a little better. Having you helps. You're a better lover for me than the *fan*, but I still miss it. I want it every day. Ray is helping. I know I'll fuck up what I have to do if I start again. I can't do that. Not now. I don't know about later."

"Are you sure you want me to stay with you at the apartment?"

Yes I do. For now. I reach out for her other hand. "I'll go *loca* if you don't."

Winnie looks like she's about to start blubbering with happiness. We've spent a lot of time crying together in the little time we've known each other. It's a good thing, maybe, when two needy people find each other. At least for a while. Eventually, I don't know. Maybe it's like two starving cannibals trying to live off each other's body parts, it only works for so long.

"When we finish our coffee we'll go to your place and pick up your things. What will you do about the apartment?"

"My room? I paid for it by the week. It's already been too long. By now there's some other Big Breasted Korean Housewife there. It's cheaper for us whores to change our names than for them to change the signs. Maybe my neighbor, Kitten Who Likes to Purr, was nice enough to keep my things for me."

"Who comes up with these stupid names?"

She puts a fake look of indignation on her face and her hands on her hips.

"Stupid? I am Korean, half anyway. And I do have big breasts. Is it so impossible that anybody would marry me and make me a house-wife?"

It feels good to be teasing each other, flirting. Crying brought us closer together, so will laughing.

"You're going to be my housewife. So it's a good name. Can I call you 'Big,' or do you prefer 'Housewife?'"

"That's Ms. Big to you Ms. Wen."

We're both tired. We've had a lot of stress. None of this is all that funny but we can't stop giggling like schoolgirls who have been smok-ing pot.

KITTEN LOOKS MORE LIKE AN OLD LIONESS that's eaten way too much gazelle. She reclines with half-lidded glazed eyes and bloated stomach on an old-fashioned Chinese Imperial-style daybed that has been crow-barred into her tiny room. A tall pile of empty food-take-away containers take up much of what little floor space there is between the bed and the door. It looks like it's stacked and waiting to be lit for a bonfire. An oily sounding French-Vietnamese chanteuse warbles from the tinny speakers of a cheap cassette player.

She's traded Winnie's music CDs for a bottle of the best quality snake bile wine. She holds up the half-drunk bottle to show us, while rubbing her belly with the other hand.

"Good for stomach."

She doesn't know what happened to the books. Winnie only looks briefly annoyed.

"That's okay. I'd already read them all. What about my clothes? I had a few pictures."

Kitten points straight down, then starts to bring her hand back up to her mouth to try and cover a belch, but doesn't get it there in time. Why is it that so many burps smell like bologna that's been left out in the sun too long?

I stoop to look under the bed and there's a lumpy red, white and blue striped bag stuffed under there. I move aside the takeout cartons and pull it out.

Winnie squats, pulls open the drawstring and looks inside. She looks up at Kitten who is looking up at the ceiling, at nothing in particular.

"That's it?"

Kitten brings her head down and nods 'yes' while shrugging her shoulders.

WE STOP AT MY APARTMENT after that and pick up the rest of my clothes. There isn't anything else I want from there.

Back at Ray's it doesn't take long to move his personal stuff out of the bedroom and for Winnie and me to fill the closets and drawers with ours. I don't know what to do with Ray's belongings. I don't want to deal with them. Sooner or later I'll have to, but not now.

I sit down to make a list. Ray used to do that all the time and it fascinated me. He never followed the lists, or if he did, it wasn't in order. A lot of the time he'd make a list, stick it somewhere, never look at it again and eventually throw it away. He said the list itself was meaningless, it was writing it down that mattered.

So I make my own list of all the things I need to do. When I'm finished, it looks like a lot less than it feels like inside.

First on the list is to get the guys who got Ray. But I'm not even sure what that means. The people who actually killed Ray are already dead. They were part of a bigger problem. But it's so big, what can I do about it? I can't fix China.

Suwandi's bank was tied up with corrupt officials, factories that used slave labor or something close to it and shipping companies. I can't do anything inside China itself. It's too much like that game at *fiestas*, the one where you hammer down heads that pop up, but they keep popping up in different places. You can score points in a game like that. You can't win it. And sometimes one of those heads pops up with a gun and shoots you.

Still, even if all you can do is score points, maybe that's worth doing. In one of our last conversations, Ray was carrying on at me about how fed up he was with people using the excuse of, 'if I don't do it, someone else will.' He said, "Of course they will, but it's got to stop somewhere, with someone."

So what am I going to do?

"MONTGOMERY." He snaps his name off crisp. It's how I used to answer the phone when I was a journalist and wanted to sound like I had some authority. I didn't. He still does, for the time being.

"Wen Lei Yue, Mister Montgomery. I'm, I was a colleague of Ray Sharp's."

"Ray spoke of you often, Ms. Wen. My deepest condolences. I liked Ray. I considered him a friend. He will be sorely missed. I understand from Bill Warner that you will be handling Ray's affairs. Should you require any assistance, please do not hesitate to call me."

I am? I guess so, but no one had made it this clear before now.

"Thanks, Mister Montgomery. I'm calling because I might need some help with something else."

"Please, call me John. May I call you Lei Yue?"

"Sure, John. Can I ask you some shipping related questions?"

"Of course. Does this have anything to do with the investigation that Ray and you were working on in Shanghai?"

"I'm following up some things on my own now."

"Ray always said that you shared some of his dogged traits."

"I'm learning, John. Do you know anything about a shipping company called BajaChina?"

"Yes, Wellfleet contracts with them for some of its freight consolidation business to Mexico from both here and in Shanghai."

"And Eduardo Garcia?"

"He's with Mexico's trade office in Shanghai. Does he have something to do with BajaChina?"

"He's a VP."

"That's not unusual. A lot of countries, particularly poorer ones, appoint people from the private sector to their trade missions."

"How many of their business cards are found in the wallet of a guy who was connected to the people who killed Ray? The man with the wallet is dead now, too. He was a member of Sun Yee On, one of the triads."

"That's why you're calling me?"

"*Si senor.* I'm trying to unravel the sweater."

"You are going to have to speak English, Lei Yue. Even when you are speaking English."

"I mean, it's like when a stitch comes loose on a knit sweater and you start pulling on the yarn and if you keep pulling, it all comes apart."

"I see, and you think BajaChina or Garcia's card in a dead bad man's wallet is the loose thread. That brings two questions to mind."

"Okay."

"Why do you want to unravel this sweater? And what is it you think I can do to assist?"

"Two good questions. First, it's a bad sweater, uglier than anything my grandmother ever gave me for Christmas. I can see it and I can try and do something about it. I owe it to Ray."

"Ray's dead."

"I owe it to his memory, then. I owe it to myself, too. You don't know what those people did to me, and I don't want to talk about it. But I want them to pay for it."

"Ray did also say you are tenacious."

"If you say anything about a dog with a bone I'm going to hang up, come over to your office and kick your ass."

"I believe you would. What would you like me to do?"

"You said that Wellfleet does business with BajaChina. I think they might be involved in smuggling from China and here to Mexico. Ray said you were a straight businessman. You wanted us to sort out that Cambodian mess for your company, because you didn't want it involved in illegal activities."

"What do you think they're smuggling?"

"Whatever they can. People, for sure. I know that much. Garcia told me as much. But if they're doing that I'll bet you they're also into drugs, guns, money, counterfeit products, anything else they can make money on. It's easier and cheaper to get anything you want to Mexico by ship. Then there's that whole long border with the U.S. that anyone can cross almost any time they want."

"Can you prove it?"

"Not yet. That's what I'm going to do."

"What do you want me to do?"

"Call Bill Warner. Hire DiDi to look into it for Wellfleet. Insist on him putting me on the job."

"Lei Yue, I'm leaving Wellfleet at the end of the year. Why should I want to uncover anything that might cause the company trouble in my final months as its managing director?"

"John, I am going to pull on this thread no matter what. If something comes up that's embarrassing to your company, wouldn't it be better if it looked like you were trying to fix the problem yourself, rather than ignore it, or at best had no idea what was going on right under your nose?"

"I have yet to meet you in person, Ms. Wen; but you must be Ray's twin sister."

CHAPTER **TWENTY-EIGHT**

L ike I said, Lei Yue, you're not going back to China, even if you can get a visa. It might be dangerous." I'm back in Warner's office and he's not happy that I talked to Montgomery.

"Suwandi and Bellevue are dead. Why would it be dangerous?"

"It's not clear what they were planning to do with you or why. They were mixed up with triads, and those bad guys haven't gone away. The police here are still investigating our murdered monk. The only thing anyone's sure of is that he was killed for something to do with the monastery's money and Suwandi's bank. The triad guy who killed him is running loose.

"So long as you're here, and not mucking around in their territory, they'll leave you alone. It would be more trouble than it's worth to them to do anything about you now, especially in Hong Kong. But if you go back there, start getting in their way… If they see you as a problem, they'll come after you."

"So, you are assigning me the job."

"Montgomery made it clear I don't have any choice. Wellfleet's too good a client to say no to. I don't know what you told him, but I'm not happy being held over a barrel on this."

"You don't think I'll do a good job?"

"That's not it and you know it. It's too soon. You're too emotionally involved. Hell, the only reason you even know anything about BajaChina is that you found that card in the wallet of someone you had to kill to escape from who the hell knows what. You've got to be a mess, maybe you just don't know it yet."

"Hell" is a pretty strong word for Bill Warner. He must really be upset.

"I didn't kill him, Mister Warner. It was Mei Lin, my friend."

I don't know what's wrong with me. One of these days I might break down and go *loca* over it. But so far I don't feel all that bad about what we had to do to get out of there. I don't like it that I had to kill the flower *Puta* to escape, but it's been a whole lot easier not letting it get to me than I thought it would be.

"Christ, Lei Yue, you know what I meant. Do I have to tick off all the reasons it's crazy for you to do this job right now, again?"

"No, you don't, Mister Warner, and I appreciate your concern. I really do. But do I have to tick off all the reasons I need to do this job right now, again?"

"No wonder you and Ray were such good friends. You're as messed up as he was. It's a damn good thing you never fell in love and had kids."

I stifle a laugh. It's not a good idea to laugh around your boss unless he knows for sure that you're laughing with him, not at him. I can't help but smile, though.

"Ray and I were messed up in a whole lot of different ways, Mister Warner. It's one of the things we liked about each other. You're right, though, we'd have made lousy parents."

He sinks his forehead into his hand, propping it up with his elbow on the desk and shakes his head back and forth.

"Keep me informed, will you, Lei Yue? Report to me before you tell Montgomery anything. Try not to get into too much trouble. And if it looks like you're going to, let me know so I can help, or cover my ass or whatever's necessary. Okay?"

"*Si Senor.*"

He doesn't say anything, raises his eyes at me then flicks them with a slight tilt of his head at the door.

I walk out feeling bad for having given him a hard time. He's a good boss, pays well, respects and trusts me, backs me up when I need it and I think his concern is real. He's got a soft spot that might have got in the way of his C.I.A. career.

But he's still the boss, and I don't tell him everything. I can't. If I told him what I have in mind he'd probably have me taken away by the nice men in the white suits.

WINNIE'S BEEN SAVING TO GET TO AMERICA. She tried to do it legally, at least on a tourist visa, but it didn't work. An arrest for prostitution near a U.S. military base in Seoul didn't help. Not that the U.S. military isn't happy to accommodate hookers near its bases; it is. But every now and then they make a show of cracking down to keep everyone in line. Being half-American didn't help either. The immigration officials assumed, correctly, that she was likely to overstay her visa, maybe permanently. So she's been saving up for a 'coyote,' as we would call them in Mexico. 'Snakehead' is what they're called here.

"How much?"

"Fifteen thousand U.S. here, fifteen more when I get there, but I can work that off."

"Doing what?"

Winnie blushes, gives me a sad look and puts a hand on mine.

"Don't be jealous, Lei Yue. It doesn't mean anything, not like us."

It's not jealousy, I don't think. Maybe it is a little.

"Wouldn't you rather do something else?"

"What? Fifteen thousand dollars is a lot of money. It might take five years to pay that off working in a factory. Working as a whore, even a cheap one in America, maybe a year."

I know a little something about coyotes. They have ways of turning fifteen thousand dollars into a lot more than that. That second payment is a trap.

"What if you pay the whole thirty here?"

"I don't think they'll let you. And it would be stupid, anyhow. Once you've paid them everything, they don't have any reason to care about you."

"How does it work?"

"I know someone here. For five thousand Hong Kong he'll introduce me to the snakehead. They give me a date. I show up at the harbor and pay them the fifteen thousand. I go by boat to California or Seattle."

"Don't a lot of people get caught?"

"Yes. But what can you do?"

"What about Mexico?"

"I don't want to go to Mexico. I can make more money here."

"I didn't mean that. It's probably easier to get into Mexico than the U.S. or Canada. Then it's really easy to get over the border into the U.S." And I know just the shipping company that can do that.

She gets a look that's a lot like young kids get when their teacher tells them to 'put your thinking caps on.' I can hardly stand it. Am I trying to use her? I don't want to. But this is what she's been saving for, right? I lean into her, turn my lips up to her. She brings hers down and we kiss, soft and loose and moist and I want to linger there and not talk anymore. I want her to know I'm not using her. I want me to know it.

I have to tell her. I take my lips away. She moves forward trying to hold on to them, but I pull back far enough to look at her. I take her hand and press it to my lips, then bring it down to my lap and hold it there.

"Winnie, I have to tell you what I'm thinking."

She looks wary, concerned. "About us? About me?"

"Well, yes." She pulls back, tenses, hunches her shoulders, worried she isn't going to like what I have to say.

"I want to be with you. I want us to be together."

Her body relaxes, not fully, about halfway, still not sure what I'm going to say.

"I won't go if you don't want me to, Lei Yue. I'll stay here with you."

I wish it was that simple. I wish we could. We can't. I can't. I used to hear people talk about their sense of duty, of honor. And I used to think that was stupid. Even Ray used those words sometimes. I always thought he was half-joking. I know now, he wasn't.

"I want to go with you, to America."

"But you have permanent residency, a green card. You can meet me there."

"I need to go with you, through Mexico if we can. I'll pay for it."

She looks wary again, pleased but uncertain.

"Why?"

I explain it to her. It doesn't sound all that convincing to me, either.

She puts her arms around me, kisses me on the forehead. Pulls back and looks at me with a very crooked smile.

"That's crazy, Lei Yue, totally crazy. No one does that who doesn't have to. Can't you find out what you need to here, then take it to the police?"

"I need to know all of it, Winnie. I need to know where it starts and where it ends and who's involved in it all along the way. I've got to understand it inside out. If I fuck them up at this end, that won't do anything. Someone else will just take over. It's true, if they're not doing it, someone else will. I've got to make as big a problem for them as possible. I've got to fuck them up here, in Mexico and in the U.S., and maybe then somebody will do something about it."

She doesn't like it. I don't blame her. Neither do I. But my mind is made up. I've got enough money saved to pay for us on this end. I can borrow the money from my parents to pay off our debt on the other end, so that we don't have to work it off. They will think I'm crazy, too. There will be a lot of yelling and screaming and my mother crying. The return of the prodigal daughter, my father's *chingada enana loca*, crazy fucking dwarf. But they'll do it.

Convincing her takes a lot more crying on both our parts. And promises that I'll be happy to keep if I can. I'll try. Winnie insists that she will pay the triad guy here for the introduction. It seems important to her, so I don't put up much of a fight.

MONTGOMERY THINKS I'M NUTS, TOO. But he doesn't try to stop me.

"It's your funeral, Lei Yue."

"Thanks. I hope not."

"Why are you informing me of this?"

"Someone needs to know and I can't tell Bill Warner."

"Because he'd stop you."

"He'd try. You can tell him, if you want, after the ship leaves."

"When is that going to be?"

"I don't know yet, soon."

"What have you uncovered so far?"

"I know we can get a snakehead to take us by freighter from Shenzhen to Ensenada on the west coast of Mexico. BajaChina's one of the only shippers that regularly makes that route. And the company's got offices in both ports."

"Why Shenzhen?"

"I could be wrong, but I think it must be easier to slip all sorts of things past the port authorities in China than it is here in Hong Kong. And Shenzhen's just across the border, it might as well be Hong Kong."

"You're not wrong. Port fees are cheaper, too."

"It's not proof of anything, yet, but it's suspicious."

"Do you think you can get proof?"

"I'm going to try. And I'll find out what they've got going on the other end."

"I admire your, how to put it, your pluck."

"You don't think I'm crazy?"

"Rest assured, I do, as a March hare. But in this instance it is, perhaps, useful."

"So you're not going to tell Bill Warner."

"No, I suppose not unless it becomes necessary. But you will be incommunicado for a time. It takes anywhere from a fortnight to three weeks to make the passage across the Pacific. He will no doubt have some curiosity as to the whereabouts of his employee."

"Maybe you should tell him, after I leave."

"Perhaps it would be better were you to write out a detailed report of everything you have learned up to the point of your departure, then post copies to myself and your boss on the day you leave. The report will arrive no sooner than the next day, at which time you will already be irretrievably out to sea."

"You should have been a diplomat, Mister Montgomery. You're sneaky enough."

"Ray thought I was a spy, MI-6."

"Are you?"

"As I said, Ray was under that impression."

I'm never going to get the question answered, so I give up trying. I'd called him to get any contacts he has in shipping in the U.S. or

Baja California in Mexico. They might come in handy once I get there. He does have several at the harbor in Los Angeles and one who is a cross-border freight consolidator in Calexico, on the California side across from Mexicali. He promises to get in touch with them, give them my name, let them know I might be calling.

I thank him and am about to hang up.

"*Bueno suerte,* Lei Yue."

"I didn't know you spoke any Spanish."

"I don't. I have made a point of learning how to say "good luck" in many different languages. It makes me feel good to say it. I don't, however, recall it ever doing much good."

WINNIE'S PUT ON HER SLUTTIEST CLOTHES and a lot of makeup. It's not a look that does much for me. I'm sprawled on the sofa in sweat pants and a t-shirt.

"Why are you dressed like that?"

"I've got to go pay the money to the triad guy for our introduction."

"Let me get dressed. I'll go with you." I start to get up.

She blushes, looks sad, moves and puts her hands on my shoulders to sit me back down.

"You can't, Lei Yue. It's not a good idea. I should go alone."

"Dressed like that?" I've got my suspicions of why she wants to go alone.

She sits down and takes my hand. Her eyes are beginning to get wet. I'm tired of all the crying we do together. I won't let myself this time, no matter what it is.

"He'll want to fuck me. I'll have to let him."

"Why? You're paying him the money. Isn't that enough?"

She looks at me, silent, the tears starting down her cheeks. I know it's not enough.

"I don't want you to have to do this for me, for us. I'll go with you. We'll talk him out of it."

"I know him, Lei Yue, He's with Sun Yee On, the boss of the area where I used to work. He won't listen. If you come, he'll have both of us. I won't let that happen. It doesn't matter what we want. He can do whatever he wants."

"*Chingate*, I can't let you do this."

She strokes my face, kisses me around the edge of my lips. Her face is so close that it's like I can't see her at all. She whispers, but it sounds loud, too clear.

"My sweet Lei Yue, I've been doing this since I was fourteen. It's nothing more than a way to get some of the things I want. When I'm doing it, it's only my body, it isn't me. The real me, the part that's with you, she's somewhere far away, somewhere that triad bastard and the others like him can't ever find."

Chingate, I wasn't going to cry. I'm sick of crying. I bury my face in her shoulder and let it flow. But only for a little before I fight it back.

"Winnie, we have to stop this, enough."

"It's the only way, now. Later, when we're in America."

"No, I don't mean that. Yes, I do mean that. I don't want you ever to have to be a whore again. But no, I mean all this crying all the time. We cry too much. When do we get to laugh?"

She takes my head between her hands and pulls my face to her. She forces my mouth open with her tongue and we kiss, long and deep and hard, as if trying to squeeze our whole beings into each other. We kiss until I think I'm going to suffocate and I won't mind because I'm kissing her. I can die happy like this.

Then she takes her mouth away, her lips, her tongue, her teeth. And she starts to get up and her smile is so big I can almost bathe in it.

"We will, Lei Yue. We will laugh soon, a lot. Just not today."

She closes the door very softly behind her.

CHAPTER **TWENTY-NINE**

Winnie comes back. She doesn't say anything, walks into the kitchen and drops a large bag of takeout food on the table, then goes straight to the bathroom, locks the door and the water runs for a long time.

When she comes out, she's beautiful, young, fresh, wet, no makeup, wrapped in a towel. I've put the food out on plates. It's something Korean, ripe with garlic and chilies. My mouth has been watering from the smell for almost a half hour.

I hadn't been hungry when I had my sweet. I'd eat sometimes because I knew I had to. But now, my appetite is back with a vengeance. Winnie made fun of me last night at dinner, she said I must be storing up for winter.

While we eat she tells me about the boat.

The Golden Chariot, a mid-sized container ship with Greek registry, leaves the port of Shenzhen in five days. It's scheduled to take sixteen days to get to Ensenada. Fifteen thousand U.S. dollars each buys us one-way passage in the cargo hold and an introduction to a coyote somewhere along the California-Mexico border.

That's it. There will be a little food. If we want to eat more than a barely subsistence diet, we have to bring our own. If we want to sleep on anything other than the corrugated metal of the floor of an empty container padded with flattened cardboard boxes, we need to bring that, too. If we want light we'd better bring our own flashlight. We should bring some extra water. And we can't bring a lot of anything, no more than we can carry ourselves.

"We go in a shipping container?"

"That's what he said."

"A regular, metal container?"

"Yeah, I think so. Why?"

"If I remember right, that's twenty feet by eight feet on the outside, a little less inside."

"Small."

"That depends on how many people are in it. Did he say?"

"He didn't know. He said they wouldn't go with less than ten."

"What about air, going to the bathroom, things like that?"

"I don't know. We can ask when we go to pay the money."

"Did you get a receipt?"

She looks at me like I've lost my mind, chopsticks holding fire engine red *kimchi* pausing halfway to her mouth.

"Receipt? He's a triad. You're joking, right?"

"We need proof of as much of this as we can get. Anything. We can always say what we've seen, what we've heard, but it's even better if we can get something on paper."

"We're not going to get anything, Lei Yue. These people are too smart for that."

"He must have given you something. You gave him the money and… and, what did he give you?"

"He gave me a place, a name and a code word. That's it. He didn't write any of it down."

"What?"

"We're supposed to go to the BajaChina offices tomorrow, ask for Danny and tell him we want to go for a picnic on the beach. We have to give him the money, fifteen thousand each, in cash."

"And he gives us tickets or something? How do we know we can trust him?"

"We don't. But a lot of people do this. And remember, they get fifteen thousand more from us on the other side. Can you get the money in time?"

"Yeah, we'll have to go to the bank in the morning."

"What are you doing with thirty thousand dollars sitting around in a bank account?"

"It was Ray's idea. I'd been playing the stock market and doing okay. About four months ago he said I should sell everything, put the money in a bank. He thought trouble was coming."

"Did you always do what Ray told you?"

"No, but he was usually right about financial stuff."

"Is that all your money?"

"Most of it." I'd been saving it for something, but I hadn't decided what. It's a fair amount of money in Mexico, or in China, but it wouldn't have gone very far here in Hong Kong.

We spend the early part of the night deciding what to bring with us and figuring out how to pack it. I've got to call my parents, let them know we're coming. It will be good to have someone there when we arrive, someone we can depend on. But I can't do that until right before we leave. I don't want to answer too many questions.

I'm not sure what to do with the rest of Ray. The box is only half empty. I know he had friends in Indonesia. Maybe one of them will take some of his ashes to that place in Bali that he loved. I go through his address book and write down some familiar sounding names and their numbers. I'll call tomorrow.

I start writing out the report I'm going to send to Warner and Montgomery, everything that's happened, everything I know, everything I suspect. The section on everything I can prove is too short, but maybe I can add to it before we leave.

I'm nearly done writing when Winnie comes up behind me and puts her arms around me, snaking a hand under my shirt and onto my breast. She holds me tight, letting me feel her soft, steady, slightly moist breath on my neck.

"Come to bed, Lei Yue. I need you to come to bed with me, now."

I drop the pen onto the yellow legal pad, stand up and let her lead me by the hand.

At first I'm awkward, tentative. This is the first time it's been so deliberate, rather than the fast hard hunger we've spontaneously fallen into before. I'm not sure I know what I'm doing. I want to be good for her. I know she's good for me. I can feel it. I'm consumed by it.

Then later I can tell that I am good for her. Her response leaves me in no doubt.

BANKS IN HONG KONG are used to dealing in large amounts of cash, and in any currency. Winnie and I wait in a short line for a regular teller in the Hongkong Bank main branch. When I hand her a withdrawal slip for thirty thousand U.S. dollars, she doesn't hesitate, just asks what denominations I want the bills in. Would anyone want anything less than hundreds?

There are three stacks, about an inch and a third thick in total. That doesn't seem like much. The teller gives me an envelope for the money. It's only slightly bigger than one you'd send a letter in. It fits easily in Winnie's purse.

In a lot of places, I'd be looking around nervously, trying to see if anyone is paying too much attention to us, if they follow us out of the bank. Not here. Asia isn't like the U.S. Most people still pay with cash, or on account, not with credit cards. Thirty thousand is more than I usually walk around with, but I rarely have less than five hundred or even a thousand in my purse or pocket, so it doesn't seem as scary as it would somewhere else.

Still, we take a taxi to BajaChina's office in Kwai Chung, rather than the subway which would be a lot cheaper, and probably faster.

The subway line divides Kwai Chung in half. On the east side are enormous housing estates. Row after row of thirty-something story buildings with eight apartments on every floor and five or six people in every apartment, rise up along the hills and from their three- or four-story shopping center foundations.

On the west side is one of the world's busiest container ports. Row after row of blue, white, red, yellow, green, purple, gray shipping containers carefully placed like an obsessive child's building blocks in neat stacks as many as twelve high. Enormous four-posted cranes on tracks, like giant versions of those children, rove the aisles between them, plucking one up here and putting it there, then another, then another, all day and night.

As our taxi drives past, the stacks of containers look huge, ominous. The containers themselves look too small to crowd a bunch of people into. I nudge Winnie and gesture out the window.

"Those don't look good."

She looks a little paler than usual.

"Why are we doing this, again?"

I reach over to hold her hand. She knows, and I know. We're doing this because we're *loca, chingada* crazy. And we've got our reasons.

Some of them even make sense. I think. I'm not like Ray. Am I? Even if I am, he made sense, most of the time.

BajaChina's offices are in a small building made from four containers with windows cut into them and a spiral metal staircase leading from behind a reception desk to a second-floor loft. There's a gigantic air-conditioning unit attached to one outside wall, with ducts like so many octopus tentacles coming off it and disappearing into holes cut in the roof. It's arctic cold inside and the whole building vibrates with a deep, almost subsonic hum that after a short while is bound to make anyone's bones ache.

The receptionist could be in her fifties. But she could also be a sour thirty year old. She looks like she started frowning twenty years ago and never stopped. She turns a palm to us, motioning us to stop a few feet in front of her desk. She looks us up and down and her scowl deepens.

"Danny." The name screeches out of her in a shrill, rising inhuman tone that sounds a lot like a hawk screeching down from the sky on its prey. If someone called for me that way, I'd run the opposite direction, fast.

Winnie and I turn our heads up when we hear footsteps coming down the thin metal stairs. A pair of fat-kid chubby little feet in flip flops comes into view. Then a short length of flabby leg, followed by a twisted torso, topped with a bulbous head that from our angle looks as big as a beachball. We're looking up at him, but I can tell he's shorter than me. By as much as a foot, maybe. Another Chinese dwarf. Is that going to work to my advantage, or not?

He stops on the fourth step and turns to face us, his head about level with Winnie's. He looks us up and down carefully, taking a full inventory. His eyes linger on me and then he flashes me what I think is supposed to be a seductive smile. His scraggly mustache turns up at the corners.

What he's thinking is way too obvious. He's little. I'm little. Maybe we can get something started, make some little babies. *Chingada cabron.* No chance of that.

But I have to play nice. I have a mini-cassette recorder in my pocket, the microphone barely peeking out at the top. If I can get him to say anything incriminating, I can get it on tape. I smile back at him. I speak English for Winnie's sake. She's picked up a little Cantonese, but not enough to follow a conversation. I do my best to talk with a Hong Kong accent. I don't want this guy wondering why a Mexican wants to be smuggled into Mexico.

"Are you Danny?"

"Yes, beautiful little lady, I am."

Now I really hate him. I can sense Winnie standing there, trying not to snicker. She's *simpatico*, she knows how I'm feeling. She knows that in my head I'm squashing him like a bug. I lock the smile on my face.

"My friend and I want to go for a picnic on the beach."

"Yes, of course. Please come upstairs to my office. We can make the arrangements."

He's got a large, tall, bright red lacquer desk. It's got three wire mesh in-out trays on it, each piled high with precisely stacked papers. All three stacks are weighted down with iron bars, but the edges of the paper riffle in the gale force cold wind from the duct vent directly overhead. Behind the desk there's a large whiteboard, scribbled with black schedule notations. On one wall there's a world map, colored push pins stuck into a dozen or so of the world's harbors, with colored string tied between them and Hong Kong, Shenzhen and Shanghai. The string between Shenzhen and Ensenada is as red as his desk.

There are two low, wooden stools in front of the desk. He motions us into them, then disappears behind the desk, reappearing as he climbs the three steep wooden steps to the seat of the antique Chinese judge's chair behind the desk. He looms over us. Winnie has worn a low cut blouse in case she needs to impress, or distract, any men. He's obviously impressed with the view, but his eyes keep returning to me. I'm the real distraction.

"Now ladies, where would you like to have your picnic?"

"We hear that Mexico is nice this time of year." I gesture toward Winnie. "And my friend has always wanted to see America."

"Ah, so I understand that you wish to picnic in Mexico and would also like to meet a good tour guide. Is that correct?"

I'm not sure what I need on my tape, but I'm pretty sure this isn't it. I hope he's just a functionary, an employee without too much of a personal stake in what goes on here. And hopefully not too smart, either. But I also hope he knows enough that I can get something useful out of him.

I broaden my smile even more, lean toward him, fiddle with the top button of my blouse. I don't have nearly as much to show off as Winnie, but I've already got his attention. I put on the 'please fuck me, mister,' voice that I hate hearing come out of women who want something. But I want something.

"Please, Danny. You must meet many people in our situation, an important man like yourself. This is frightening for my friend and me. We don't know what to expect. It is a lot of money. When we get there, we won't know anyone. Can we please not talk in code anymore? It will be so very reassuring, it will help us to be more comfortable. You do want us to be comfortable, don't you?"

His smile widens and his eyes focus on the buttons of my blouse.

"What is it you would like to know, Miss…"

"Lei Yue, please call me Lei Yue."

"Of course, Lei Yue. I will be happy to do what I can to make you and your friend feel more comfortable."

"Thank you, thank you so very much. Please do not be offended if I want to make everything as clear as possible. May I ask you some questions?"

Danny puffs himself up. He wants to look impressive, the man with the answers. It's a common weakness of *cabrones* like him, clerks and bureaucrats. He unfolds a hand toward me by way of invitation.

"We've got thirty thousand U.S. dollars, fifteen each. That's the right amount, isn't it?"

He smiles and nods yes. That doesn't do my tape any good.

"That gets us from Shenzhen to Ensenada, right? And then we owe fifteen thousand more, each, when we get there?"

"That's right."

That's a little better.

"That's a lot of money for girls like us, Danny. What if we don't have the full amount when we get to Mexico?" I put a pout on my face, hopefully one he finds attractive.

"My associates in Mexico will help you find work. It will not take long to pay off the money."

"But we want to go to the U.S., Danny. We can make more money there."

"We can introduce you to the right people for that, also. We can make all the arrangements you need. But you will have to ask about that when you get to Mexico."

"What's the ship we're going on like, Danny? Is it safe?"

"It's a regular cargo ship. The last I heard there will be about twelve, maybe fifteen of you in a container. It is not so bad, but no, it is not deluxe. You should bring some things with you. It is not a pleasure cruise."

"What about food and water?"

"There will be some rice, a two hundred liter barrel of water. If you are nice to the crew, they might be nice to you and make it more comfortable." I don't at all like the way his eyes rake over both Winnie and me when he says that.

I can see that he's getting impatient and I still don't have anything much. I lean further forward, undo the top button of my blouse, move my hand down to the next button and start playing with it. His eyes follow.

"I'm so sorry to be a bother with all these questions, Danny. It is a big person's world and I am always very nervous if I don't know everything about what I am going to do. Especially when it is so expensive."

I have to get something soon before I can't stomach this any longer. I'm already going to need a very long, very hot shower. How does Winnie do it?

"Please, please, of course Lei Yue, ask me what you want."

"Is it safe, Danny? Is our money safe? Do we get tickets, or receipts or anything to prove we have paid the money? The man who gave us your name was a triad member, and I can't help but worry about that."

"Yes, Lei Yue, it is safe. It is illegal, but for our customers it is one of the only ways to start a new and better life. BajaChina is a legitimate company. Shipping is a very difficult, very competitive business. This extra service helps people who need help, and it is also profitable for the company. It is a 'win-win' situation. That is why you can trust us to take care of you. If we didn't, word would soon get around and we would lose the business."

He has a smile like an advertiser you can't trust on late night television. I keep smiling back.

"When we get to Mexico, who will meet us? Who will help us cross the border?"

"There will be a man from our office in Ensenada who will meet you at the harbor. He will give you all the help you need. But that is enough questions for now. I am sorry, I have another meeting before long. Do you have the money for the two of you?"

Winnie takes the envelope out of her purse and stands up to hand it to him. She has to lean far across the desk to reach. His horrible, over-sized bug eyes nearly pop out of his head when she does.

It doesn't take long for his grubby little hands to count the money. We don't get anything in return other than the dock number for the ship and the time to be aboard. I get that on tape, too.

CHAPTER **THIRTY**

I don't know how you do it."

"Do what?"

"You know, like I did with that, that, little weasel back there."

Now that we aren't carrying around a large envelope of cash, we're taking the subway back to Central. Winnie throws back her head and rolls out a loud, sharp laugh. The train car isn't too crowded yet, the hordes will start getting on around Sham Shui Po, but the people who are sitting around us all stare.

"Little? You hate it when anyone calls you little."

"He was the sort of *pinche cabron* who would be little even if he was tall and handsome. I hated having to flirt with him. How do you…?"

"I told you, it's not me, I'm not there. My body does it, but I go somewhere else."

"I don't know how you do that."

"I've had a lot of practice."

"I feel like I need a shower, and I didn't even have to touch the *cabron*."

"You got what you wanted, though. Didn't you? And I can take a shower with you. You'll feel a lot better soon."

"It's that easy?"

"It can be."

"Don't you worry about it fucking up your head?"

Winnie looks concerned, serious, puts a hand on my arm.

"Lei Yue, do you think I'm messed up? What do you really think of me?"

I don't know the answer to that. Winnie acts like she's made peace with herself, with what she does. Maybe she has. I don't know about myself though. I wish I knew what I really want from her. I don't want to need her, but I feel like I do. I hate it that I need anybody. It makes me feel small. She needs me too. Is that better?

Do I need her the way Ray used to need his whores? Do I feel bigger around her because of what she does? Am I that fucked up? I hope not. But maybe. It feels good being with her now. That ought to be enough.

Ray used to say that prostitution is all about the illusion, at least for the person doing the buying. And that relationships with lovers aren't all that different. That sounded cynical to me, but I'm beginning to see his point. If it feels good, why question it until you have to, until the bubble bursts? The illusion's probably better than real life anyhow, so why beat on it with a bat like a *piñata*?

I'm pretty sure I don't feel about Winnie the way Ray felt about Irina, the Russian woman. She was a prostitute, too, but I don't think he had too many illusions about her. Still, she broke his heart. My heart's safe from Winnie, I think. But I like her. And I need her for now. And I don't want to hurt her. I just paid fifteen thousand dollars for her. Maybe she'll pay me back, maybe not. Does that change anything? I don't know.

It's no wonder I love the sweet. One simple poke in the arm from my lover and I don't have to think about any of this stuff.

"Yeah, Winnie, you're plenty fucked up. So am I."

She relaxes, leans against me, almost knocking me into the elderly man dressed in smiley face pajamas and black kung fu slippers sitting next to me. He's got his nose buried in a translated Japanese comic book full of sex and violence. She rests her head on my shoulder, sighs and looks up into my eyes.

"Do you think we'll ever get over it?"

"No." She tenses again, wipes the smile off her face. I feel like shit for having said that. But it's the truth.

THERE'S A LOT TO DO OVER THE NEXT FEW DAYS before we leave. I call Ray's friend Juli in Indonesia and spend the first twenty minutes listening to Juli's assistant, Iris, sob and reminisce over the phone. It almost sets me off again, but I've done so much of it already. I'm taking a break.

When Juli gets on the line she only sobs for five or so minutes, then gets angry that Ray put himself in the kind of predicaments in which he might get killed.

"He was no superman. Even he knew that. He was smart and loyal and kind-hearted and very lucky. But the jerk kept testing his luck. We all knew it was going to run out someday. I just wish it had taken a while longer."

I don't know Juli, but her saying Ray was no superman opens the floodgates. We spend the next hour on the phone talking about all the ways that Ray was a plain old mess, a fuckup, a jerk. It makes me miss him all over again. And then I start crying again, which I swore I wasn't going to do.

She's happy to take some of his ashes to the valley he loved in Bali. He'd told her that he'd never go there again after Irina. But she knew he didn't mean it. I'll send her a couple of film cans of Ray, express post.

Winnie and I take more of Ray on a trip to Macau. A little gets thrown off the side of the ferry as it hydroplanes across the silt brown spill of the Pearl River entering the South China Sea. Some is sprinkled over the gaping maws of the giant carp in the pond at the Lou Lim Iok gardens.

There's a 15th Century Portuguese cannon at the Monte Fortress that looks like it's pointing right at the new Bank of China Building. Ray used to go there sometimes and sit on it and try not to think about Irina and a friend of hers who he thought he might have got killed. He told me it didn't work—that he would sit there and think about them and get maudlin. I feel maudlin myself when I pour some of his ashes into the mouth of the old gun.

We have dinner at Fernando's, Ray's favorite restaurant. We buy two extra bottles of *vinho verde* and take them for a walk along the beach nearby. We sit on the black sand and I try to explain to Winnie what it was that I loved about Ray. But I give up about halfway through my bottle. Some things don't require, or can't be explained.

There's about half a film canister of Ray left. There's more back at the apartment, but we didn't take all of him with us. It's almost time to get back to the ferry.

I hold up the gray plastic container with its black lid and shake it.

"What are we going to do with the rest of you, *cabron*?"

"Doesn't *cabron* mean asshole? Why do you keep calling him that? First you're telling me how much you loved the guy, now he's an asshole."

"It's one of those things, Winnie. Some people really are *cabrones*. And some people you love are *cabrones*, too, but in a nice way."

"If you ever call me *puta*, or *cabron*, I won't like it. I don't care how you mean it."

I push her back on the sand and give her a deep kiss by way of an answer. I come up for air pretty quick. There are people around, and in this part of the world, two women kissing like this are frowned upon unless they're surrounded by a hooting and hollering crowd of men who've paid to watch.

Winnie picks up the film can. She holds it up, then touches her wine bottle to it, then touches the bottle to my bottle.

"To your friend, Ray. He was not a *cabron*." She throws her head back and takes a long swallow. I do the same.

"So, Lei Yue, what should we do with the rest of him? Did he like the beach?"

"Not particularly, he got sunburned too easily."

"What then?"

"There was a massage parlor he liked."

She looks like she's about to say something not very nice, but then she shrugs her shoulders.

"Is it on the way to the ferry?"

It is. Winnie won't come up the stairs to the Darling Massage Parlor with me. She waits on the sidewalk below. I push open the door and am confronted with the 'fishbowl,' the big picture window behind which sit dozens of Thai women in brightly colored bikinis with red number badges pinned to the tops. An older Chinese woman in a spangly blue ball gown, the *mamasan*, comes out from behind the front desk, her palms in front of her as if ready to push me back out the door.

"No ladies, no ladies. Man only."

I look around the reception room. There's a ratty sofa, a coffee table littered with porn magazines and in the corner a small shrine to Tin Hau, the goddess of the sea. There's a brass brazier in front of the shrine. It's filled with sand, smoldering incense sticks stand upright stuck into it.

I turn away from the *mamasan* and kneel in front of the shrine. I don't turn around to look at her, but I don't hear anything. She doesn't want to interfere with this, even if there are no ladies allowed in the place. I ease the film can out of my pocket, keeping it in front of me so no one can see what I'm doing, open it with one hand and upend it over the brazier. It won't be long before the ash from the incense covers the ash from Ray. I wonder how often they clean out the brazier.

FIGURING OUT WHAT TO PACK ISN'T EASY. Water's the big problem. It's heavy. One liter, which is about the minimum we'll each need per day for drinking, weighs a little over two pounds. That's thirty-two liters for the two of us. If there are twelve to fifteen people sharing the two-hundred-liter barrel, we'll need to bring extra. Food, too.

Rolled up blankets are also heavy. I don't care what the other people on the boat will think, I go to a camping store and buy two lightweight sleeping bags and blow up pads to put under them. I buy us each a backpack, so that our hands will be free to carry the eight-liter plastic water jugs I also buy. Flashlights, extra batteries, Swiss Army knives with a bunch of gadgets; the clerk almost sells me a small gas stove, but I decide against it.

He's whip thin, with a big lopsided grin and a terrible complexion. As he rings up my purchases, he wants to know where I'm going camping. He can tell me about some great places in Yunnan Province if I want.

"No thanks, my friend and I are going to Mexico."

"That's a long way for a camping trip."

I smile back at him. "It's a long way for a lot of things."

EVERYTHING'S LAID OUT ON THE FLOOR of Ray's apartment when Winnie gets back from picking up our passports with the visas we'll need to get into China. Warner was wrong, there was no problem with mine. She looks all the gear over, tries on one of the backpacks, opens and closes all the gadgets on the knife. She looks at me and raises an eyebrow.

"That's a lot of stuff. When I was a kid I went on a school trip to Sorak National Park. We went camping for three days. It was beautiful."

I look her up and down and the last thing I can see her as is a kid.

"It's hard to picture you as a child."

"I was, once. Most of it wasn't very good, though."

"Yeah, me, too."

"Isn't it going to look strange, us getting on the boat with all this?"

"Why? We might as well be as comfortable as we can."

"Oh no, I'm glad to have it. But aren't we supposed to be poor immigrants, going to America for a better life."

"Poor immigrants with fifteen thousand U.S. each to pay the snakehead. This stuff is nothing compared with that."

We spend the rest of the afternoon trying out the packs with different things in them, filling up the water bottles and seeing if we can carry everything. I might be smaller than Winnie, but I'm stronger. I can carry my water bottle, she can barely pick hers up when she has the pack on her back. If we have to, we'll pour some of her water out before we get on the ship.

I want to bring an extra pair of shoes. I decide not to and use the space for what's left of Ray and two books that he used to try and get me to read.

"What are you going to do with the rest of Ray's ashes?"

"I don't know. He always said he loved Los Angeles. I might take some there. Maybe burial at sea. Isn't that what most people do?"

She puts an arm around me, leans down to kiss my neck.

"You're not most people, Lei Yue."

"Neither was Ray. I can't just leave him here." I don't want to talk about it anymore. Sooner or later I'll know what to do.

We're both exhausted. It hasn't taken as much work to get ready to go as I thought it would, but the whole thing is making my brain hurt. I've wanted my sweet a lot over the last few days. It would be so nice to sink into her arms, float away and not think about any of this. But I can't. I can't because of Ray, because of Winnie and maybe even a little because of myself.

We have to be in Shenzhen by tomorrow evening. The boat leaves early the next morning.

We go to bed early. I fall asleep fast but spend a terrible night dreaming, then waking up, then falling back asleep and dreaming some more and over and over again. I get up about three in the morning. Winnie is sleeping peacefully, lightly snoring. I pace around Ray's apartment, looking at everything, touching everything, not sure what I'm leaving behind. And not sure where I'm going.

I dig out one of the yellow legal pads that Ray used to buy by the dozen and finish writing my report to Warner and Montgomery. My handwriting is bad. I have to concentrate as much on keeping it legible as I do on what I'm writing.

I still don't have much. The tape of Danny is something. It's enough to bring down one *cabron*, maybe even the local office of BajaChina. But I want them all. It might be enough to get the police on the case, at least here in Hong Kong. It's enough for Montgomery, and he'll push the investigation. But I've got to get to the end of it. That's what Ray would do, or try to do. It's the last thing I'll ever be able to do for him.

The report fills up six pages. I can't stand writing it over again. I'll use a copy machine at the post office when I mail it in the morning. I prepare two envelopes. Wrap the mini-cassette tape in a protective layer of newspaper for the one addressed to Bill Warner. I've got to try and go back to sleep.

I take Ray's bottle of vodka out of the freezer. There isn't much left. I pour myself two full shots, one in each of the small, souvenir 1997 Hong Kong Handover glasses that Ray had bought before the ceremony because he thought they were funny. I steel myself, because I know the *mierda* burns and I don't like it. Then I toss them back in quick succession and feel the hot pain in the back of my throat and down my esophagus and into my stomach.

And when the pain subsides and my stomach cools and I've made one more circuit around Ray's apartment, I go back to bed. I slip in under the sheets without waking Winnie and curl up against her.

CHAPTER **THIRTY-ONE**

It's dark and hot and the relentless rumble of the big engines sends vibrations burrowing into every part of the ship, every part of me. The crew member who led us here, who flirted with Winnie, told us we'd get used to it. It's been three hours since the gas powered chug of onshore generators gave way to the *whomp* of onboard pistons and the slight whine of turning screws, and I'm not used to it yet.

We've laid out our blow up pads, unrolled our sleeping bags and are huddled together in our black corner of the container. There are fourteen other people in here with us and it's already humid and close with their breath and their sweat. Everyone has brought a light of some kind, but no one wants to risk using it up early in the voyage. I'm thirsty already, but I'm holding off on drinking our water for the same reason.

I alternate breathing between my nose and my mouth. Through my nose is more even, calmer. Except for the smells, which is why I switch to my mouth. It's not that they're bad, it's that they're intense and mixed-up and confusing. There's diesel and oil from the engines. The sharp, salty, metallic odor that seems to come from the paint on ships. A dry, grassy smell that might be part of the cargo or whatever it's packed with. A hint of green wood from shipping crates, a sheen of light grease, maybe from the hinges on the container's doors. The food that we've all got with us. The smell of the others.

I nuzzle my face up into the nape of Winnie's neck to smell her. I love the scent of her. It relaxes me, helps me breathe easier.

The last time I was in the dark like this was different. It was worlds away. She wasn't there. No one was there until near the end, when Mei Lin came. There was only my lover and my sweet and I still miss them, but every day I miss them a little less.

We haven't been talking much, lying here adjusting to our surroundings. I can hardly hear her whisper over the thrumming of the ship.

"Lei Yue, did you bring any money?"

I did. I've got about twenty-five-hundred U.S. in twenties hidden in five different places. It wouldn't be hard for someone to find all of it, but I'm hoping that if they find the first batch they'll think that's it and stop looking.

"Yes, why?"

"We might need it."

"I know, that's why I brought it. I don't know what's going to happen when we get to Mexico. I called my family, but it's not like I was able to give them arrival information or anything, like if we were flying into Mexico City."

"No, we might need it here, on the ship."

"What for?"

"Remember the crew guy who told us we'd get used to the noise?"

"Sure." He was young, Filipino. He looked shy until Winnie smiled at him when we were getting on board. Then he was all over her, like she'd given him the big come on. He pulled her aside and I could see he wanted her. I could imagine the whole thing. I wanted to go over and kick him in the shins, pull her away. But I didn't.

"He's going to help us."

"How?"

"They don't usually let people out of the container until they get to where they're going. He'll let us out for an hour or two every night, let us up on deck. And he'll give us food, some of what the crew eats, extra water."

"Is this like the triad guy who introduced us to the snakehead? Are you going to have to fuck him?"

I can't see her in the dark, but she pulls away from me. I can picture the sheepish look on her face. I put my hands up and lightly press them against her cheeks. She's nodding yes.

"Winnie, we don't need this guy. We'll get through this without him."

"Maybe. We'll get through it better with him. It's no different than before."

"I want it to be different."

"Me, too. But right now, here, it's not. I'm doing this for us, for you and me."

I don't want her doing this for us, for me. But a part of me does want her to—anything that will make this easier. And I feel like a *cabron* for thinking that. And I could start fighting myself in my head about it. And I could fight with Winnie about it. But now's not the time.

"He wants money, too?"

"It's for his friend."

"Why should we pay his friend?"

She pulls further away, turns her head away from me. Her cheeks flush, I can feel them warming. I turn her face back toward me.

"Winnie, why?"

"He only wanted to help me. I told him I wouldn't do it if he didn't help you, too."

"What about the friend?"

"He said it was too much trouble for him to help two of us. If you wanted help, he'd have to get his friend to help you."

"And the friend wants money?"

"That or, well, you know…"

I know. And I don't want to. I offer, but it's because I know she won't take me up on it. And I've got money.

"If you can do it, so can I."

She reaches up and puts her hands on my cheeks, brings my face up hard against hers, then pulls it back a little.

"No, you can't. I won't let you."

Her voice is firm, strict. There's no opening for argument. That's fine with me.

"How much does he want?"

"Five hundred U.S. Do you have that much?"

"Why can't we pay your guy, too? I've got enough."

"I asked. He won't take money."

"Why don't we ask his friend to help both of us?"

"It's too late. I already said yes. How would we find his friend, anyway? We can't get out of this container whenever we want and walk around the ship. They have to come get us."

A HALF HOUR LATER there's the sound of a metal bolt sliding and one side of the container's door swings open with a piercing, long squeak. Dim light flows in from outside. Everyone in the container sits up straight, wary, not sure what's going on.

A flashlight snaps on and eerily spots a grinning face sticking up a little above the floor. We're three containers up, in a stack of eight. We climbed up here on a ladder that they took away after everyone was inside.

It's Winnie's Filipino sailor. Winnie nudges me.

"Get the money, we need to go."

The easiest stash to reach is buried in the thick plastic bag with what's left of Ray. I smiled when I did that. He would have appreciated it. I discreetly sneak it out of my backpack.

I don't have much choice but to leave everything else behind. I can't do anything other than trust our fellow container-mates. Just like they have to trust me.

Winnie and I scuttle across the legs of our fellow passengers to the front of the container.

Her sailor tries to kiss her. I'm happy to see she turns her head away, letting him have only a slight peck on a cheek. He boosts himself into the container. He's got a bucket filled with cold, cooked rice. He sets it on the floor a few feet inside the door, waves an arm to take in everybody in the container, then points to it. He turns back toward us and tells Winnie and me to climb down the ladder first.

"Are you going to leave the door open after we leave?"

Winnie's voice sounds loud echoing off the metal walls. There are air holes that have been punched in the sides of the container, but it's a lot better with the door open.

"I'm supposed to close it, Ma'am."

He's polite enough. But it's hard to imagine anyone calling Winnie, "Ma'am."

She moves up to him, strokes him with her fingertips from his face down his neck and his chest and his stomach, stopping above his crotch.

"Please, it is much nicer with the door open. We would all be so thankful if you could."

With her fingers lightly drumming over his belt buckle, he doesn't think for long, and agrees.

We climb down the ladder and he leads us through a warren of stacked containers to an exposed, narrow, metal staircase leading the long way up to the deck. As we near the top, the air gets fresher, cooler. I take deep breaths and it loosens my body, the tension exhaling out of me.

Winnie's sailor leads us to a corner by the rail along the edge of the deck, away from the lights of the bridge and the cabins. The wind comes off the ocean, whipping back at us and I get cold, but it feels good. It wakes me up. We stand there, not talking, hands in pockets except for my one hand that's holding the bag of money and Ray.

I hear someone coming up behind me and turn around to look. It's another Filipino sailor. He could almost be the twin of Winnie's guy, only he has bleached strawberry blonde hair and doesn't look too happy when he sees me. He's carrying a stacked metal lunch pail, the kind with compartments set on top of each other, and a large thermos.

He puts them down at my feet, then stands closer than I'd like. I wonder if I can turn him around, use him as a windbreak. He sticks out a hand.

"Have my money, Ma'am?"

It doesn't sound polite coming out of him, just business.

I unknot the top of Ray's bag and dig for the roll of twenties. I shake them off in the bag before taking them out and handing them to the surly sailor. He unrolls them inches from my face and slowly counts. He grunts when he finishes, puts them away in a pants pocket, then points down to the lunch pail and thermos.

"That's for you and the other one. Don't take them down the hold with you. Eat and drink here. When you're done, he'll take you below." He turns and walks away toward the back of the ship.

I'm glad I paid him and didn't have to do the other thing. Maybe he would be nicer if he was having sex with me. He didn't seem all that interested anyway. I'm happy that I don't have to find out.

Winnie and her sailor are standing, watching. When my guy walks away, Winnie stoops down to pick up our food. She takes it over to a place where the railing will protect us from the wind. I follow and we sit down on the hard metal deck.

Her sailor stands over us, tapping his foot impatiently. Winnie looks up at him.

"I'm sorry sweetie, my friend and I are hungry. I'll eat quick, then I can show you a good time. Okay?"

He looks around nervously, then squats down next to us, out of the wind. We ignore him and dig into the food. There's barely warm rice, a couple pieces of greasy fried chicken and some mixed vegetables. We'd eaten a good dinner before going to the boat. We're eating now only because we know we'll regret it if we don't take every chance to eat that we can. By tomorrow night, and the nights to come, this will seem like a feast. The tea in the thermos is bitter and hot. We pass the one tin cup back and forth.

Winnie's had enough before I do. She stands up and pulls her sailor to his feet. She bends down to me.

"I'll be back as soon as I can."

I don't want her to go. I want to throw myself at her sailor's legs, catch him off-balance, toss him overboard. I want Winnie to help me. I want her to take me in her arms, kiss me, tell me she loves me. I don't want her to leave me alone.

And I hate that I'm not strong, that I want to keep her here by kissing her back and for us to laugh and make love in the cold wind off the sea. All I can do is nod as she takes the sailor's hand and leads him away.

I'm not hungry anymore. I don't want them to think they can bring us less food, so I get up and empty what's left over the side. I drink another cup of the tea while standing, leaning into the harsh wind.

I can hear Winnie and her sailor. There's whispering, deep intakes of breath, a light slapping sound and a rhythmic *unh unh unh*. And I look up and out and around me, trying to silence it in my head.

There are only a few lights on the boat. Above, and curving down to the horizon wrapped all around me there is a plush, sparkling blanket of stars. More than I've ever seen.

All the fiery pinpricks above. All the deep cold dark liquid flowing below, teeming with unseen life. On a boat heading away from so much and to, to what? I don't know. And this is as good a place as any for the rest of Ray.

I place the cup of tea down on the deck and balance the plastic bag on one hand. I bounce it gently up and down. There's not much left. A pound, maybe.

I untwist the top of the bag, pinch the bottom between two fingers to hold it on my palm and then lift it out and high as I can over the edge of the ship. It flops open and the ashes begin to sift out. Ray is taken by the wind and I look up into the enormity of stars as I let the empty bag go.

And I feel so small, so insignificant, so unimportant. And then it's like Ray is standing behind me and I can feel his chill breath.

And I turn around and of course he's not there. He can't be. But it's like I can hear his voice, soft like a whisper, but almost pleading, like he's trying to convince himself of something and maybe talk me into it, too.

"If you don't do it, Lei Yue, who the hell else will?"

And if he was there. And if I was standing here and taking cover behind him from the wind, I could poke my head out around him and catch a glimmer of the sun rising in the east. Rising where I'm going.

ACKNOWLEDGEMENTS

No writer is any good without readers. Those of you who are reading this have four others, in particular, to thank. Emily Bronstein, Bill Krauss and Ashley Ream (as well as Eva Eilenberg, who the book is dedicated to) read and critiqued early drafts of this book. They were all intelligent, insightful, eagle-eyed, diligent, conscientious and most important of all, brutally frank.

The same is true of my frighteningly smart, witty, charming and hell-on-skates editor, Alison Janssen.

Ben Leroy, my publisher, has put together a publishing company that I am very proud to be writing for, and he's also a whole lot of fun on a late night taco truck crawl around Los Angeles.

Janet Reid is my beleaguered agent and trusted scout. Her guiding and trail-blazing services through the dark and scary wilderness of the publishing world are invaluable.

Madeira James (www.xuni.com) makes me look good online, could not possibly be any better to work with, and I am pleased to count among my close friends.

Sheri Rowe of the Houston P.D. is a great pal and comes in very handy when it comes to keeping it real with the details of crime scenes and guns. Get to work on your book, girl. You're a damn fine writer and I want to read it.

In 1978, and again in 2006, I stayed in the Peace Hotel in Shanghai. It is one of my favorite hotels in the world, for its location, rundown charms and a variety of quirks. It is, apparently, being rennovated by the Fairmont Hotel Group. While it could use the work, it will almost certainly become too expensive for me to stay in again.

On July 1, 1997 I watched the celebratory, handover fireworks display over Hong Kong Harbor from a suite of offices with a spectacular view, at the invitation of Alan Zeman, my ex-wife's now ex-boss. The canapes and booze were excellent. I had mixed emotions about the occasion. My host didn't. A Canadian by birth, he recently became one of the very few naturalized citizens of the People's Republic of China.

The graphic depiction of heroin addiction in the book springs from close, too close at times, observation of a number of friends during my teenage years. Several of them made it out of the '60s alive and went on to do okay. One didn't. And one other, I hope she's okay, I don't know. I lost track of her after she and her girlfriend tried, I think, to run me over with their car. Thanks for missing.

Photo by Misha Rasovich

ERIC STONE worked as a writer, photographer, editor, publisher and publishing consultant. He is the author of the novels *Living Room of the Dead, Grave Imports,* and *Flight of the Hornbill,* the first three titles in the Ray Sharp series. Additionally, he wrote the non-fiction book *Wrong Side of the Wall.* He lives in Los Angeles. Visit him at www.ericstone.com.